Praise for *To A[lice]*

"*To Alice* is a compelling, compassionate, h[eartfelt] story of the amazing caregivers that work in our towns everyday. The author's detailed knowledge and respect of those in need of care and those doing the care through home health services creates a cast of characters true to life. Most of us will end up in these professional hands and we can be grateful for this eloquent and complex story of the burdens and blessings of caring so well."

—Virginia Lynn Fry, author of *Part of Me Died Too: Stories of Creative Survival among Bereaved Children and Teenagers*

"Barre author J. Peter Cobb vividly captures the details of hospice workers moving through rural landscapes and balancing a life of caring for others while trying to escape their own demons. In Alice's case, those include a traumatic experience in med school and the expectations of a family who doesn't understand her struggles. It's no surprise how accurately Cobb portrays that world, considering his former role as the executive director of Vermont's Visiting Nurses Association. In *To Alice*, he shows the perils of putting your heart into something that just might not return the favor."

—*Seven Days*

"There is beauty amid the grittiness in Cobb's novel. And readers care about Alice and the Vermonters she serves, and her reluctance to establish boundaries between them. The tagline asks, 'Is caring too much a bad thing?' There is no clear-cut answer; a mark of a realistic novel."

—*Montpelier Bridge*

TO ALICE

TO ALICE

J. PETER COBB

Rootstock Publishing

Montpelier, VT

To Alice Copyright © 2021 J. Peter Cobb
All rights reserved. Second Printing.

Paperback ISBN: 978-1-57869-182-1
eBook ISBN: 978-1-57869-183-8

Published by Rootstock Publishing
an imprint of Ziggy Media, LLC
info@rootstockpublishing,com
www.rootstockpublishing.com

This is a work of fiction. Names, places, characters, and events are fictitious. Any similarities to actual events and persons, living or dead, are purely coincidental. Any trademarks, service marks, product names, or named features are assumed to be the property of their respective owners and are used only for reference. If any of these terms are used, no endorsement is implied. Except for review purposes, the reproduction of this book, in whole or part, electronically or mechanically, constitutes a copyright violation.

Cover Design: ColbieMyles.com. Cover Images: sad and tired woman on porch by LoloStock (Adobe Stock); white king and black queen in a game of chess by Meindert van der Haven (iStock, GettyImages).

Connect with the author: www.jpetercobb.com, Instagram @jpetercobb, Facebook.com/JPeterCobb

Printed in the United States of America.

This book is dedicated to all the home care and hospice nurses, therapists, social workers and home care aides who help millions of people have better lives.

CHAPTER 1

CLYDE NASON

ALICE HAMMOND PASSES the third of six switchbacks on Beckley Hill Road, three more to go. Even in good weather the road is treacherous. One hundred yards beyond the fourth switchback the road surface changes from cracked tar to loose gravel and the moderate incline steepens to resemble the initial climb of a roller coaster. In April, especially the day after a hard rain and rapid snow melt, the gravel turns to tire-sucking mud.

Yesterday, it rained for nearly three hours. Before the rain, the snowpack in the woods along the side of the road was four feet deep. It is less than two feet deep now. The bottom of her Ford Focus is rubbing against the mud. The tire grooves in the road were made by much bigger vehicles with much larger tires. She has only a quarter mile to go. She chokes the steering wheel with both hands. "I can do this," she says to herself.

Alice is a home health aide for the Providence, Vermont Visiting Nurses Association. Her patient is Clyde Nason, a former logger who hasn't left his house without assistance in over five years. She helps him bathe and checks his pulse and blood pressure. She stopped recording his weight three months ago when he topped the two hundred eighty-five pounds maximum on his scale.

Today is Clyde's fifty-fifth birthday. Alice has a *Far Side* card for him, a bouquet of flowers, mostly red carnations, two cupcakes with pink frosting and the DVD *True Grit* with John Wayne. She has scrubbed Clyde's body clean twice a week for thirty-one months. He needs her because he can't get in and out of the tub without help and he can't reach most of his body. The first few weeks his nakedness embarrassed both of them. The embarrassment is long gone. Now, when she pushes aside his drooping stomach to clean the rolls of his skin, she and Clyde continue their conversation as if they were two friends sitting on kitchen chairs chatting about the weather.

She parks her car on the side of the road, opens the door and searches for a dry spot. A muddy soup surrounds her car. She grabs her nursing bag, the cupcake bag, the birthday card, the DVD and the flowers from the passenger's seat. She steps to the ground. Her left leg sinks five inches into the mud. She lifts her foot. Her foot is free but her boot is buried in the muck.

"Damn," she says. When she reaches down to pull the untied boot out of the mud, she drops the cupcakes and the flowers. She grabs her boot, opens the car door, sits on the driver's seat, puts her muddy boot back on her foot and ties the laces on both boots extra tight. She slogs the fifty yards to Clyde's house. Each step sounds like the plop of a toilet plunger.

Clyde's dog Ella is barking. The dog is several pounds lighter than Alice's cat. "Shut up," she tells the dog. The dog barks louder. "Shut up you stupid dog." Her words wouldn't insult Clyde. She tells him just about every day his dog isn't a real dog but a yappy, rat dog and he tells her, her cat is fat, lazy and useless. He has seen pictures of her cat.

Ella is at the front door barking even louder than before and scratching madly on the wood. "Relax Ella, I'll be in there in a minute." She turns the doorknob. The door is locked. She knocks hard. "Clyde, it's me, Alice." There is no response from him. Ella's barking continues. She pushes her face against the living room window and shades her eyes to see inside. The only thing she can see clearly is the television. Steve Harvey is rolling his eyes in mock disgust. A tall, Black woman wearing a tight, red dress, has said something stupid on Family Feud. Her family members and the audience are all laughing at her.

"Clyde, it's me, Alice." Still no answer. She taps the glass and scans the room. She can see better, her eyes are used to the dark room. Clyde is laying face down on the floor in front of the couch. Ella is on his back, barking.

She pounds on the front door with her fists. It doesn't open. She pushes against the living room window frame. The window doesn't move. She swings her nursing bag into the window and smashes the glass. She kicks the glass shards still attached to the frame and crawls through, careful not to cut her back. The room smells like rotten cabbage. Ella licks the mud on her ankles. "Good dog Ella," she says. She tries to roll Clyde over onto his back but he is too heavy. She grabs his arm. His skin is cold. She checks for a carotid pulse. There is none. He is not breathing. She calls 9-1-1.

Clyde's logging days ended eight years ago when a tree fell the wrong way and landed on his legs. He was working alone. No one found him until the next morning. His right leg was shattered and couldn't be totally repaired. His left ankle needed a six-inch long, metal rod and four screws. Eight months later he could walk with a cane but with great difficulty.

Clyde was Alice's first patient. It was obvious to him that she didn't know what to do. She told him, "I have no clue what I am doing."

"No kidding," he said.

Her twice-weekly visits were the high point of his week. As best he could, considering he couldn't reach most of his body, he tried to sponge bathe himself clean before her visit.

The only person who visited him on a regular basis was his younger brother Bill who brought him food, mowed his lawn, took his trash to the dump, plowed the driveway in the winter, bought clothes for him and helped him pay his bills. Bill was often annoyed with Clyde and frequently told him so.

Clyde watched the news every night to make sure he could talk to Alice without embarrassing himself and he read books he thought would impress her. But mostly he talked about his passion for logging. When he described the sound of the wind blowing through the trees she would close her eyes and imagine the cool breeze on her face and smell the pine needles and rotted leaves. One afternoon, three black bears walked so close to him it was as if they were lost and needed directions. The day he was pinned under the tree, he was afraid he would die. "I don't want to die but I'd rather die here than anywhere else in the world," he said to himself as he looked up at the night sky.

On his fifty-fourth birthday Alice brought him the book, *Poetry of Robert Frost*. She read him the poem where the woodcutter cuts off the boy's hand.

"Why did you read me that poem?"

"I thought you'd like it."

He thought for a minute. "I do like it, not sure why, but I do."

After her work was completed, she and Clyde would play chess for ten minutes, sometimes a bit longer. Each match took eight to ten visits to finish. She has been warned several times by Susan Young, her work supervisor, that her visits to her patients take too long and cost the agency too much money.

The chessboard is on the kitchen table. Alice is white, Clyde black. She looks at the board. The white king is laying on its side, checkmate, her fourth loss in a row. She remembers when she taught him how to play. This is a foolish game he told her. He learned quickly. She won the first six games easily but he got slightly better with each match. By the second year he won most of the time. One day she found the book *Modern Chess Strategy* hidden under a towel in the laundry basket. She held the book close to his face.

"You cheat, you sly son-of-a-bitch," she said.

"You're just jealous of my superior skills."

She swatted the top of his head with the book. That memory makes her cry.

She opens the front door and looks for the birthday gifts she had left on the porch, under the kicked-in window. She brings them into the house and places them on the kitchen counter. *His birthday would have been a very good day*, she thinks.

Ella trots to the kitchen, to her empty food dish, and whines.

"I guess I better feed you."

Ella does a happy dance around her feet.

CHAPTER 2

ALICE HAMMOND

ALICE IS ASLEEP on her couch wrapped in the bedspread from her bed. Clyde's dog Ella is sleeping with her. The dog's head is under the blanket, resting on Alice's right foot. Alice couldn't sleep in her bed because every time she closed her eyes, she pictured Clyde's dead body on his living room floor with Ella on top of him, barking. She is convinced the smell of his rotted flesh is still in her nose.

In her dream she is driving her father's Lexus and Clyde is sitting in the backseat doing a crossword puzzle. He is young, thin and handsome, the Clyde from a picture with his brother Bill taken when they were teenagers. In the picture, Clyde has Bill in a headlock and is rapping Bill's head with his knuckles. He is much bigger and stronger than Bill. Their mother Eileen is in the background laughing. In Alice's dream, the car is belching smoke from every vent. There is so much smoke inside the car she can barely see the road. "Where the hell are we going?" Clyde asks her.

There is a banging noise from the engine, almost as if someone was pounding on the motor with a rubber mallet. Alice wakes up from her dream. The banging continues. She shakes her head clear, rubs her eyes with her thumbs and checks the clock on the table next to the television. It is three in the morning. The banging noise is stronger than it was in her dream. Alice hears a woman say, "Left, left, yes, right there, right there, yes." She now knows what the banging sound is, it's her neighbor's headboard banging against their shared wall.

Alice's three-room apartment is in an old Victorian house on Main Street in Providence. The apartment is too cold in the winter and too hot in the summer. Half of the windows open and half are painted shut. The faucet handle for cold water from the kitchen sink is broken. Alice uses a wrench to turn the water on and off. The wall-to-wall carpet in the living room is worn through to the floorboards. The tub and sink in the bathroom are green porcelain and the linoleum in both the kitchen and bathroom is cracked and buckles along all four walls of each room.

One hundred years ago Main Street was home to Providence's power families, but not now. Both sides of the road were lined with maple and elm trees and all of the houses were the biggest and finest houses in the town. The elm trees are long dead. Most of the grand, old houses have been torn down and replaced by gas stations, rent-to-own stores, or fast food restaurants. A homeless man sleeps under the porch of her building and steals returnable cans and bottles from the recycling bins throughout the neighborhood. Everyone in her building calls him Can Man.

Alice presses a pillow over her head to muffle the banging sound. "Third time this week," she says to her dog. Ella licks her feet. The banging and moaning stop. Ella is whining, she has to go out. "Please dog, not now." Ella continues to whine and tap dance across the floor. "Goddammit dog." The dog cowers as if it had been slapped. Alice picks it up, hugs it and kisses the top of its head. "So sorry my little buddy," she says in adult baby talk. She stumbles through the apartment to find the dog's leash, a bathrobe and her slippers. Ella is at her ankles the whole time. "All right dog, let's go."

In the hallway, her neighbor is sitting on the floor in front of his door, in boxer shorts and a white T-shirt, smoking a cigarette. "Didn't mean to wake you up, Judy's real loud, sorry about that."

"No problem."

"I'm Brian."

"Alice."

"Who you talkin' to?" Judy shouts from inside Brian's apartment.

"Nobody, none of your damn business."

"Not that stuck up bitch from next door, you been lusting after her for months."

"No, I haven't," he says, his lips almost touching the door. He stands up and crushes his cigarette against the wall. "Don't mind her, she's an idiot."

"I heard that," Judy says.

The tip of his penis has slipped out of the slit in his shorts. He turns away from Alice and tucks it back in behind the cloth and returns to his apartment.

The air outside is damp and cold. Alice ties the bathrobe belt tighter around her waist and hugs herself to get warm. Ella is sniffing her poops from the last three days. Every time she finds a new poop she looks up at Alice as if to say, "That was me."

"Come on Ella, hurry up, it's cold out here." She pulls the robe belt even tighter and rubs her runny nose with her right sleeve. She tugs on the dog's leash, "Come on dog, get it done."

"It sure is cold," Brian says. His comment surprises both Alice and Ella. Ella growls at him.

"Stop it," Alice says to the dog. She tugs the leash. The dog bows its head in shame.

Brian is wearing jeans and a sweatshirt but no shoes or socks and is standing on the front porch, his back leaning against the door. He steps off the porch and walks toward Alice. "Don't listen to that bitch, she doesn't know jack shit."

It takes Alice a few seconds to realize who he is talking about. He grabs a pack of cigarettes from his back pocket, pulls one from the pack, lights it, takes a deep drag and exhales the smoke over his head.

"Want a cigarette?" He holds the pack toward her.

"No, I'm fine."

"I really am sorry. The freakin walls are like tissue paper."

"Tell me about it."

"Not neighborly. It won't happen again."

Alice laughs. "Not a big deal. You're pretty active, I got to say".

"True. You're not, either that or you're wicked quiet."

"Not."

"Too bad. You're so quiet, sometimes I forget you live next door. Judy calls you The Silent Monk."

"I'm here. I've been here for almost six months."

"Six quiet months. Can I ask you a question?"

"Sure. Can't guarantee I'll answer it but go ahead, shoot."

"Are you gay?"

"What? No. What?"

"Are you gay? Are you a lesbian?"

"No, why would you ask me that?"

"Because you wear flannel all the time, too much flannel not to be a lesbian."

"Good to know. I'll have to start wearing something else."

"And drop the hiking boots while you're at it, worse than flannel. Nothing says lesbian more than big, brown leather boots." He flips his cigarette to the grass. "I'd stay and chat but my balls are freezing."

"I bet they are. If I had any, mine would be too."

He laughs, turns away from her and walks back to the house. At the door, he stops and turns to her. "Remember, drop the flannel and get new shoes."

"Got it. Tank top and Daisy Dukes from now on."

"Daisy Dukes?"

"Tight, really short, jean shorts."

Brian gives her thumbs up and disappears into the hallway. Back in her apartment she checks Facebook, Instagram and Snapchat. Nothing new from the last time she checked three hours ago. She switches to YouTube and watches a clip from the Daily Show. Trevor Noah is interviewing John Krasinski. Krasinski is imitating his wife's British accent. Both men and the audience laugh. Alice has watched this clip several times before.

Next door, Brian and Judy are arguing. Judy grabs one of Brian's shoes and throws it at his head. The shoe misses him but hits the common wall between the two apartments so hard a picture from Alice's wall falls to the floor. The glass on the frame cracks.

"You're a fucking loser, that bitch wouldn't fuck you on a bet, she's outta your league you dumbass," Judy says. She stomps across the bedroom, gets dressed, stomps through the living room, to the apartment door, opens that door, and slams it shut.

"Good riddance bitch," Brian says.

Judy stomps through the hallway, opens the door to the building and slams it shut, even harder than she had slammed the door to Brian's apartment. Alice's front door rattles.

Alice retrieves a photo album from her bookshelf Clyde had given her on her twenty-seventh birthday. The first photo in the album is a picture of her and Clyde sitting on his porch. The sun is reflected in the window behind them. Both of them are squinting. It was a hot spring day. Clyde's shirt was soaked with sweat. He had a blue can of Bud Light in his right hand.

Clyde had placed his camera on the hood of her car and had used two paperback books under the lens to get the camera into the right position. It took him three tries to take the picture. On the first try he forgot to set the timer to the ten-seconds delay. The second try failed because the camera slipped off the books. "Goddammit," he said after the second miscue. Alice had never heard him swear before. When he finally got a picture he showed it to her. "Beauty and the beast," he said.

"Who's the beauty?" she said.

The best picture in the album is a picture of two beavers in a pond in the fall. The beavers are swimming across the pond, one beaver is swimming slightly behind the other. The colors of the fall foliage are reflected in the water.

Alice falls asleep. The photo album tumbles from her lap and nearly hits Ella as it slips off her knees. Her cell phone rings and wakes her from a deep sleep. "What?" she says to Ella. "What time is it?" She checks the time on her phone. "Oh damn." She answers the phone. "Susan, I'm so sorry, I overslept, I can't believe it's eight o'clock."

"I figured as much. Sounds like you're still asleep," Susan Young says.

"Who's my first visit?"

"Danny Myers."

"Grand View Drive?"

"Yes."

"Don't forget, he's the one with the vicious dog. If the dog isn't on a leash, don't go in."

"I hate that dog. I'll be there in fifteen minutes, twenty at the most." Alice ends the call. She dresses quickly, wets and combs her hair with her fingers, and brushes her teeth. Ella is whining.

"Dammit dog, not now. She grabs the leash and takes the dog outside. "Do it fast today, please dog." Ella starts to sniff her old poops.

Brian is sitting on the porch, smoking a cigarette. His legs are dangling over the side and he is kicking the dirt. Alice pulls the dog to him. "Could you do me a favor? Could you watch my dog as she poops and then bring her back into my apartment? The door's open, it will lock when you shut it."

"Sure. Sorry about the yelling last night, won't happen again, she's out of my life."

"I got that, something about good riddance bitch."

"Not my finest moment."

"No, not really."

"I thought you were going to can the flannel and the shit-kicker boots."

"Tomorrow, for sure."

Alice's car doesn't start. "Damn, damn, damn." She pounds the steering wheel with her fists.

"Take my truck and give me your car keys," Brian says. He hands her his keys.

"It's kind of big, I've never driven a truck before." His truck is a Dodge Ram.

"You'll be fine," he says.

"Thanks, I owe you one."

When the engine starts, the muffler roars.

"You'll get use to the noise," he says.

"I doubt it."

She checks her morning schedule on her laptop, Danny Myers, then Charles Burke and then Harold Doty. "Tough morning," she says out loud.

Two months ago she cracked Burke's dentures when she stepped on them. They were on the kitchen floor. He is still angry. Medicaid doesn't pay for false teeth and he doesn't have the money for a new set.

"I'm eating mush because of you," he tells her every week.

CHAPTER 3

HAROLD DOTY

IT'S A CHALLENGE for Alice to navigate through the debris scattered throughout Harold Doty's house. On the left side of the entrance hallway, from the front door to the kitchen at the end of the hall, are endless piles of newspapers, magazines and empty boxes stacked from the floor to the ceiling. Several piles of dirty laundry are on the floor in the living room and the kitchen. Next to the couch there are four cardboard boxes filled with photo albums, a metal toolbox stuffed with rusted tools, and four boxes of odds and ends. The open space in the hallway between the newspaper piles and the right wall is less than three feet wide.

Doty's house wasn't always a total mess. From when he was first married, at twenty-six, until his wife left him, thirty-four years later, the house was spotless. His wife Donna took pride in having the cleanest house and neatest yard in the neighborhood. She mopped all the floors every third day, dusted above the door sills every Saturday morning and washed the outside of the windows four times a year. In her front yard she had a flower garden that was so big and beautiful, tourists, especially during foliage season, would take a picture of themselves in front of her flowers.

Harold was nearly as persnickety as his wife. Everything he owned was in perfect condition. His tools were neatly arranged on hooks on a brown pegboard that was nailed to the back wall of the garage, above his workbench. The screwdrivers were hung on the pegboard in height order, the longest screwdrivers with the fattest heads on the left and the shortest and thinnest on the right. The same arrangement was repeated for his wrenches, saws, paint scrapers, hammers and the rest of his tools. The saws were always razor sharp. Hoses and extension cords were coiled neatly, never tangled. Spare nails and screws were in labeled jars on the shelf just under the pegboard. The chaos and mess of his house didn't happen overnight but was accumulated gradually over twenty-six years.

Donna left Harold because she couldn't tolerate Vermont winters. She told him many times, starting her first winter in Vermont, her body couldn't handle below zero weather. She frequently warned him when the last of their three children graduated from high school, she would move back to Tucson, Arizona and join her family. He never took her threats seriously, he considered them just background noise. The day their youngest son Stephen graduated from Providence High School, on the drive from the gymnasium back to their house, she told him she was leaving at the end of August. He could join her or not, either way she wasn't going to scrape ice off the car windshield ever again.

The two met when Harold was in the army at Fort Huachuca near Tucson. When she married him, she didn't expect Vermont winters would be so depressing. It wasn't just the snow and the cold that drove her crazy, what was worse was the constant, steel gray, winter sky.

Harold drove a snowplow for the city of Providence in the winter and mowed the lawns at the three town cemeteries and at the town parks during the rest of the year for the Parks Department. "They need me to plow the roads," he said to her when she told him she was leaving Vermont.

"They can find somebody else," she said.

When she left Providence she took just two suitcases of clothes and three photo albums with pictures of her children. The rest of her clothes are still hanging in their bedroom closet. Her three children did not try to change her mind. They had heard her complain for two decades and they always believed her. Her eldest son Ron drove her to the airport.

Harold hasn't seen any of his three children in over nine years. The last he knew his son Stephen was living in Arizona, five blocks from Donna. His daughter Betty has four children he has never met and probably will never meet. Ron is serving a life sentence in Dannemora prison in upstate New York for killing his ex-wife's lover. He caught the two of them in bed at a roadside motel in Plattsburgh and beat the man to death with the desk lamp.

Donna and Harold wrote letters to each other almost daily for the first few months after she left him. By the end of the first year the letters were down to two or three a week and then weekly and by the third year the letters were sent monthly. By the tenth year the only communication between them were Christmas and birthdays cards. In each letter sent the first year Harold told her how much he loved her and he greatly missed her and he wanted her to come back to Vermont. The last line of each of his letters asked, When are you coming home? She never answered his question and never wrote that she loved him. When he retired at sixty-nine he considered moving to Arizona but decided to stay in Vermont. On her seventieth birthday he flew to Tucson. He hadn't seen her since she left and hadn't talked to her since he called her on her sixty-fifth birthday. She met him at the baggage section of the airport. They walked to an airport restaurant and ordered coffee. She asked him if he was still driving the snowplow. He laughed. "I'm too old, I retired seven years ago," he said.

"We never divorced," she said.

"Probably too late now."

She agreed.

When his coffee cup was empty, he kissed her on her forehead, grabbed his bag and walked to the United Airlines ticket counter and exchanged his ticked for a flight leaving in four hours for Atlanta, Georgia and then to Burlington.

"This isn't meant to be," he said. He had planned on staying at least a week, maybe forever. He lost contact with her six years ago. He is pretty certain she is still alive but he is not sure.

. . . .

ALICE IS RUNNING late. She should have been at Harold Doty's house ten minutes ago. She checks the gas gauge. The gauge needle is on empty. "Damn," she says. She has been late six weeks in a row. This will be seven.

Every Tuesday she washes his feet, checks his vital signs, and helps him exercise. If there is a problem she calls his nurse, Jen Mason. Mason cuts Harold's toenails every Friday, checks the various sores and age spots on his body, monitors his breathing, takes his blood pressure and pulse and makes sure he has been taking his insulin.

Harold can't clean his feet or cut his toenails because when he bends over he gets too winded and he gets dizzy. His feet are in bad shape. It hurts him to walk more than fifty yards. All ten toenails are yellowed, thick, brittle and cracked.

He is a smoker. He has smoked since he was twelve, three to four packs a day when he was younger, a chain-smoker by the time he was twenty-five. He smokes only a pack a day or less now. At fifteen bucks a pack, he can't afford more. In every picture of him, from his wedding pictures taken on the steps of the First Baptist Church of Tucson, to the last picture of him, taken eight years ago, there is a cigarette in his hand or in his mouth, almost as if the cigarette were a body part. He has a smoker's barrel chest, thick suck lines on his lips, pale tired blue eyes, yellowed teeth, nicotine stains on his right thumb and index finger, thinning gray hair and stick thin legs. He has a penchant for profanity and racial and ethnic slurs. Every other word is damn, goddamn, fuck, or Jesus H. Christ, not usually spoken in anger but rather as a pause between thoughts.

He spends the first twenty minutes of each morning coughing phlegm from his lungs. When he is done coughing, he walks to the kitchen and grabs a cigarette from one of the packs he keeps in the drawer next to the sink. With the room still dark, he turns on the front stove burner, waits for it to glow red, lights the cigarette on the burner, sucks in deeply and blows a cloud of smoke into the air. In late spring, summer and early fall, after he lights his cigarette, he walks to the porch, in his sweat-stained undershirt and boxer shorts, sits on the top step, and waits for the newspaper. When the weather is cold or raining, he stands in the hall, leans against the wall, stares out the window, and blows smoke rings into the air while he waits.

Twenty years ago the newspaper was delivered by a boy on a bicycle who rode from one house to the next. Eight years ago the paperboy was replaced by a very short woman who drives a rusted Grand Marquis, which had been a cop car in its previous life. She tosses the newspaper, wrapped in a plastic bag, out of the window of her car, to the end of his driveway. Harold is the only person on the street who still gets the newspaper delivered. It takes him nearly ten minutes to walk to the end of the driveway and back to the house because, after every four or five yards, he has to stop, cough up more phlegm, wipe the slime on his pants, and catch his breath for another five yards.

"You're late," he says to Alice as he opens the front door for her. He taps his watch three times with his right index finger. He points to the end of the driveway and asks her to get the newspaper. She pulls it from her nursing bag and hands it to him. "One step ahead of you as usual old man."

He grabs the newspaper from her, pulls it from the plastic cover and scans the front page headlines. "Nothing in this damn rag anyway, never nothing worth reading, what a goddamn waste of money."

"You say that every week. If you don't like it, stop getting the paper."

The house is musty. "When was the last time you opened a window? How can you breathe in here?" she asks. She walks by him, steps over the cats' litter box, walks through the living room, opens the curtains and pulls up the blinds. She tries to open the window but it won't budge.

"Haven't opened it ten years," Harold says.

Harold sits down on the chair facing the television, tosses the newspaper to the floor and takes off his shoes and socks. He tells Alice the big toe on his right foot hurts. He stubbed it on the leg of the kitchen table three days ago and it still hurts.

She grabs the washbasin on the kitchen counter and fills it with warm water. She walks slowly from the kitchen to the living room, careful not to spill any water. When she enters the living room, she looks at the television. Maury Povich is smiling. A bony, white man with very bad teeth, wearing a green muscle shirt and arms covered with tattoos, is nervous. The text under his picture says he is awaiting the DNA results of a paternity test. The audience is chanting, "Baby daddy, baby daddy, baby daddy."

"I seen this one, he's not the father, his brother's the father," Harold says.

"Good to know," Alice says. She places the washbasin next to her feet. She lays a towel on the floor in front of his chair and tells him to lift his feet onto the towel. She kneels on the floor in front of him and puts on a pair of rubber gloves. She dips a cotton towel into the warm water, spreads soap on the towel and gently rubs the soapy cloth against his right heel.

"You're just like Christ, washing the feet of the Apostle Harold."

"I don't think Christ wore rubber gloves."

Harold's toes are black and there is a wound the size of a fifty-cent piece on the ball of his foot. Alice shakes her head. "This is not good, not good at all."

"It's nothing, I bumped my toe, no big goddamn deal."

"It's probably nothing to worry about, but just to be sure, I'm going to have Jen stop by this afternoon."

"It's nothing. A bumped toe. Don't make a goddamn federal case out of it. I'll be fine, it's a minor bruise. I've had worse, a lot worse. Jen doesn't need to come." His voice cracks.

Alice is pretty certain the infection is gangrene. Harold's foot is swollen and foul-smelling and brownish pus is oozing from the wound. She kneels at his feet, washes his toes and dries them with a hand towel she had draped over her right shoulder. She rubs foot cream on his heels. He tells her the lotion feels good. He tries to glimpse down her shirt.

"Mr. Doty, stop it."

"Stop what?" He laughs.

"It's not funny. I've told you a dozen times you can't do that."

"Do what?"

"If you look down my shirt again, I'm going to leave and not come back. I'm tired of it."

"Sorry, I won't do it again." He shakes his head no.

"Don't forget, I am going to send Jennifer this afternoon. Either she will come or someone else will come, depending who's on today, but definitely someone will come this afternoon to check your foot."

"I won't forget, you've told me ten times."

"No, I've told you only twice."

"Even if I forget, where am I going to go? Take that back, I have a dinner date in Paris at seven tonight. I need to leave in ten minutes so call Jen and cancel."

"Make sure you visit museum d'Orsay, it's better than the Louvre."

"I'll add that to my must-see list."

She lightly swats the back of his head with a dry towel. "Very funny," she says. She grabs the TV remote on the floor next to him. "Why do you watch this garbage?" She turns the channel to the Price is Right.

Harold grabs the remote from her and returns to Povich. The audience has just learned the father is the bony man's brother. "I told ya so," the bony man says.

The real father walks on to the set. "I knew it weren't me," the bony man says. The real father also is wearing a tight green muscle shirt. The audience is chanting, "Baby daddy, baby daddy," to the second man as he walks across the stage. Povich is amused. The real father gives the audience the middle finger. His hand is blurred from the television viewers.

"As I said before, total garbage. What's next, Jerry Springer?"

"He's not on 'til noon."

"Can't wait." Alice takes the washbasin and towels to the kitchen. She rinses the basin and places it on the counter and throws the towels into a basket in the broom closet.

Harold is watching the Price is Right. "Happy now," he says.

"Yes, much better."

One of Harold's seven cats has left a mouse head on the porch floor. Alice kicks the head off the porch, to the grass. She backs Brian's truck into the road without checking for traffic. A garbage truck nearly hits her. Her heart pounds hard from the near miss.

"Look where you're going you moron," the truck driver yells. He shakes his fist at her.

It takes several minutes before her pulse is back to normal.

CHAPTER 4

ALICE HAMMOND

WHEN ALICE WAS was fourteen she won a short story contest for middle school students sponsored by the *Providence Herald*. The year she won was the fifteenth anniversary of the contest. Her story and picture were printed in the entertainment section of the Sunday newspaper. She was interviewed by Vermont Public Radio and the local television station. The judges marveled at her story. There were several letters to the editor praising her, especially praise for her clear, crisp and efficient writing style.

What the judges didn't know was she had plagiarized the story, pretty much word for word, from a story her grandmother had written twenty-seven years before. Her grandmother, Pat Hammond, had been a prolific writer. She wrote for two to three hours every night after her three children went to bed. She wrote so often her children had a hard time getting to sleep without hearing the clack, clack, clack of her typewriter. By the time she died, when Alice was ten, she had written five novels and one hundred eighty-six short stories. Fourteen of her stories were published, most in journals few people had ever heard of and she was paid almost nothing for them. One of her stories was featured in *Saturday Evening Post*. *The Providence Herald* ran a story about her passion for writing. None of her novels were printed although her last novel would have been if she had opened the envelope. She thought it was just another rejection and tossed it in her box of rejections.

Everything Pat wrote was stored in cardboard boxes in the attic of the garage at Alice's house. Alice found the boxes when she was twelve. She had heard about her grandmother's stories but hadn't given them much thought until one rainy day in May when she had nothing to do and all of her friends were out of town. She spent the whole afternoon reading. What she liked best about the stories was when she recognized one of her uncles or her father or her mother as one of the main characters in the story. Some of the stories were so close to what had actually happened, they read more like family histories than fiction.

Alice never planned to plagiarize her grandmother's story. She tried writing her own story but everything she wrote displeased her. Before eighth grade she always had been the best student in every subject, in every class. Her math and science knowledge were several grades above her peers and her spelling and grammar were always perfect. She was the best, not because she was the smartest kid, but because she worked harder than everyone else, much harder. Even in first grade she was determined to excel beyond all her classmates. Her drive to excel was not forced by her parents. Many Fridays in the winter, when the weather was good and the snow deep, her father would tell her to skip school and go skiing with him but she always refused. 'It's not right, I can't skip school' she'd say.

Creative writing was the first time she was not first in her class. The course, which was taught by a local author who had four crime novels in print, was open only to the twelve best students in eighth grade. Alice was an easy pick, not only because she was first in every subject but also because she was quiet and well behaved, the perfect combination for an honors student.

Writing well didn't come easily to her and working overtime, like she did with every other subject, didn't help. What she wrote was always competent, her grammar was correct, her paragraphs ended when they should have, and her vocabulary was extremely advanced for a fourteen-year-old. But her stories were boring. She tried very hard to write interesting stories but no matter how hard she tried, nothing helped. It bothered her that the stories written by one of the boys in the class, who didn't seem to try at all, were so much more entertaining and funnier than her stories.

The short story contest was the high point of the year for the creative writing class. A student from the class had won the contest seven years in a row and nine of the past ten years. Alice was determined to win. She sat down with her laptop and tried to write an interesting story. She wrote four different stories. Much to her dismay, all of them were dull. *I'm not going to lose this competition.*

Most of her grandmother's stories were not suitable because they were clearly written by an adult with adult themes. When she read the story about a simple, old man and a group of annoying boys who constantly ridiculed him, she knew she had the perfect story. The only words she had to change were outdated references which made no sense to her. One of the boys in the story wore a T-shirt with the words 'Think Different' on the chest. She took that reference out of her story.

Her teacher praised her. "Alice, this story is very good. Much different and much better from anything you've written before. I'm very impressed."

"Thank you."

The teacher announced her victory to the class. Everyone applauded her. The annoying boy who wrote the funny stories came in second. His story was about a boy who could burp the first twelve notes of the 'Star Spangled Banner'.

Alice did not sleep the night before the awards ceremony. She tossed and turned in her bed and paced, back-and-forth across her room, for over an hour. At two in the morning she threw up. She used the downstairs bathroom so no one would hear her. Her father heard her and greeted her at the bottom of the stairs. "Are you okay?" he said.

"I'm fine, I'm just a little nervous about tomorrow."

"About the awards ceremony?"

"Yes."

"We need to talk." He guided her to the living room couch. "I loved your story, I really did, but I also loved it when your grandmother wrote it thirty years ago."

Alice started to sob. "I so sorry Daddy, I didn't mean to copy grandma's story. I don't know why I did it. I'm the worst person who ever lived."

Her father pulled her to him and hugged her. "Alice, you are not the worst person who ever lived, not by a long shot, I think Hitler's got that pretty much sewn up." He hugged her hard and laughed at his joke.

"I'm glad you think it's funny. When everybody finds out, I will be humiliated."

"It will be hard but you'll survive."

"Why didn't you say something before now?"

"I didn't figure it out until about an hour ago. When I heard you pacing and sighing, I wondered, why are you upset, you wrote an amazing story and everybody is proud of you. I am so proud of you and then I remembered grandma's story." He hugged her again. "I've been laying in bed and listening to you and asking myself, 'What I should do?' I should have come to you an hour ago."

"Are you going to tell Mom?"

"No, you need to tell her."

"I can't do it, I just can't do it. This is so awful."

"Yes, it is awful but remember we still love you, this doesn't change anything."

"I wanted to be the best. I tried, I really did but I couldn't do it."

"Alice, I want you to listen to me and listen carefully. You don't need to be the best at everything, just do your best, that's all that matters."

"Do you think Mom will be mad?"

"Probably."

"Are you?"

"No, I'm not mad. I'm disappointed."

"That's even worse."

"You did a stupid thing. We all do stupid things. The world is not going to end."

"Easy for you to say."

He lifted her up from the couch and walked her to her room. "Get some sleep, we'll figure this out in the morning."

CHAPTER 5

TIM ROGERS

TIM ROGERS IS sitting on his bed, his hands are locked behind his neck. He is staring at the digital clock across the room on the clothes dresser. It is eleven-fifteen. The morning sun is streaming through the bedroom window. Dust is floating in the sunbeam. A *Time* magazine is next to his right thigh and a bowl of Corn Chex cereal is on his lap. Some of the milk from the bowl has spilled onto the sheets. His home health aide, Alice Hammond, is fifteen minutes late. Tim doesn't expect her for at least another fifteen minutes. Earlier than that would be unusual.

He grabs the cereal bowl, leans over the side of the bed and places it on the floor. He slides off the bed and walks six steps to the window. His ankles creak with every step. The bright light at the window burns his eyes. He squints and rubs his eyelids with his thumbs. He closes the window shade and turns on the ceiling light. He searches through the back of his closet for his army uniform from nineteen fifty-five. Today is Memorial Day. Every Memorial Day, Independence Day and Veterans Day he wears his uniform with pride. It doesn't fit him anymore but he wears it anyway. He had marched in every holiday parade, even when it rained or snowed, from nineteen fifty-six until two years ago when his legs hurt so much after the first half mile he had to stop and get a ride back to the high school parking lot where the parade started. His legs hurt so much now he can't leave his apartment without help.

Tim had hoped to go to Korea but he never made it past Fort Benning in Columbus, Georgia. He was a barber on the base. Several officers, who liked the way he cut their hair, routinely blocked his transfer requests. When he returned to Providence he spoke with a thick, southern drawl and said words like fixins and piddling and druthers and y'all. He didn't drop his newly acquired accent until a family from Atlanta moved to Providence and it was clear to everyone in town that his accent was preposterous.

Alice finds an open parking space ten feet from the front door of Tim's apartment building. Usually she parks three blocks away in the Maple Street parking garage. Good thing she is closer today because she has extra baggage. In addition to her nursing bag, she has a small, heavy, Cinderella record player her father gave her on her eighth birthday and a shoulder bag filled with a half-dozen vinyl albums, slow dance music from the nineteen forties and fifties. She borrowed them, without permission, from her father's prized collection. He has over a thousand records from the forties through the eighties, stored in plastic milk crates in his den. When he plays them, which is rare, he handles the records with cotton gloves as if they were evidence at a crime scene. He has specifically barred Alice because she has an amazing bent to drop and break expensive things. He will never miss them, she thought when she took the records.

Rogers lives in a four-room apartment on the second floor of the Blanchard building on North Street in downtown Providence. One hundred years ago the building was the busiest of the three downtown hotels. By nineteen eighty-five all three buildings were vacant eyesores and homes for the homeless and hangouts for bored teenage boys. The Blanchard Hotel closed in nineteen sixty-eight and was empty from then until nineteen ninety when it was renovated as part of an effort to save the dying downtown. Federal funds paid for the renovations. The plan was to build one hundred fifty affordable apartments, eighty in the Blanchard Hotel and thirty-five each in the other two buildings, which supposedly would bring young families and shoppers to the few remaining downtown stores. Only twelve apartments were rented the first year in the Blanchard building and fifteen total in the other two buildings. Most of the current tenets, in all three buildings, are clients of Providence County Mental Health or poor families who can't afford anything else or single men just out of prison. About once a month someone from the Blanchard Hotel is arrested, usually on a drug charge or domestic assault or public intoxication or disturbing the peace or a combination of all four.

The stairs have not been painted since the nineteen ninety renovation. The air in the stairway has a salty taste. The stairs to both the second and third floors are wide but very steep. Most of the wood is dried and cracked. The handrail is loose and wobbles under Alice's right hand. Halfway to the top, she stops, lays the record player on the stair one step above her feet, and rests her tired, left arm.

"Need some help," says one of the tenants of the building, who is sitting in the dark, on the top step, smoking a cigarette. All Alice can see is the red glow of her cigarette and the dark outline of her body. Only eight of the eighteen ceiling lights in the second floor hallway work and none in the stairway.

"No, I'm fine."

The woman ignores her, steps down the stairs, and grabs the record player. "I got this."

Alice pulls the record player away from the woman. "I'm fine, really."

"Bitch, I was just trying to help." She drops the cigarette butt onto the step under her feet, crushes it out with the toe of her right shoe, and steps down the stairs to the ground level and mumbles "fucking bitch" three times.

Alice continues up the stairs, rests at the top, and walks sixty feet to Tim's apartment. A man and a woman are arguing loudly in the apartment across the hall from his door. The man calls the woman a no good, fat, ugly whore and she calls him a lazy, useless, son-of-a-bitch, worthless piece of shit. She tells him to get the fuck out of her apartment or she will call the police. "I'll get a goddamn restraining order," she says.

"Fuck you," he says. He opens the door and steps into the hallway. "I ain't coming back."

Alice turns to look at the man. He is thirty-five, maybe forty, at least six-feet tall and very thin, one hundred fifty pounds or less. His feet are too long for his body and his large ears and exceedingly long nose remind her of Goofy from the Disney cartoons. The woman is standing in the doorway wearing a gray sweatshirt that says, 'I'm with Stupid' with an arrow that points to her left. She is very short and chubby. "He's worthless," she says to Alice and slams her door shut.

"What ya looking at?" the skinny man says to Alice.

She says nothing. She turns away from him and lifts her right hand to knock on Tim's door. Before her knuckles hit the wood, Tim opens the door. "Don't mind him, he's harmless," Tim says.

The skinny man, who is now halfway down the hallway, stops, turns around to face her and Tim. "Fuck you old man," he says.

Tim looks at the record player and the canvas bag filled with the albums. "What's all this?" he asks.

"You'll see. Love your uniform." She touches the arm of the jacket with her left hand and rubs the fabric between her thumb and index finger.

"Me too." He lifts a Johnny Mathis album from her tote bag and holds it up to the light. "Johnny Mathis, his voice was velvet. He should have been the velvet fog not Mel Torme, no comparison."

"My father agrees with you."

"He knows his music."

Alice's task today is to help Tim exercise his legs. His legs are pencil thin and very weak. His ankles are blue and fat. The skin on his legs feels like an air-dried cloth and he has gnarled, enlarged, varicose veins on each leg. He was a barber for forty-four years. Alice looks at his tired legs. "Forty-four years of standing on my feet did this," he says.

Alice walks to the living room, places the record player next to the television and drops her nursing bag and canvas tote to the floor. She plugs the record player cord into the wall socket and opens the top. She selects an album from the bag, pulls the record out of the cardboard sleeve and places it on the turntable. She lifts the needle arm to the fourth track. "It's unbelievable the way you thrill me," Nat King Cole sings.

"I need you to teach me how to dance," Alice says.

"Why?"

"No reason, I want you to teach me how to slow dance, how to waltz."

"Why?"

"Because I don't know how to dance, that's why."

"What do you mean you don't know how to dance? Everybody knows how to dance."

"Not everybody, not me."

"You've never danced?"

"I've danced but not really. Mostly I just shuffle my feet as if I were trying to sand the floor with the soles of my shoes."

"Not ready for Dancing with the Stars?"

"No, not even close."

When Tim was a young man he and his wife Beatrice frequently won dance contests. They were the waltz champions, five years in a row, from nineteen sixty-four to nineteen sixty-eight, at the annual midwinter dance gala at the West Providence American Legion. They won ten straight New Year's Eve waltz contests at the Elks Club and ten Providence Ballroom Dance Club championships in fourteen years. Every September, for seventeen years in a row, they drove four hours to Providence, Rhode Island to compete in the New England Ballroom Dance championship. "Providence to Providence," Tim said at the start of each trip. They competed in both the waltz and the foxtrot. One year they came in third in the waltz, only the eighth Vermont couple ever to win a medal. The third place trophy sits in the china cabinet against the West wall in the living room. On the wall, to the left of the cabinet, there are five pictures of Tim and Beatrice dancing and a framed newspaper article about their fifth Legion win. The headline says, 'Providence's Own Fred and Ginger Win Again.'

Alice pulls her stethoscope and blood pressure cuff from her nursing bad and takes Tim's vital signs. "Looks good," she says.

"What did you expect?"

Alice stuffs her gear into her bag. "What we are going to do today, instead of walking around your apartment, is we're going to dance." She grabs Tim's left hand with her right hand and gently guides him to the center of the living room. "What do I do?"

"Well, mostly you do the opposite of what I do. When I step forward with my left foot, you step backwards with your right foot. And when I move my right foot to my right, you slide your left foot to your left. The slide is important. It makes you look classy. It's really pretty simple."

He grabs her left hand and places it on his side, just above his right hip. He grabs her right hand with his left, interlocks their fingers and lifts their hands so their palms are shoulder high. "All right, let's begin," he says. Nat King Cole is singing, "If you're happier without me, I'll try not to care."

Tim steps slowly forward with his left foot. Alice does not move her right foot. His foot steps on her toes. "Remember, when I step forward with my left foot, you have to step backwards with your right foot, the same distance," he says.

"Got it."

He tries again and steps on her right toes again. He lets go of her right hand, lifts his hand off her hip and steps three paces backwards. "Watch what I do." He takes several dance steps, making elegant circles as he dances and says "One, two, three," with each three-step move. "Got it?"

"Got it."

He grabs her left hand with his right hand and places it on his right side, just above his hip and rests his right hand on her left side, his fingers on her back. "Grab my hand." He holds his left hand shoulders high. She grabs his left hand with her right hand and steadies her left hand on his right side, her fingers clutching his shirt. "Ready?"

"Ready."

He moves his left foot slowly forward, watching her feet to make sure he doesn't step on her toes again. Alice is looking at her feet. She slides her right foot backward. Tim steps to his right. Alice follows with her left foot. He slides his left foot to his right foot. She follows his lead again. He steps backward with his right foot, she steps forward with her left.

"Perfect. By George, Eliza, I think you've got it," he says in a phony English accent.

"Eliza?"

"Eliza Doolittle. My Fair Lady."

"Who?"

He shakes his head in mild dismay. "Don't you young people know anything?"

"Nope."

They dance for five minutes at a pace that is somewhat slower than the music. "It's so loverly," he sings.

"What's so loverly?"

"So loverly, from My Fair Lady, check the album. I am sure your father has it."

"I'll check the internet."

He scratches his nose and steps away from her. "All I want is a room somewhere, far away from the cold night air, with one enormous chair, oooooh, wouldn't it be loverly?" He sings in a low whisper. His voice waivers on the word loverly.

"I'm not sure you're quite ready for Broadway, maybe next year."

"Not this year, next year for sure," he says.

They dance for fifteen minutes more. Nat King Cole is singing, "The party's over, it's time to call it a day."

"I think I need to call it a day. My legs are very tired." His forehead is covered with sweat.

"Oh, I'm so sorry."

"Don't be. It was fun. I haven't danced in years, since Beatrice and I waltzed in our living room the day we sold our house. She was the best dancer in the world. She made me look good. Without her I was just a clod with two left feet. She was Ginger Rogers. I was more like Herman Munster thumping across the dance floor."

"I find that hard to believe. You're as smooth as a duck on the water."

"A very old duck."

She guides him to the recliner and helps him sit. She takes his pulse. It is one hundred forty-seven beats per minute. "Maybe this wasn't such a hot idea," she says.

"It was a great idea. I can't remember the last time I had this much fun. You need at least one more lesson, minimum, maybe a dozen more, just to be on the safe side. Next time, how about some classical music, Strauss would be good, 'Blue Danube' would be perfect."

"I don't think my father has any classical music, just geezer rock and lounge singers."

"I do. And you don't need to lug that heavy old thing up the stairs. The sound is terrible." He points to his CD player on the end table, next to the couch.

"It's a plan." She rechecks his pulse, eighty-one beats per minute. She tells him the number. "Much better," she says.

"Were you worried?"

"No, but if you had a heart attack, I'm not sure how I would have explained the Cinderella record player."

"Doesn't every eighty-nine-year-old man have a Cinderella record player?"

"Sure, that would work." She packs her bags, lifts them onto her left shoulder, unplugs the record player, grabs it with her right hand and walks to the door. She turns to Tim. "See you next week."

"Bring your dancing shoes."

"Are you trying to tell me my boots aren't made for dancing?"

"Yes."

The woman, who was sitting on the top step smoking when Alice ascended the stairs an hour ago, is back, sitting on the top step, smoking another cigarette and comforting Tim's angry neighbor who had kicked out her boyfriend. The angry woman is crying. The smoker woman is cradling the sad woman's head in her lap and is stroking the woman's back. "Let him go, he's not gooden nuff for you," the smoker woman says to the crying woman.

"But I love him so much," the sad woman says.

"You're too good for him," the smoker woman says.

When Alice gets near the two women, they stop talking and don't resume their conversation until she leaves the building.

A parking ticket is stuck under the driver's side windshield wiper. She checks the fine, ten dollars. She opens the car door and tosses the ticket to the passenger's seat. There are seven other tickets on the seat. Before she enters her car, she takes six dance steps on the sidewalk.

"One, two, three; one, two, three," she sings softly to herself, "isn't it loverly."

CHAPTER 6

ALICE HAMMOND

ALICE IS AN hour late for her mother's sixtieth birthday party. She has been reading birthday cards at Walgreens for thirty minutes. She has read every card at least twice. She grabs a card with Snoopy and Woodstock on the cover. Snoopy and Woodstock are doing a happy dance. Both of them are wearing birthday hats and are being showered with confetti. The words above the two dancers say, 'Happiness Is'. The message on the inside says, 'Sixty!' Snoopy is blowing on a party horn and Woodstock is flying upside down, just above Snoopy's head. Alice had rejected the card twice before. "This is just right," she says out loud. A tall woman at the end of the aisle looks toward Alice to see if she is talking to her or to someone else.

Alice is in no hurry to get to the party. Her brother David and sister Laura will be there. David is a fourth-year student at Columbia University medical school in New York City. He is being recruited by so many hospitals for his residency he has lost count, he says when asked. Laura is in her last year at Suffolk University law school in Boston. She is being aggressively recruited by three Vermont law firms and three law firms from Boston. Her senior year she was the editor of the *Suffolk University Law Review*. The pay in Boston is much higher but so is the cost of living; her new friends are in Boston but her old friends are in Vermont. She does not know what to do.

Both of them will tell funny stories about their perfect lives. All of David's colleagues, at least in his stories, have one or more laughable physical or emotional anomalies. One of his professors has a facial tick and is slightly cross-eyed, the office secretary in the surgery department belly laughs at every joke, no matter how lame, and often farts when she laughs. At his Christmas break, David told a story that was so funny their father, Dan, snorted wine through his nose. The story was about a patient who had slithered off the operating table onto the lap of one of the nurses. She was pinned and could not move. David and the surgeon had to roll the man off the nurse. The surgery was successful and all was well. The next day everyone at the hospital, from the janitors to the CEO, had a great laugh. The only person who didn't laugh was the hospital's lawyer. That line made Dan laugh hardest of all. David's story was filled with hilarious details, especially about the look on the nurse's face when she was pinned to the floor.

Alice could tell them, but she probably won't, that yesterday, when she entered a patient's apartment, the woman's overly friendly, very large Great Dane surprised her by jumping, paws first, up to her chest, which forced her backwards. She tripped over a vacuum cleaner, fell hard, and hurt her wrist. That's why she is wearing a wrist brace.

Three-and-a-half years ago, when Alice had only four months left at Johns Hopkins medical school, she packed her bags and left. Her father was furious. On her daily rounds at the hospital, one of her professors often would lightly bump into her and each time pretend it was an accident. He frequently implied to the other students that the two of them were having an affair, which was not true. Even casual comments to her, especially if there was an audience, were spiked with sexual tension.

One evening he showed up at her apartment with a draft copy of an article he said he was writing for a major medical journal, and a bottle of red wine, two long stem wine glasses and a single red rose.

He said he wanted her opinion on his article. "I think I'll submit it either to the *New England Journal of Medicine* or the *American Journal of Medicine*," he said. He was wearing too much cologne and had on a new, tight-fitting, red sweater and an Apple watch. He said his arms were sore from his workout. He had bench-pressed one hundred sixty-six pounds, that's why his arms were so sore. He rubbed his flexed, left arm muscle with his right hand. She told him to leave the article because she was not feeling well, she would read it later. He said, no, let's read it together, that way I can get a better idea about what you really think. He tried to push his way into her apartment.

"Please leave," she said.

"Don't flatter yourself. I just wanted you to read my article."

She left school the next day.

Three years later, Dan is still greatly disappointed Alice left medical school. He is head of surgery at Providence Regional Medical Center. Her grandfather was head surgeon there when the hospital was called Providence County Hospital and her great-grandfather was head surgeon when the hospital, which back then had twice as many patients but was a third the size, was called Providence Hospital. The Hammond Surgery Center was named for Alice's grandfather but most people today think it was named for her father. When Dan's patients make that mistake, he politely corrects them.

Dan always considered Alice's life, like his, to be preordained. She would go to the University of Vermont for her undergraduate study, as had her father, grandfather and great-grandfather, then to medical school and a residency at Johns Hopkins, then a surgical residency in Boston, spend a year doing charity work, either in an American inner-city or in Africa, and then come back to Providence where she would join him at the Hammond Surgery Center. Until her last year at medical school, Alice agreed with him.

When she arrives at her parent's house, her father meets her on the porch. "So you couldn't be on time for your mother's sixtieth birthday."

"Dan, you promised," his wife Lesley says from the dining room.

"Your sister drove four hours from Boston and your brother drove six hours through terrible New York City traffic and they were both here on time," he says so loudly everyone in the house hears him.

"I was busy. I was at work."

The four Hammonds had finished their meal twenty minutes before and were waiting for Alice for the cake and gifts. Lesley fills the plate in front of Alice with three pieces of chicken, a scoop of mashed potatoes and four, cold, limp, asparagus spears.

"Eat, you're so skinny," she says.

"I'm fine Mom, one of my patients fed me. I'll just have cake."

"You need to eat."

Alice tells her mother again she is fine and is not hungry.

Laura retrieves the cake from the kitchen. "I got the cake at this fabulous bakery in the North End," she says. Everything she buys in Boston is fabulous. There are only two candles, the numbers six and zero.

Lesley closes her eyes and blows the candles out. "I've made my wish."

"What is it?" Dan says.

"Can't say, if I do, it won't come true."

Dan scrapes the frosting off his piece of cake with his fork and places it on the edge of his plate. Laura watches him remove the frosting. "Alice, how long do you expect to work as a home health aide? I thought you would have moved on by now, it's a pretty physically demanding job," he says.

"It is, for sure. I don't know how long I'll last, Dad, I really don't. Some women do it their whole lives. I don't know how they do it. I love my patients. They need me. Some of them barely know who their doctor is. But they know who I am and they know who their nurse is and they know who the other home health aides are and they know they need their feet washed and their wounds dressed and their muscles rubbed. Most of them could go months without seeing their doctor but if I miss one day, they're in trouble."

"Excuse me, Mother Teresa, I didn't know we were in the shadow of a saint," David says.

Laura hands her mother a red envelope. "Open it," she says. Inside there are two tickets to *Ragtime* at the Bosch Theater in Boston and a gift card for two nights at the Omni Parker House. "Bob and I saw it last week, it's a great play."

"Oh how wonderful," Lesley says. She holds the tickets and gift card in front of her chest as if she were posing for a picture for the newspaper.

"We've seen the play. It was all right, a little preachy," Dan says.

"I can exchange the tickets for another play," Laura says. Her voice cracks.

"No, no, no, it's just perfect. I would love to see the play again. I don't even remember what it was about," Lesley says.

David's gift is two tickets to a game between the Red Sox and New York Yankees at Yankee stadium, two airline tickets from Burlington to New York, and a voucher for three nights at the Gramercy Park Hotel.

"Thank you David. How could you afford this?"

"Relax Mom," he says.

"Now we're talking," Dan says.

"I can't match them but I think you'll like this book," Alice says. She gives her mother *Sing Unburied Sing* and the Snoopy card.

"Didn't your book club read that last month?" Dan says to Lesley.

"No, we did not." She says the words, 'you did not' as if each word were its own, angry sentence.

"I can take it back, no problem," Alice says.

"Don't listen to your father. I have not read this book. It is a wonderful gift."

David reaches across the table and lightly taps the wrist brace on Alice's left arm. "What's with the wrist, get in to fight with one of your patients? Joining WWE?"

"I tripped over a buckle in the rug in my living room."

"That place is a dump. I told you I'd help you buy a condo," Dan says.

"I'm happy where I am."

Dan grabs the book from Lesley and reads the plot summary on the book's cover flap. "Sounds boring," he mumbles. He places the book on the table, next to his dinner plate. "I heard you got really stuck in the mud recently," he says to Alice.

"Yes, I did."

"Thank god for your triple A card," Dan says.

"It was a great present Dad, for sure." She shakes her head, annoyed.

"I heard you found one of your patient's dead, face first on his living room floor, and he was so heavy you couldn't roll him over."

"I don't know where you heard that, Dad, but it's none of your business." One thing Alice has learned at her job is there are no secrets in Providence. She checks the time on her phone. "Sorry all, but I have to go."

"You just got here," Lesley says.

"I know, Mom, but I've got to go. I have a very early job tomorrow morning." She is a bad liar.

Dan walks with her to the sidewalk. "Alice, I am not trying to be a jerk. I just want what's best for you. What you're doing is great work, I really do get it. Mom was a home care nurse."

"I know she was. Why did she quit?"

"She stopped when you were three, when David was born. Two kids and a full-time job was too much. It didn't help that I was never home." He hugs her. "Alice, you can do much better than a home health aide, you've got to know that."

"I don't know if I can or not."

"Anything I can do to help you?"

"Not really."

"Did something happen to you in Baltimore? You haven't been the same since you came home."

"I just wanted out. I was tired of being number one, really tired of being number one."

"I love you, you know that, right?"

"I know, Dad." She hugs him. "And just so you know, I don't plan to be a home health aide forever. I don't know how much longer, maybe another year, maybe less. I'm in a fine place now. I love the work, I really do. But I can't do this forever. Even if the money were better, I'm not sure how much longer my back will hold out. When I tried to roll my patient over I wrenched my back, it hurt for days."

"I take it the wrist injury was work related?"

"I tripped over a vacuum cleaner when one of my patient's dog jumped on me."

"Ouch."

At her apartment Ella greets her at the door. Her cat Boo is sitting on the top of the refrigerator watching her feed the dog. The cat is not happy the dog has moved in. She checks her calendar. Clyde Nason's funeral is tomorrow.

CHAPTER 7

ALICE HAMMOND

THE DAY ALICE left Baltimore she took the Amtrak train to Providence. The drive time from Baltimore to Providence is just under eight hours. The train takes eleven hours when it runs on time.

She packed her clothes and shoes in a small suitcase and three garbage bags and stuffed her laptop, two novels, her phone, two sweaters and a set of earphones into her backpack. She left her college books in the apartment and everything else she owned, which wasn't much, a Bluetooth speaker, two concert posters, several framed pictures of her friends, a sleeping bag and a tent, some dishes, glasses, cups, pans and silverware, her bathroom essentials, and her bicycle and bike helmet. She left a check for two hundred sixty-seven dollars on the kitchen table with a note to her roommate.

'Nicki, I'm going back home to Vermont. Sorry I couldn't say goodbye. It's complicated. This $267 should cover what I owe for the rest of this month. You can have my bike. Use it, sell it, give it away, it's yours now. As for my books, get rid of them, throw them away, burn them, sell them, I don't care, just get rid of them. You've been a good friend, I will miss you.'

When she got in the taxi to go to Penn Station the cabdriver wouldn't give her a ride until she showed him a credit card. "I wasn't going to pick you up, you look homeless," he said.

The message board said the train would be two hours late. She bought a *Marie Claire, Elle* and *Vanity Fair* at the newsstand. The lead story in Vanity Fair was about Frank Sinatra and the Rat Pack. Except for Sinatra, she had never heard of any of the others.

A short man with a long, gray beard sat next to her. He also had a backpack and several garbage bags full of clothes. He was wearing a red winter parka, wool pants, and a blue baseball cap, and he smelled like wet wool. He removed his right boot, pulled off his sock, and cleaned the dirt under his big toe with the blade of a pocket knife. Alice moved to a different seat. He followed her. One of the station cops, who had been watching the man, walked up to them and said, "Hey buddy, time to move on." He grabbed the man's shoulders and lifted him off his seat.

"Thanks," Alice said to the cop. Her phone rang. It was Nicki. She did not answer it. She sent her roommate a text: 'When I'm ready, I'll call you.'

Before she entered the train, the porter asked to see her ticket. He had not asked any of the other passengers for their tickets. Stepping up to the train car was difficult with the three garbage bags and a suitcase. At the top step she dropped one of the bags to the ground. It split open. She got off the train and gathered the clothes that were splayed across the cement. The passengers behind here were annoyed at the delay.

At Penn Station in New York City the train detached most of the cars. There was a half-hour wait until departure. She left the train, walked to a newsstand, bought a Hersey bar and a chocolate milk, and returned to her seat. The man in the seat across from her pointed to one of her garbage bags that had fallen from the overhead storage to the aisle floor.

"Is that yours?" he said.

She grabbed the bag and stuffed it back on the rack. "Yes, and no, I am not homeless."

She tried reading an article in *Elle* about Selena Gomez but she couldn't concentrate. All she could think about was her teacher, Marshal Thompson. She closed her eyes, put on her earphones and listened to the music on her phone. *I should have said something, I should have complained, what was I thinking, why didn't I say something. Modern women don't just give up.*

"Hey, young lady, you realize you're thinking out loud," said the man across the aisle. "We get it, you should have said something."

She remembered the first time Thompson touched her. She had gotten a perfect score on his test. He called her to the front of the classroom. "Come here, next to me," he said. He stretched his right arm across her back and pulled her to him. Her left side was flush against his right side. He gently squeezed her right shoulder. "Ladies and gentlemen, fellow students, your classmate Alice Hammond not only got one hundred on my very difficult test, she is the only person who has ever gotten a perfect score. She knows more about cancer than I do." He laughed, squeezed her shoulder a second time and then released his grip. He and the other students applauded her.

Four days later she and several of her classmates were eating lunch in the cafeteria. The chair next to Alice was empty. "Do you mind?" Thompson said to the group. He dominated the discussion for the next fifteen minutes. He told them he had been a consultant for the HBO show The Wire. "David Simon, what a piece of work," he said. None of the students knew who David Simon was.

"Do you guys like DJ Blaqstarr?" he asked them.

"He's all right," one of the men said who was sitting across from Thompson.

"I bet you didn't know he was Charles Smith before he was Blaqstarr, the bad boy rapper." He squeezed Alice's left thigh. "How are you doing Alice?"

"Fine."

When he left the group, he used Alice's shoulder to brace himself as he rose from his chair.

"It's been real, ladies and gentleman, see you tomorrow," he said. Two weeks later he found her studying in a secluded section of the library. She studied in the same spot every day, a location so private most students didn't know it was there.

"Fancy meeting you here," he said. His words startled her. He had followed her from the cafeteria to the library and had waited a half-hour before he approached her. He grabbed a chair from the cubicle next to hers and dragged it to her chair. "Is everything going well?"

"Yes."

"Are you enjoying my class?"

"Yes."

"You're a great student."

"Thank you."

He pulled his chair so close to her, their knees were touching. He leaned to her and grabbed both of her shoulders.

"It's such a pleasure having you in my class."

Alice did not respond.

"You're looking exceptionally fine today," he said. He massaged her shoulders for a few seconds. His thumbs flicked her bra straps under her shirt. She pushed her chair away from him and checked the time on her cell phone.

"I just remembered, I have to meet someone in fifteen minutes." She stuffed her books, pens and laptop into her knapsack.

See you tomorrow," he said as she walked away from him, "looking good."

When she got back to her apartment she tried to study but could not. She ran to the bathroom and threw up. The vomit burned her nose.

The train jolted forward. Alice opened her eyes and removed her earphones. She looked out the window of the train car.

"Where are we?" she asked the man across the aisle.

"We entered Vermont about ten minutes ago. I should tell you, you continued to think out loud, either that or you've been talking in your sleep. I know a lot more about you than I should."

"Sorry about that."

"Don't worry, it's just me, look around, there's no one else in this car," he said.

She stood up, scanned the car from front to back and saw he was right. She walked through the train car toward the club car. There were four passenger cars in all and fifty, possibly sixty people total. In the dining car two men were playing cards and a young boy and his father were watching a movie on a laptop. She bought a tuna fish sandwich and a Coke. She took a bite from the sandwich and felt sick. She threw the food and the soda into the garbage.

She walked back through the three coaches to the last car. The man sitting across the aisle was asleep. She went into the bathroom and wept.

The porter knocked on the door. "Are you okay in there?" he said.

"I'm fine," Alice said.

"Are you sure?"

"Yes, I'm sure," she said as she opened the door. She and two others got off at the Providence station.

He father met her at the loading dock. "What happened Alice?"

"Nothing happened, I don't want to be a doctor."

"I wasn't born yesterday, something happened, you wouldn't have just quit," he said.

"I did just quit, it's that simple."

"Don't take me for a fool."

"I'm not taking you for a fool, Dad. Nothing happened, I was sick of it."

He grabbed the two garbage bags and the pile of clothes from her and carried them to his car. "I called the college. You can go back whenever you're ready."

"I'll never be ready, it's over."

CHAPTER 8

CLYDE NASON

CLYDE NASON'S FUNERAL is at the Providence Congregational Church. Everyone in town calls the building The White Church. During the Vietnam War it was the church where a young man, regardless of denomination or religion, could get counseling on how to become a conscientious objector. Today, it is known mostly for the funny sayings that appear weekly on its announcement board.

Alice parks her car in front of the message board. The sign says: Seven Days Without Jesus Makes One Weak. She smiles at the sign. She checks her phone. There is a text from her mother. She deletes the message without reading it. She turns her phone off, wraps it in her sweater, and tucks the sweater and the phone under the passenger's seat. She tries to lock the car doors but the locks don't work.

The minister is standing at the front door, at the top of the eight steps from the sidewalk to the landing. One of the steps is cracked and should be replaced. He is not wearing a jacket and he looks cold. "Greetings," he says to Alice as she climbs the stairs.

"Clyde Nason?" she asks.

"Yes." He points to the door. On a card table at the entrance to the nave there is a picture of Clyde. He is young and strong. He is holding a chainsaw in his left hand. His T-shirt says: Vermont is for Loggers. There is a golden retriever resting on his feet.

Nine people are sitting in the pews. Jennifer Mason, Clyde's nurse, is in the last pew on the left reading the prayer card given to her by the usher. Alice joins her. Jennifer stands up and hugs Alice. "Very sad," Jennifer says.

Eight people enter the church including Clyde's brother Bill and his wife Charlotte.

The minister walks to the front of the church and turns to the congregation. "Welcome. We are gathered here not to mourn the death of Clyde Nason but to honor his life," he says. Everyone stands. "Please sit," he says.

He reads a passage from Revelation. "He will wipe away every tear from their eyes, and death shall be no more, neither shall there be mourning, nor crying, nor pain anymore, for the former things have passed away." He looks to the eighteen people in the pews for a reaction but there is none. "Clyde was a throwback to another era, a mountain man, a man with an indomitable spirit."

One of the two men sitting in the last pew on the right whispers to the other man, "What does indomitable mean?"

"I don't know, strong, I think," the second man says. They are the loggers who found Clyde the day after he was pinned under the fallen tree. When they found him, they thought he was dead.

The minister gives several facts about Clyde that aren't totally correct. The taller of the two loggers shakes his head in mild amusement. The minister can tell from the reaction of the few who are assembled he has lost them.

"All right, I'll be honest, I never met Clyde. I understand he was a wonderful man but I did not know him. I wish I had, but I did not. Would anyone like to add something about Clyde that tells his story, he deserves more than what I can give," the minister says. There is no reaction. "Please, someone, anyone, what made Clyde special?"

Clyde's brother Bill is checking emails on his phone. One of the loggers is checking his watch.

"I will say something," Alice says. She stands up, grabs the top of the pew in front of her with both hands and squeezes the wood. "You are right, he was a wonderful man. He was kind, and gentle, and funny and he loved the forest. His descriptions of the woods were so vivid you felt like you were there with him. He wasn't a religious man but he was very spiritual. The forest was his church. And he was a damn good chess player. I was lucky to know him."

"I'll second that," Jennifer Mason says. She stands next to Alice and places her left hand on Alice's right shoulder. "One time he told me a story about the time he found a small bird that had fallen out of its nest. He climbed forty feet up the tree to put the bird back in the nest. The mother bird just watched him from ten branches above the nest as if it were normal for a big, burly logger to save a tiny bird. I was lucky to know him too." She wipes tears from her eyes with her left shirtsleeve.

"Anyone else?" the minister says. There is no reaction from the other sixteen. He opens his Bible to a page he had saved with a green ribbon. "In my Father's house are many rooms. If it were not so, would I have told you that I go to prepare a place for you? And if I go and prepare a place for you, I will come again and will take you to myself, that where I am you may be also." He invites them to the undercroft. "We have sandwiches and snacks and coffee. Please join me. My name is Reverend Ron Cady. Thank you all for coming. Please sign the guestbook at the back of the church." He silently counts the number of people in the pews and sighs.

"What's an undercroft?" the shorter of the two loggers asks the other logger.

"The cellar, I think," the taller logger says.

Bill Nason turns off his phone and puts it in his right, back pocket. The service took just twenty-eight minutes. "I suppose we should go downstairs," he says to Charlotte. She nods.

The stairs to the undercroft are narrow and the ceiling is low. All the men have to stoop slightly so as not to hit their heads; not a problem for Jennifer, Alice or Charlotte. The undercroft smells like burned coffee and Lestoil. The room is much darker than the upstairs. It takes everyone a few seconds to get used to the low light. On a blackboard, at the far end of the room, someone has printed, in dark blue chalk, 'Love is our true destiny. We do not find the meaning of life by ourselves alone.' Under the quotation is the name Thomas Merton, written in cursive script as if Merton had signed it himself.

A very short, older woman, possibly in her eighties, wearing a blue apron, is standing next to a table that has a platter of egg salad sandwiches and a second platter of ham and cheese sandwiches, all on white bread, cut in small triangles, and the crust has been removed. A coffee pot, napkins, cups and paper plates are next to the food platters. The loggers each grab a sandwich triangle and a cup of coffee. The taller logger pours the contents from five Sweet'N Low packets into his cup.

"Have a little coffee with your fake sugar?" his friend says.

The minister offers his right hand to the loggers. "Glad you could come. Take more food, we have plenty." He shakes the taller man's hand. He turns to Alice and shakes her hand. "Thank you for bailing me out. I should have done better. I am so sorry."

"No problem. I'm Alice Hammond. I was Clyde's home care aide."

"Jennifer Mason." She shakes his hand. "I was his nurse and his friend."

"Sounds like Clyde was a pretty good man," Ron says.

"He was a very good man," Alice says.

Bill Nason steps behind Alice. She does not see him or hear him. "Kind and gentle, seriously?" he whispers directly into her ear and taps her right shoulder. His words and touch startle her. "My brother was a lot of things but kind and gentle, I don't think so," he says so loud that everyone in the room hears him. He is too close to Alice. She steps back and bumps into the food table.

"He was kind to me," Alice says.

"Of course he was, you're a young woman, who wouldn't he be kind to you."

"That has nothing to do with anything. Your brother was a good man," Jennifer says.

"Yes, he was a good man, a very good man," Bill says. He grabs an egg sandwich and rips it in half with his teeth. He walks to the stairway, turns to Alice, and mumbles to himself as he walks up the steps to the main floor. "Kind and gentle, what a joke."

Charlotte pushes him up the stairs, shakes her head and sighs.

Clyde never married. He came close several times but there was always something wrong. One woman talked too much, another talked too little. One sniffed constantly, which drove him insane, and another had sour body odor. One woman kept comparing him to her ex-husband and another compared him to her father. In either case he didn't measure up well. The only perfect woman for him died in a boating accident when Clyde was thirty-six. She died the same day he had bought an engagement ring for her. He learned the news when he got home from the jewelry store. He placed the ring in his toolbox. He considered selling it many times but he never did.

Clyde started logging right out of high school. He was six foot four, two hundred four pounds of solid muscle. He had earned two football scholarships, one to the University of New Hampshire and the other from the University of Rhode Island, but he wasn't interested. He knew from when he was a little boy, he wanted to be a logger.

When he was twenty-eight he set a New England record for the caber toss at the Highland Games in Lincoln, New Hampshire. He had a near perfect throw. A picture of him, with a long caption, was in the Providence Herald. In the picture, his left foot is resting on the caber and the trophy is cradled in his arms. The headline said, 'Providence Man Sets Caber Toss Record.' Alice found the clipping one day when she was searching for his medical records. She asked him about the trophy. He grabbed the clipping from her. "It was a long time ago," he said. He crumbled the clipping into a ball and threw it toward the wastebasket.

Alice checks the time on her phone. It's only eleven-fifty. She thought the funeral service would run longer. She has an hour until her next home visit. She will buy Ella a bag of dog food. She has a text from her boss, Susan Young. 'Don't forget, your evaluation is at four today. It's important!' Alice shakes her head. *Most likely I will get one more lecture about personal boundaries with my patients.*

In the glove compartment in her car she has the news clipping about when Clyde set the caper toss record. The day he crumbled the article into a ball and tossed it against the wall, she retrieved it and stuck it in her nursing bag.

"What are you going to do with that?" he said.

"Not sure. It's a great picture."

She opens the glove box, grabs the clipping and rereads the caption. *Goddamn he was handsome.*

CHAPTER 9

SUSAN YOUNG

SUSAN YOUNG DRAGS the eraser end of a green pencil so hard across her laptop screen she cracks the wood. Today is the start of the annual evaluations of her staff, the worst three weeks of her year. She must meet with all twenty-four home care aides individually, tell them what they did right and wrong over the past year, write a two-page evaluation for each aide and have each woman sign her evaluation, even if she doesn't agree.

She hates evaluations. They are time consuming and totally useless. It's a no-win situation for her and for them. If she adds anything negative, that is all the employee sees, even if ninety percent of the evaluation is positive. If all her comments are positive, the evaluation will be used against her should she need to fire someone.

Susan is the supervisor for the home health aides. In a perfect world she would replace about a half dozen of them but it is not a perfect world, at least not for the home health aide division at the agency. She needs twenty-eight aides and could use thirty. She has only twenty-four and is not likely to get more anytime soon. Most of the aides are fifty or older, seven are over sixty, and three are over seventy. Finding young people willing to work as hard as they do for thirteen bucks an hour is nearly impossible. If any of her current staff retires, she will be in big trouble.

Her first evaluation is at four this afternoon with Alice Hammond. Alice is both her best employee and her worst. Best because she never misses a day of work, she fills in on her days off when needed, the patients love her, and the quality of her work, especially her carefully crafted wound dressing changes, is the best at the agency. Worst because her visits take way too long, she gets too involved with her patients, and she is blowing through the department's overtime budget.

When Alice started at the agency several of the veteran home care aides held a betting pool on when she would quit. No college graduate had ever lasted more than nine months, most less than three. The winner of the pool bet Alice would last eleven months. Her bet was four months longer than the second place bet. She won forty-four dollars.

Before Susan was promoted to home health aide supervisor, she had absolutely no idea the job would be so difficult. It is a rare day when all the home health aides scheduled to work actually show up. Their cars break down, their kids are sick, they are sick, their parents are sick or their kid's teacher needs to see them immediately. So many reasons not to work Susan has lost count. And it has not helped that four months ago the agency got new laptop computers for all the staff and most of the aides, even some of the RNs, can't figure out the new coding program. Several of them have threatened to quit.

Agency CEO Charles Connor has given Susan two more months to get all her staff up to speed. "How hard could it be?" he said to her at the last staff meeting. Alice is the only home health aide who is under thirty, the only one who went to college, and the only aide who learned the new coding system in just one day. What does typing data have to do with giving a bed bath? Not much, Susan thinks every time one of her best aides screws up the coding.

The day Susan got the job as supervisor was a very good day, no more weekends, no more nights, no holidays, she could take a vacation whenever she wanted to, no more angry barking dogs, no more worried spouses or adult children of her elderly patients watching her every move and telling her what she had done wrong, and best of all, more pay for less work. She and her husband Conrad celebrated with champagne and flowers. She posted a message about the promotion on Facebook. All of her friends liked her post and most sent happy comments. She thought her new job would be wonderful. She was wrong. Her days start very early, usually well before seven, and don't end until five p.m. or later, and that doesn't include the time she spends reading work emails at home. She has never calculated her per-hour pay but most likely it is less than when she was a staff nurse. If she could go back in time she probably would reject the promotion. Middle management is terrible. She gets complaints from all sides but has almost no power to change anything.

Later this morning Susan meets with agency CFO Charles Potter. In private, all the aides call him Little Charles and they call Connor, Big Charles. Susan knows what will happen at the meeting today with Potter. He will tell her the productivity in her department is too low and show her a colorful graph that proves what he just said. He will call her patients, clients or customers, and somewhere in the conversation he will use the word cohort and tell her she needs to think outside the box. He will show her the trend line for her department and tell her the trend is troubling and ask her what she plans to do to fix it. She will tell him, as she has once a month for the past eight months, she is doing the best she can with the staff she has. That's not good enough, he will tell her. She won't say anything. Instead she will bite her lip, walk away angry and think, four more years until retirement, I can do this.

. . . .

SUSAN GUIDES ALICE past the four hallway cubicles to the agency's conference room which is directly opposite the CEO's office. There is a poster in the conference room of a kitten hanging from a trapeze swing. The caption says: Hang in There. One of the first things Connor did when he took the job was to hang inspirational posters throughout the building. His favorite says: It's not about being the best, it's about being better than you were yesterday. On that poster there is a picture of a woman climbing a steep cliff. Her body is surrounded by the setting sun. She is young, thin and fit and is wearing black tights and a tight-fitting black top.

The conference table has six, leather chairs on each side and two chairs at each end. The table and chairs take up most of the room. The agency's board of directors met earlier this morning and no one has cleaned up the mess. Susan points to the far end of the table, which is clean. She is holding Alice's personnel folder in her left hand. She drops the folder on the table and removes two copies of this year's evaluation. The chairs squeak when the women sit down.

"Alice, you've been here almost three years, nobody thought you'd make it this long," Susan says.

"I know, I was tempted to bet on myself in the when-will-Alice-quit pool. I could have won easily. I'm the Tom Brady of home health, I'll never quit."

Susan laughs. "You knew about the betting pool?"

"The ladies aren't very good at keeping secrets."

"I'm embarrassed to admit it but I was in the pool. I bet you'd last six months and fourteen days. Obviously I was wrong." She pauses. Alice smiles. "Don't take this wrong but why are you still here?"

"I love it here. I love my patients, even the ones who drive me nuts, well most of them, and I admire the nurses and the aides and therapists and everybody here. Before I was hired I had no idea what you all do. My mother was a home care nurse and until the day before my interview I had never asked her what she did. I can't believe that. I was so focused on becoming a doctor, I never considered anything else."

"I don't know what more to say, you're a good worker. You're never sick and you fill in on your off days. I could use two more like you," Susan says. She hands both copies of the two-page evaluation to Alice. "I need you to sign here." She points to the original document. She taps the bottom of the second page with her right index finger.

Alice reads the evaluation. It says the same as it did last year, she is a great employee and she does quality work, but she has boundary issues with her patients and she is often late for her visits.

"I agree," Alice says. She signs the paper and hands both copies back to Susan.

"Any questions?" Susan says

"Not really."

Susan tells her she must retake the on-line course on patients, staff boundaries.

"That will be my third time. The third time must be the charm." Alice laughs. "I'm a pretty slow learner."

Alice, you must take this seriously. You spend way too much time with your patients. You're not their friend, you're their caregiver. Don't cross that line. When you do, it confuses them."

"I know. I will change."

"I've just learned about the chess games with Clyde Nason. Please don't ever do that again."

"I won't. It wasn't the chess, it was his stories. His stories were so funny and so interesting. When he'd tell me one I'd literally lose my sense of time."

"I'll get you a watch."

"No need, no one else tells stories like he did."

"Alice, we don't pay you to listen to stories. If you listened less you'd be on time more. Getting to work on time is a skill you don't have. You need to improve your on-time record this year."

"I will, I promise."

"When your job is done, leave. If it would help, say that to yourself ten times every morning on your way to your first visit." Susan hands Alice a copy of her evaluation.

When the two women exit the conference room, Charles Connor, who is standing in the hallway, summons Alice to him with a finger curl. "So how'd it go?" he said.

"Fine."

"Not ready yet to go back to med school."

"No, not yet."

"Your father will be upset. He's not a happy camper."

"No, he is not."

"Despite what he thinks, we're very happy to have you here."

"Thanks."

At her apartment her dog Ella has taken a dump behind the toilet and looks ashamed. She pets the dog's head. "At least you did it in the bathroom little buddy," she says to the dog. Ella licks her ankles. Her cat Boo is clawing the couch.

CHAPTER 10

MARIA GALLO

ALICE FILLS A yellow, plastic washbasin with water from the kitchen faucet. She checks the temperature with her elbow. The water is warm and soothing. She carries the washbasin to the living room and places it on a side table next to a hospital bed. The bed barely fits in between the couch and the television. Maria Gallo is laying on the bed under a thin, pink, cotton blanket and a white sheet, staring at the ceiling. Her husband Tony is watching her and half reading a magazine. He is sitting on a kitchen chair next to the bed. He has read three pages of an article on global warming but does not remember one thing from the story. Maria notices a spider walking across the ceiling at the far corner of the room. She considers telling Tony about the spider but decides not to bother.

Their thirteen-year-old daughter Celeste is standing in the doorway, leaning against the door frame. She is angry that her mother is in the living room. Three months ago Maria moved from her upstairs bedroom to the living room when it became too difficult for her to climb the stairs to the second floor. Celeste watches Alice walk across the room with the filled basin. If Alice spills any water on the floor she will tell her to be more careful and to pick up the mess, this isn't your house. Alice does not spill any water so Celeste has nothing to say to her this time.

Maria has cancer. The cancer started in her breast two years ago and has spread throughout her body. Until four months ago, her husband Tony and her father Patrick Bove were sure they would find a cure for her. They have spent hundreds of hours searching the internet and comparing notes. Every time Maria's doctor said there was no hope they forced her to change to a new doctor. Five months ago they traveled to Juárez, Mexico and met with a physician who said he had a cure for her but he needed fifteen thousand dollars up front and five thousand more when she was cured. His cure has an eighty-six percent success rate, he said. They told him they would go back to Vermont and get him the money. You have one month, he told them. Maria stopped them. "I am sick. I am dying. Don't waste one more cent on this foolishness," she said to them when they explained their latest cure for her. "None of your damn cures have worked, this one won't either."

Alice lowers the left side rail. She grabs a pair of latex gloves from a box of gloves in her nursing bag and tugs them onto her hands.

"If it doesn't fit, you must acquit," Tony says to her. He laughs and she smiles. He has told this joke several times before. She offers him a pair of gloves but he declines. She pulls the blankets down to Maria's knees.

Tony removes Maria's hospital gown, rolls it into a ball and places it on the table that holds the television. He slowly rolls his wife onto her right side. Alice places two towels under Maria's torso and pulls the bed covers up to her chin. Maria is very light, just eighty-four pounds at last check. When she was the assistant principal at Providence Middle School she was one hundred forty-eight pounds of pure power. Her main job was to enforce discipline. Most of the students were afraid of her, not afraid of her like the fear of a stranger, but afraid like the fear of disappointing a parent. When she left school last October the students were so upset Principal John White had to call in grief counselors to talk to them.

"How are you doing Mrs. Gallo?" Alice asks.

"It's Maria. I've told you that before." Her voice is so soft Alice has to place her right ear near Maria's lips to hear her.

"What did she say?" Tony says.

"She said she's fine," Alice says.

Tony doesn't believe her.

Alice wets a washcloth, wraps it around her right hand, softly wipes Maria's eyelids, and pats them dry with a hand towel.

"You're rubbing too hard, you'll hurt her," Tony says. He grabs the wet towel from Alice and repeats what she had just done. His stroke is so light the cloth barely touches Maria's skin. "That's how you should do it."

"I will try to be more gentle." Alice rinses the wet cloth and squirts a gob of soap on it, careful not to get any soap into the rinse basin. She washes and dries Maria's face, neck and ears. There is a thick wad of ear wax in both ears.

"Better," Tony says.

Maria catches Alice's eyes with her eyes, blinks a message to her and nods her head to let Alice know she has something to tell her. Alice lowers her head to Maria's face, so close her right ear is touching Maria's lips. "He means well, he really does," she whispers.

"I know."

"I know what?" Tony asks.

"Nothing, the warm water feels good," Alice says.

"No secrets," Tony says.

Maria smiles. "No secrets."

Alice pulls the blanket and sheet down to Maria's waist and washes Maria's left side from her head to her waist. She repeats the same progression, from the shoulder to the hand, for Maria's right side. She rinses the cloth and washes Maria's front. She lifts Maria's shriveled breast with her left hand and gently washes the skin under her breast. She grabs a new towel and pats her dry. The room is silent except for the sounds made when Alice rinses the washcloth. When she finishes washing Maria's torso she covers her upper body with two towels. She lifts Maria's legs and places a towel under each leg. She washes and dries Maria's hips, legs, and feet. She checks for redness and sores.

Alice removes the towels from Maria's chest, rolls her onto her side, grabs the damp towels from under her and drops the washcloths and towels into the rinse water.

Tony pats his wife dry with a towel, retrieves the hospital gown, puts it on his wife and pulls the blankets and sheet to her chin. Alice raises the side rail, walks to the kitchen, throws the towels into the laundry basket and dumps the water into the sink. She returns to the living room with fresh towels and the basin filled with clean water. Maria's cat Diablo saunters through her legs and nearly trips her. Celeste watches for a water spill but again nothing is spilled.

Alice places the towels and water basin on the side table, drops the side rail and pulls the blanket and sheet down to Maria's knees to expose her genital area. Tony steps away from the bedside. "I can't do this," he says. He walks to the kitchen, fills a glass with water and drinks the entire glass in three, hard gulps.

Alice pulls the bottom of the hospital gown up to Maria's stomach and washes Maria's genital area from front to back. She rolls Maria onto her side and washes and dries Maria's back and buttocks. She checks for skin sores. "Looks good," she says to Tony.

She removes her gloves and tosses them into the wastebasket next to the bed. She squirts lotion on her right palm. Before she applies the lotion, Tony, who is back standing next to her, grabs her hand. "Let me do that." He covers his palms with lotion and rubs the cream onto Maria's arms, legs, feet, torso and neck. Tony applies the lotion to Maria's back. Tony ties the back strap of the hospital gown and resets the side rail.

Maria blinks at Alice and nods her head. She is sending Alice another signal. She has something more to tell her. Alice drops her right ear to Maria's lips. "Promise me you'll help him when I'm gone. He is a good man but he's useless. He can't even boil water."

"I promise," Alice says.

"Promise what?" Tony asks.

"Nothing, just girl talk."

"No secrets," he says.

Maria says something that neither Alice nor Tony hears.

"Do you believe in God?" Tony asks Alice.

"I don't know, sometimes I do, sometimes I don't."

"Do you pray?"

"Not usually."

"Will you pray with me?"

She nods her head.

Tony kneels at the side of the bed. "Please kneel," he says. She kneels next to him. "God, please take away Maria's pain," he says. His eyes are closed and his forehead is resting against the bed. "Please, please, please take away her pain."

Celeste, who is watching them from the doorway, shakes her head, turns her back to them, and walks up the stairs to her bedroom. She is angry she hasn't had a friend at her house since her mother moved downstairs. She is angry her friends are too kind. She wants them to insult her like they do everybody else. She wants them to tell her she's a fool when she says something stupid, to laugh at the awkward way she runs in gym class, to stop treating her as if she were the one who was dying. Her teachers are even worse. They want her to confide in them, to tell them how they can help her, to share her pain with them, to tell them something she has told no one else. *If you want to help me, leave me alone,* she thinks every time a teacher asks her how she is doing.

Alice grabs the bed's control panel and raises the top end of the bed six inches. She leans over the side rail and says to Maria, "You're doing fine."

Maria blinks and nods her head. She has another message for Alice. Alice drops her head as close as she can to Maria's lips without touching her. "Tony'd be a good man for you, a really good man, a good husband," she whispers.

"I'm sure he would," Alice says.

"Sure he would be what?" Tony asks.

"More girl talk," Alice says.

"No secrets," Tony says.

"Think about it," Maria says to Alice.

"I will."

"I will what?" Tony says.

"Nothing," Alice says.

"I'm doing great for a dying woman," Maria says as forcefully as she can. She and Alice laugh.

Tony shakes his head. "Not funny."

"I thought it was," Maria says.

Alice packs her nursing bag and lifts it onto her left shoulder. Celeste has returned and is standing in the doorway. When Alice walks past her, Celeste says, "It isn't fair, my mom is only thirty-eight. Why did this happen?"

"I don't know why. I wish I did but I don't. You are right, life isn't fair." She drops her nursing bag to the floor and hugs her.

"When my mom dies, will you show my father how to cook? I'm so sick of sandwiches and pizza." She rolls her eyes.

"I would but I'm not a very good cook."

"You got to be a better cook than he is. He can't even boil water."

"Your mom just said that."

"I heard that," Tony says, "and yes, I can cook."

"No, you can't," Maria says. No one hears her.

"No Dad, you can't cook, not even close."

Maria blinks her eyes yes in agreement.

Celeste follows Alice out the door, to the front lawn. "He cooked chicken yesterday. He boiled it for a half hour. No spices, nothing, just a chicken boiled in water. It was like eating rubber, except rubber would have tasted better. You've got to be better than that."

"I wouldn't bet on it." She drops her nursing bag to the grass and hugs Celeste a second time. "I do know how to cook some Italian meals. Do you want to learn how to cook eggplant Parmesan?"

"Okay. I think so. I've never actually had it."

"First time for everything."

Alice checks the time on her phone. She is only ten minutes late for her next home visit. I'll be almost on time, not too bad. She hugs Celeste one more time.

CHAPTER 11

CHARLES CONNOR

CHARLES CONNOR IS pacing across his office throwing wads of paper against the wall. He kicks his desk and jams his big, right toe. "Damn that hurt," he says. He rubs his foot. The agency's revenues are in the tank and he doesn't know what to do. He was hired to pull the Providence VNA into the twenty-first century. What he didn't know when he took the job was how difficult that would be. Before he was hired the agency ran annual operating deficits of around fifty thousand dollars a year. The losses were easily covered from donations, especially from the families of the hospice patients. The operating deficit this year is nearly a quarter-million dollars, well beyond the annual gifts. If nothing changes, he won't be able to meet payroll in six months.

Connor blames poor management. Before he was hired, except for the hospice program, the agency operated Monday through Friday, days only, even though the competition was running seven days a week, evenings, nights and holidays, and was gobbling up more of the business every day. When he added evenings and weekends to the schedule, his third month on the job, he had no idea how hard it would be to find new nurses or how resistant the current staff would be to working weekends and nights. Five of the thirty-eight nurses quit and several of the others are still grumbling.

The new coding system has been an even bigger problem. The

laptops, software, and license fees cost the agency three hundred and fifty thousand dollars and that doesn't include the cost of the time spent training the staff how to use the program. The vendor promised the program would raise efficiency so much so that the average number of visits made per day by all the staff, the nurses, home health aides and therapists, would increase by one or more visits and the system would pay for itself in less than a year. The salesman, who is not a nurse and has never made a home visit, said the program was so simple the nurses would learn to use it in less than a month.

But that's not what happened. Five months later, half the nurses are still having trouble, the physical therapists and speech therapists say it doesn't work for them, and the social workers refuse to use it. Revenues are down and costs are up and there is no end in sight.

Last August, Connor and Charles Potter presented a full color, PowerPoint presentation to the board of directors that proved purchasing the new program was a good investment. Connor told them the old program was so out-of-date the company that sold it was no longer in business. In his presentation, the costs and benefits graph lines crossed at the eighth month and after that the program savings would pump thousands of dollars into the agency, money that could be used to pay for long neglected projects such as fixing the pothole-filled parking lot.

Connor checks his work schedule. Mike Dean is coming at eight-thirty, fifteen minutes from now. Dean is President of the Board of Directors and a total pain in the ass. He is sure he could run the agency better than Connor and he tells him so on a regular basis.

Dean is one of three members of the fifteen-member board who has been on the board for over thirty years. In private, when Connor and Potter are alone and are sure no one can hear them, they call the three veteran board members The Walking Dead. Dean, the youngest of the three, is sixty-eight. He has been on the board, off and on, since nineteen eighty-six. The other two, both women and both in their eighties, are so deaf they can barely follow the board's deliberations. The three of them are routinely out voted.

Before Connor moved to Vermont he had never worked with so many women. He had no idea working with them would be so much different from working mostly with men. Every decision, even decisions that don't matter, is made by consensus. He would love to get rid of all the committees but that's not going to happen unless he wants a full scale rebellion.

Mike Dean is standing in the doorway of Connor's office. He has a coffee cup in his left hand and a Red Sox baseball cap in his right hand. He blurts a fake cough to alert Connor he is there. Connor looks up from his desk. "Busy day?" Dean says.

"They're all busy days."

"You're probably wondering why I am here."

"No, I can guess, the finances are in the toilet and you want to know what I am going to do about it."

"True, but that's not on my agenda for today. We need to talk about Alice Hammond."

"Who?" Connor says.

"Alice Hammond. She's one of your home health aides."

"I know who she is. Why her?"

"What do you know about her?"

"Not much. From what I hear she's a pretty good employee." He opens the employees' file on his computer and checks Alice's file. He taps his fingers on the computer screen.

"Do you remember Clyde Nason?" Dean says.

"How could I forget? He was so fat we had to rip out the door frame to get his body out of his house. It cost the agency four thousand dollars in repairs. Not sure why we had to pay. His brother Bob . . ."

"Bill."

"His brother Bill threatened to sue the agency if we didn't fix the door. I didn't want to pay but our attorney..."

"Doris Lang?"

"Yes, Doris Lang, said pay the damn repair bill, that would be cheaper than going to court, so we paid. It was nuts."

"I've got news for you that is even more nuts," Dean says. He leans toward Connor as if he were telling him a secret he doesn't want anyone else to hear. "Clyde left all his property, a house, a barn and two hundred acres, and one hundred twenty-five thousand dollars in cash, to Alice Hammond. His property is some of the best land in the county, probably worth close to two million dollars. He also left twenty-five thousand to the agency and another ten thousand or so in stocks. And he left his brother Bill nothing, zip, nada."

Connor gets up from his desk, walks to the window, and presses his face against the glass. "That is nuts," he says. He lightly raps his left fist against the window pane.

"Yes, it is, how could you let that happen?" Dean says.

"Let what happen?"

Dean steps behind Connor's desk to read Alice's file. He scrolls down the screen and reads the documents. He takes a sip from his coffee cup. The coffee is cold. He spits it back into the cup. "What do you know about the relationship between Alice and Clyde? Did she do anything inappropriate, did she take advantage of him?"

"I have no idea. I doubt it but I don't know one way or the other. How do you know about his will?"

"I was Clyde's lawyer. I wanted to tell you when he wrote it but I couldn't. I can now because his instructions to me were to meet with you and Alice before I read the will to Bill. One thing I can tell you is Clyde was pretty insistent about leaving the property and the money to Alice. I told him Bill would be furious, and would sue the agency, and he said he didn't care."

"Bill's going to go nuts."

"No kidding. I know him pretty well. We've faced off in court several times. He'll say Alice took advantage of a lonely, old man. He'll say Clyde was simple, which I assure you he was not. He'll say the agency fucked up big time and should have fired her. He'll go to the Providence Herald right away, probably as soon as tomorrow afternoon. He tends to try his cases in the press, even minor cases. I read the will to him and Alice and you tomorrow morning. If we're lucky he'll have a massive heart attack when he hears the news."

Connor laughs. "What do you want me to do?"

"We need to meet with Doris Lang this morning. She needs to know what's up and you need to get her and Alice here at four o'clock today. One thing for sure, no one from the agency speaks to anybody about this nonsense. Put a gag order on the staff, especially on Susan Young, she tends to gab."

"What a mess."

"A royal mess. I'll see you at four o'clock. Make sure Alice and Doris Lang are here."

CHAPTER 12

BARBARA FERMONTE

BARBARA FERMONTE IS standing with a walker, at her kitchen sink, holding her right hand under a stream of cold water. She burned her finger tips on the side of a hot pan. She was frying red and green peppers, garlic cloves, and onions in olive oil. She burned her hand when she grabbed the hot side of the pan instead of the pan handle.

There is a hard rap at her door. "Mrs. Fermonte, it's me, Alice."

Barbara does not hear her.

Alice opens the unlocked door, walks to Barbara and taps her shoulders. The tap startles Barbara. She nearly falls to the floor. "Alice, one of these days you are going to kill me."

"I doubt that Mrs. Fermonte. You're going to outlive me." She grabs Barbara's burned hand and examines it. The burn is minor. "This is the fourth time this month you've burned your hand. You really need to stop cooking on the stove."

"It's only the third time. I've burned myself only three times, not four, you're as bad as my son."

"You need to stop cooking on the stove top. You promised." Alice reminds Barbara that lunch and dinner are available for nine dollars in the cafeteria on the first floor of her building and she has a microwave which is much safer than the stove.

Barbara grabs a menu from her refrigerator and gives it to Alice.

"Read the meal for today," she says.

"Beans, ham, coleslaw, apple crisp, roll, sounds good," Alice says.

"Good! Store brand canned beans, coleslaw that was made a week ago and is smothered in mayonnaise, a thin slice of overcooked ham and a roll as hard as a rock. I could play hockey with it. The only thing good is the apple crisp and that's just Sarah Lee."

"It can't be that bad?"

"It is and today's meal is one of the better ones. Tomorrow we get chicken pot pie. It looks like wallpaper paste and tastes like chalk."

"At least it's safe chalk and you won't burn the building down." Alice smiles. Six weeks ago Barbara fell asleep while watching television, just ten minutes after she had fried two peppers, a half of an onion, and three garlic cloves in olive oil. She thought she had turned the burner control to the off position but instead had turned the dial to medium heat. The next thing she knew she was being carried out of her smoke-filled apartment by a fireman. There was only minor damage, mostly from the smoke and from the water from the firehose and the sprinklers.

The fire spooked her neighbors. Eighty-four of them, eighty-four out of the one hundred eight residents at Pine Manor Senior Living Center, signed a petition to have her evicted. There had been other minor fires at the facility but this one was different. Barbara had moved to Pine Manor because she had burned her own home to the ground and all the residents in her building had read the story in the newspaper. She had smoked a cigarette, had placed it on the window sill above the kitchen sink, forgot about it and left the building with the cigarette still burning. By the time she got back, her house was fully engulfed in flames. The firemen were sure she was dead somewhere inside the building.

Barbara doesn't miss the house, what she does miss are the pictures of her grandchildren and her two dozen porcelain angel figurines that were destroyed. After the fire she lived for four months with her son Paul and his wife Cindy. It was awkward for everyone, especially for Cindy, who felt like an intruder in her own home.

Barbara was married at eighteen and had seven children and four miscarriages by the time she was forty. After her fourth miscarriage she told her husband Angelo she couldn't take it anymore and was planning to tell her doctor to make sure her fourth miscarriage was her last. "You can't do that, it's a sin," he told her.

"I'll let God judge me," she said.

Angelo was a quiet, mild mannered man, so quiet that twenty years out of high school most of his classmates weren't sure if he had graduated with them or with a different class. He was a kind husband, if somewhat dull, and rarely lost his temper. Their three-year-old son Dennis died on the Fourth-of-July, nineteen fifty-one. Even now, sixty-eight years later, that day sticks in her head as if it were yesterday. Dennis drowned in their neighbor's pool. He had crawled under the lilac bushes that separated the two properties and had slithered through a small hole in the fence around the pool. The hole was so tiny no one was concerned.

They were hosting an Independence Day barbecue. There were twenty-six people at the party, ten parents and sixteen children. The chaos was overwhelming. Barbara thought Angelo was watching Dennis and he thought she was watching the boy. No one noticed the baby was missing until Angelo took a head count to determine who wanted what for dinner. When Dennis couldn't be located, Barbara immediately sensed the worst, crashed through the bushes and ran to the pool. She frequently had imagined one of her children would drown in the pool. She found her son facedown, floating in the water. He was so tiny he looked like a rag doll.

Barbara paid for a mass for him once a month for the next five years and would have paid for five more if Father Caplin hadn't stopped her.

"It's time to put this death behind you, no more Masses for your son," he said to her when she tried to give him a check for sixty more. He reached toward her to touch her shoulder. She pushed him away.

"You don't get it, you don't have any children, you'll never have any children," she said. She tried purchasing Mass for Dennis at the other two Roman Catholic churches in town but the priests at those churches also refused her money and also told her it was time to move on.

Barbara and Angelo bought a small, granite gravestone of a lamb for Dennis. The lamb statue was the size of a cat. The words on the base of the stone said, 'Dennis Fermonte, 1948-1951, Our beloved son.'

Alice tosses her nursing bag to the couch. She grabs a stethoscope and places it around her neck. "Mrs. Fermonte, you turn one hundred in less than a month, you must be very excited," she says. She takes Barbara's pulse.

"Excited, why should I be excited? It's just another day."

"Just another day, one hundred is huge, the biggest day of your life."

"No, I think that would be my actual birth day, without that day I wouldn't have any big days or little days or any days at all for that matter." She looks at Alice to see if Alice gets the joke. Alice smiles. "To tell you the truth, I don't care if I live till then or not. I can barely hear, my vision is even worse, it hurts to walk, three of my seven children are dead, my husband is dead, all my friends are dead. I think about them every day. Everyone in this building hates me. I sleep more hours in the day than I'm awake. What's to live for?"

"You don't really mean that, do you?" Alice says.

Barbara does not hear her so Alice repeats what she had just said.

"I don't know, some days I do, some days I don't. One thing for sure Alice, don't live to be one hundred. It's very frustrating." She scratches her head and pulls a lock of hair from her scalp. "I need you to promise me something."

"Depends on the promise."

"On my birthday I want you to take me out of here."

"Where do you want to go?"

"Anywhere but here."

"Why not here?"

"Because I don't want to be here. There is going to be a party for me. I don't want a damn party. They'll drag out all the residents for a party no one wants to attend. Someone from the staff, probably Martha, the fat girl at the front desk, will strap a tiara on my head and everyone will blow those annoying New Year's Eve party horns and a reporter for the paper will take my picture and I'll look like I'm dead in the picture and a troop of girl scouts will sing happy birthday to me and my son Paul will tell everyone in the room that I am one hundred years young. I don't want the girl scouts to sing to me and I won't be one hundred years young, I'll be one hundred years old, nobody is one hundred years young."

"I can't take you out of here Mrs. Fermonte," Alice says.

"Yes, you can. Just walk me to your car and we're gone."

"It's not that simple. I think my supervisor would be pretty upset with me. Have you talked with Paul? He could take you out."

"He's an asshole. He's the one planning the whole damn thing. He thinks it will be a big surprise. How stupid does he think I am?"

"I'm sure he means well."

"Means well my ass. If he meant well he'd cancel the damn party. I've asked him to, a hundred times. He says, 'Mom, there's no party' and then he smiles. He couldn't lie when he was a kid and he still can't lie. Does he think I was born yesterday? Nobody listens to old people."

"I'll talk to him." Alice softly touches Barbara's shoulder.

"It won't do any good."

Alice slowly walks Barbara to the bathroom, closes the toilet lid and helps her sit on the toilet seat. She turns on the tub faucet, fills the tub and checks the water temperature. It is too hot. She adds cold. She pulls Barbara's nightgown over her shoulders and places the gown on the sink counter. Barbara steps into the tub and trips on the top edge. Alice catches her and pulls her upright. "Be careful," Alice says.

Barbara settles into the water. "This feels wonderful."

Alice wets and soaps a cloth and washes Barbara's back. Barbara grabs the washcloth from Alice. "I'll wash my possible," she says.

"Your what?"

"My possible. My vagina. When I worked in the nursing home my boss said wash as far as possible. I was a nurse's aide like you, two days a week for twenty-one years."

"My possible, I like that," Alice says.

Barbara points to the bathroom closet next to the sink. "I want you to get me something from the closet. I want you to get the electric razor on the top shelf, on the left side, behind the sheets."

Alice finds the razor. The blade covers are rusted. She hands it to Barbara. Barbara flips open the head to expose the three gears that turn the blades. She points to the gray whiskers inside the razor.

"That's my husband's beard hair. He died twenty-eight years ago this October, October third, at nine-fifteen in the morning. He had a stroke. He was watching television, Matlock I think. I was in the kitchen washing the dishes. I thought he was sleeping so I didn't hear him when he slipped off the couch. When I realized what had happened it was too late. If I'd done something earlier, maybe he would have lived. Who knows? I don't know why but I've kept the razor with his beard hair all this time. I should have thrown it away."

She dips the razor in the tub water. "I guess this is our last swim together Angelo." She stirs the floating bits of hair with both of her hands. "That man could swim. He was so fast. His arms and legs barely made a splash. I could barely swim. I'd stroke and stroke and get nowhere. My kids laughed at me and taunted me. They'd swim circles around me and say, you can do it Ma, you can do it, and then they'd laugh at me some more. They drove me crazy but it was wonderful."

"Sounds wonderful."

"When they were teenagers, they'd hide under the raft at my uncle Vincent's camp. I'd think they were dead. I'd run down to the beach screaming their names. They'd swim out from under the raft and mock me. They did that a dozen times each summer. I fell for it every time. Paul, he was the worst of them all," Barbara says.

Alice finishes the bath, helps Barbara out of the tub, and walks her to her bed. She dries Barbara's back and helps her dress. "I think we're done for today," Alice says.

"I am serious about leaving here on my birthday. I don't want to be here. You're the only person I can ask."

"I'll think about it but no guarantees."

"It would mean everything to me."

"No guarantees."

Barbara's son Paul is standing in the doorway to the bedroom. Neither woman had heard him enter the apartment. "No guarantees for what?" he says.

"There are no guarantees in life, Paul, absolutely none," his mother says.

Paul hands Alice a five dollar bill. "Take this, you deserve it, they don't pay you enough."

"No thanks."

"I insist, it's a tip."

"We don't take tips Mr. Fermonte."

"Donate it to the agency."

"If you want to donate, you can send the agency a check," Alice says.

He stuffs the bill back into his wallet.

Alice packs her bag and walks toward the door. "See you Thursday. No more cooking," she says.

Barbara brushes her away with a hand wave.

Alice checks her face in the rear view mirror. Her hair is frizzed from the heat of the bathroom. She grabs a brush from the glove compartment and brushes her hair.

CHAPTER 13

MARIA GALLO

MARIA GALLO ROLLS her head slightly to her left to watch her husband Tony walk across the living room. He has been pacing, back-and-forth across the room, for the past half hour. She turns her head. The inflatable shampoo basin under her neck squeaks like a rubbed balloon. "It sounds like we're at the beach," she whispers to Alice. Alice doesn't hear her. A glob of shampoo oozes into her right eye. She blinks several times to remove the soap. Alice dabs the shampoo from Maria's eye with a dry towel.

"Don't rub too hard," Tony says from across the room, "you'll hurt her." He is checking messages on his cell phone. Maria smiles and winks at Alice as if the two of them were in on a cherished secret. Alice winks back.

"She's not rubbing too hard, Daaaaad," Celeste says. She is standing next to Alice, so close their hips are touching.

Alice's phone in her nursing bag, rings. She ignores the ring and dries Maria's face and neck.

"Shouldn't you answer it?" Tony says.

"No, it's probably just my mother. Either that or someone trying to sell me a timeshare or a car warranty."

The ringtone stops and restarts a few seconds later. Alice ignores the phone. Tony reaches into her bag, grabs it and hands it to her.

"We can finish up," he says.

Alice takes the phone from him and walks to the front porch. The word on the call screen says: Work. She taps the answer tab.

"Alice, it's me, Susan. I've cancelled the rest of your visits for today. You need to be here by four."

"Why?"

"I don't know why. Connor asked me to get you here."

"Did I do something wrong?"

"Not that I know of, it's all hush, hush."

"Am I getting fired?"

"I don't think so."

"What else could it be?"

"I have no idea. Just make sure you're here on time."

"If I get fired will you write me a letter of recommendation?"

"Of course I will but you won't need it, you're not getting fired."

Alice hits the 'end call' icon on her phone and slips it into her shirt pocket.

"Are you getting fired?" Celeste asks her. She had followed her to the porch.

"I don't think so, maybe, I don't know."

"It's not fair," Celeste says.

"What's not fair?"

"If you get fired, it's not fair."

"I'm not getting fired."

"If you do, it's not fair. You're the best nurse, by far, nobody else is even close."

"I'm not a nurse, I'm just a home health aide."

"Then you're the best home health aide."

"Thank you but I find that hard to believe."

Alice starts to walk back into the house. Celeste grabs her arm. "Life isn't fair," she says.

"No, it's not."

"My mother shouldn't be dying. She's too young, way too young. She never smoked, she never drank more than one beer at a time, I don't think she ever got drunk, never. She jogged every day, she ate healthy food, why her?"

"I don't know why," Alice says.

"Because life isn't fair that's why."

"You're probably right,"

"I know I'm right." She grabs Alice's arm even harder. "I don't want my mom to die, I really don't but I don't want her to live like this. She's in pain all the time. She says she isn't but I know she is. Every day she takes more and more drugs. Nothing works. She doesn't even look human. Her skin looks like wax. She is so skinny. How can anybody live who is that skinny? She's too weak to sit up by herself. I am afraid to touch her. I'm afraid if I grab her too hard I'll break her bones. My arms shake when I get near her."

"Don't be afraid. It makes her feel good when you touch her."

"Can I tell you something I don't dare tell anyone?"

"I guess so."

"You promise you won't tell anyone, especially my father or that nosy social worker, she's always trying to get me to come to grips with my emotions, she even uses the words come to grips with my emotions."

"I don't know if I can promise to keep your secret or not, depends on what you say."

"You're just like the rest of them."

"All right, I promise, what you tell me will be our secret."

Celeste lets go of Alice's arm, walks quickly to the end of the porch, slaps her cheeks with both of her hands and walks back to Alice. She is standing so close to Alice she feels the warmth of Alice's breath. She grabs Alice's arms and shakes her hard. "Sometimes I want my mother to die. I lay in bed and imagine suffocating her with a pillow. I can't believe I think like that. I am an evil person."

"You're not an evil person."

"Yes, I am. I think about killing my mother. You can't get more evil than that."

"What you're really thinking about is ending her pain."

"No, what I am thinking about is suffocating my mother with her pillow. I will go to hell. When she sleeps her eyes don't shut. That gives me the creeps. I hate it. I'm living in a horror movie that won't end."

"Celeste, listen to me, you will not go to hell, you are a good person, a very good person. Your mother is dying and you're only thirteen, that's not fair, not fair to you, not fair to your father and definitely not fair to your mom. You are right, life is not fair," Alice says.

"What should I do?"

"Do what you're doing now, show her you love her. Continue to bathe her and feed her and help your dad. Just be there for her. And maybe you should talk to a therapist."

"I do, every Thursday morning. She's useless. She wants me to keep a journal and draw stupid pictures. I don't want to keep a journal or draw stupid pictures. My life sucks, I know that already."

"Have you told her what you told me?"

"No."

"You should."

"Why?"

"You just should. It will help her help you."

"I don't want her help."

"You need her help, you really do."

Celeste is crying. She drops her head onto Alice's shoulder. "I love my mother, I don't want her to die."

Alice hugs her. "I know you don't."

"I love my father too but he is driving me crazy. He's always here. He follows me around like a hungry cat. Every time I turn around, he's right there, five inches from me. It's so damn annoying. He hasn't gone to work in over three weeks. He could lose his job, we could lose our house. Where would we live if we lose our house? I don't want to live with my grandparents, they fart too much, all four of them."

"Your father isn't going to lose his job and you're not going to have to live with your farting grandparents."

Celeste smiles at the farting grandparents comment. "How do you know that?"

"I just do."

"No, you don't, you don't know anything."

Tony is listening to their conversation. He is standing inside the entranceway, hiding in the shadow, to the left of the door. When Alice and Celeste separate he scampers back to the living room, sits in the chair next to the hospital bed and acts as if he had been there ever since they left the room. He is holding his phone to his right ear pretending he is talking to someone. When they enter the room, he speaks loudly into his phone. "Listen John, I'm not sure if that's a good idea or not, I'll look over the plans and get back to you this afternoon." John Gladding is the owner of Gladding Construction where Tony works. Tony is the work crew foreman.

He taps the center of his phone, as if he were shutting it off, and places it in his back pocket. "Glad you two could make it back. I've finished everything. I put all the towels into the laundry basket. I've totally dried mom and gave her a clean nightgown. You'd think I was the one being paid, maybe I should bill the agency." He smiles.

"I'll send you my paycheck for today. But I must warn you, it won't be worth much," Alice says. She packs her bag and leans toward Maria. "They love you," she whispers.

"I know, sometimes too much." Maria says.

"Hey, no secrets," Tony says.

"No secrets, isn't that so Celeste?" Alice says.

"Absolutely, no secrets," Celeste says.

Sitting in her car, Alice checks a recent text message on her phone from Susan Young. 'I think it's something about Clyde Nason and you, not sure. I heard his name and yours mentioned in the same sentence. Connor looks like he's seen a ghost. Don't know if it's related to you or not. You didn't hear any of this from me.'

Maybe he left me the chess set or some books or his camera, that would be nice.

She checks the time on the dashboard clock. She has two-and-a-half hours before the four o'clock meeting. She looks for her gym bag in the back seat. It's there. The gym clothes have been worn several times. She opens the bag and sniffs her shirt. Not too bad. She drives to the gym. There is a help wanted sign in the window. If I get fired, maybe I can work here.

CHAPTER 14

ALICE HAMMOND

CHARLES CONNOR IS bouncing a tennis ball against the glass on the entrance door to the agency. The repeated thump of the ball is annoying Lisa Parker, the woman who answers the agency's telephone. Her desk is seventeen feet from the door. She grabs three aspirin tablets from a bottle next to the phone and swallows them without water.

Connor sees Alice drive her car into the parking lot. He checks his watch. It is quarter-after four. He shakes his head and opens the door for her.

"Alice, how are you?" he says, leaning toward her. His breath smells like coffee and breath mints.

"Fine."

"You're a bit late."

"Sorry about that, I got stuck in traffic."

"No problem, you're here now." He bounces the tennis ball on the floor, catches it and tucks it into his right, front pocket. The bulge from the ball looks wrong to him so he removes it from his pocket and holds it with his left hand.

"Am I getting fired?" Alice asks.

"No, why would you ask that?"

"I don't know, you've never asked to meet with me before."

"That's true but no, you're not getting fired."

He guides her toward the conference room. Standing at her work cubicle, Susan Young gives Alice a timid wave and a strained smile, and silently mouths the words 'good luck.'

Mike Dean is sitting on the top of the conference table swinging his legs back and forth as if he were a child pumping his legs on a swing. Charles Potter is next to him, leaning against the table, fiddling with a pencil. Alice and Connor enter the room.

Dean jumps off the table, walks toward them and offers Alice his hand. "Mike Dean, president of the board. Glad to meet you. You know Charles Potter, agency CFO?"

She nods.

"I've heard a lot of good things about you. I remember when your mother worked here, she was a great nurse," Dean says.

"Thanks," Alice says

Potter waves to her to sit at the table.

"Hi Alice," Doris Lang says. She is sitting at the far end of the table reading the third of the three annual evaluations about Alice and marking certain sections with a highlight pen.

"You're probably wondering why we're all here?" Connor says.

He pulls a chair out from under the conference table and points for her to sit down. "Do you remember Clyde Nason?"

"Yes, I do. How could I forget him? He was a good man."

"So good he would leave you two million dollars in property and one hundred twenty-five thousand dollars in cash?" Potter says.

"Are you serious?" Alice says.

"Yes, we are serious," Dean says, "very serious." He picks up a copy of the will from the conference table and hands it to her.

"That's nuts, why me?"

"That's what we're trying to find out," Dean says.

"I can't believe this," Alice says.

"Neither can we," Connor says.

"Clyde left all his property, two hundred acres and his house and barn, and one hundred twenty-five thousand dollars in cash to you. That doesn't make any sense to me. Does that make sense to you Alice," Lang says. Her voice is stern, like a teacher scolding a student.

"No. Why would he do that?" Alice says.

"We have no clue why. The property and money go to you because Clyde left them to you. He was very clear, he wanted you to have the money and property and he wanted Bill to get nothing. Why would Clyde Nason leave you everything he owned, to you? You were not his daughter. You were not his wife. You weren't even his niece. You were just his home care aide," Lang says.

"I have absolutely no idea why. Bill must be furious."

"Bill doesn't know anything, at least not yet. He won't know anything until eleven o'clock tomorrow morning. That's when I read the will to him and to you and to Connor," Dean says. "He will be furious, blood spitting mad furious."

Lang holds up one of the evaluations. "Alice, according to your evaluations, you have serious boundary issues. It appears you spend way too much time with your patients, you get too close to them," she says.

"I do not."

"Yes, you do, at least according to these evaluations."

"That's not true."

"So what you are saying is all three evaluations are wrong?"

"No, what I am saying is you didn't read the entire evaluations. Each one says I'm an excellent employee and I do quality work."

"That may be so but they also say you have serious boundary issues." She drops the document on to the table.

"You can't do this job without boundary issues, especially for long term care patients like Clyde," Alice says.

"How close is the question. It's one thing to care, it's another to care too much," Lang says.

"He was my friend."

"No, Clyde Nason was not your friend. He was your patient," Connor says.

"Why did Clyde leave the property to you and not to someone else? You saw him weekly for three years but so did Jen Mason. Why did he leave his property to you and not to her?" Dean says.

"I don't know why."

"Was he attracted to you?" Lang asks.

"What?"

"Was he sexually attracted to you?"

"No!"

Was he in love with you?"

"No. That's a ridiculous question."

"Maybe, maybe not. Alice, you should get a lawyer," Lang suggests.

"I don't even know any lawyers."

Lang hands a business card to Alice. "Your father has a lawyer, Bill Keough. Here's his card. He's a good man. In fact, I told him you'd call him today. I suggest you make that call."

"Do yourself a favor, do the agency a favor, do me a favor, call Bill Keough," Dean says.

Alice tucks the business card into her right pocket.

Lang packs all the documents on the table into her briefcase. "That will be all for today. We'll need to meet again, probably first thing next week. In the meantime, you need to be at Mike's office tomorrow at eleven, not eleven-fifteen. Take my advice, get a lawyer, you definitely need one, this is going to get messy, real messy. And don't be late tomorrow."

"Why do I need a lawyer? I did nothing wrong."

"I'm not saying you did, all I'm saying is get a lawyer for your own protection. Don't tell anyone about this, not your boyfriend, not your cat, not Susan Young, we'll tell her, not anyone," Lang says.

. . . .

ALICE ENTERS SUSAN'S cubicle. Susan hugs her. "Did you get fired?" she says.

"No, at least not yet."

"What happened?"

"I can't tell you."

"Yes, you can. I'm your boss."

"No, I really can't."

Susan hugs Alice a second time. "Don't worry, I've got your back."

"Thanks, I appreciate the support."

Gail Rivers, the scheduler for the homemakers, is standing next to Alice. Neither Alice nor Susan had seen her leave her cubicle to join them. "What cha do?" she says.

"Nothing," Alice says.

"Lang only comes here when something big's up. You getting fired?" Rivers says.

"No, she's not getting fired," Susan says. She shakes her head.

Sitting in her car, Alice pulls Keough's business card from her pocket and calls him. Her heart is pounding hard.

"I've been expecting your call," he says.

CHAPTER 15

ALICE HAMMOND

ALICE IS SITTING in her car reading the three evaluations about her that were written by Susan Young and signed by both her and Young. She has read the documents so often she can almost recite them from memory. "I'm a good employee," she says out loud, trying to convince herself she is in fact a good employee. She couldn't sleep last night. She relived every conversation she has ever had with Clyde. I did nothing wrong. By two in the morning she was sure she had done everything wrong. She took two sleeping pills. The pills had no effect.

She checks the time on the dashboard clock. It is five minutes before nine, time to meet Bill Keough. She has been parked across the road from his office for nearly an hour. He saw her pull her car to the curb, considered fetching her, but decided against it. "She'll come in when she's ready," he said to his secretary, who was watching him watch Alice.

Keough is much younger than Alice thought he would be, forty-five, possibly fifty. "Hi, I am William Keough."

"You sounded much older on the phone," Alice says.

"That was my father. I am William Keough the third. My father is Bill."

An older man enters the room. "You must be Alice. I'm Bill Keough." The two men escort Alice to Bill's office. On the wall behind his desk is a framed picture of him with George W. Bush and two other men. He and Bush are sitting in a golf cart and the other men are leaning against it. Bush is checking his scorecard. Keough's golf cap says Pinehurst No. 2.

"That's when he was running for president the first time. Cost me ten thousand bucks to get in that foursome, a total waste of money. Descent guy but not much of a golfer. You golf?" Bill asks.

"No."

"Your father doesn't either." He laughs.

Alice gets the joke. Her father plays two to three times a week and never misses a Saturday, even when it rains.

Bill sits at his desk, grabs several papers from a file next to the phone, and places them on the desktop. "I've read Clyde's will and I've read the evaluations of you and, earlier this morning, I met with your boss, Susan Young. Yesterday, I talked to Mike Dean. You're on solid ground here. The property and money are yours."

"I'm not sure if I want them or not. I really haven't had much time to think about it. This hit me like a ton of bricks."

"Miss Hammond, you realize we're talking about two million dollars in property, maybe twice that much, and one hundred twenty-five thousand dollars in cash. You could go back to med school," Bill says.

"I don't want to go back to med school, you need to stop talking to my father."

"Have you read the will?" Bill says.

"Not really. I've skimmed it but I haven't actually read it."

"Well, you should. Clyde was very clear. Pretty interesting will, actually, reads like a short story." He hands Alice a copy of the will. "Turn to the last page, third paragraph, second line. Please read it to me."

Alice turns to the page. "The bulk of my estate goes to Alice

Hammond because she was kind and generous. She made me a better person."

Tears form at the corner of her eyes. She takes in a deep breath and places the will on Bill's desk. She exhales and wipes her eyes dry with the left sleeve of her shirt.

"Please read the next paragraph," Bill says.

"If my brother Bill wonders why he gets nothing it is because he treated me like he was ashamed of me." She drops the will onto the desktop.

"The will is very clear, Clyde wanted you to have the money and not his brother," William says.

"Why me? Why not Eva Driscoll, she spent as much time with Clyde as I did, or Jennifer Mason, she was his nurse, she worked with him for a year before I even got to the agency."

"I don't know why. What matters is Clyde left the bulk of his estate to you. He wanted you to have it," William says.

"That doesn't make any sense," Alice says.

"Don't overthink this, sometimes wills don't make sense," William says. He is sitting on a couch under the window. "In the meantime, what we need from you is a detailed summary of all your encounters with Clyde, everything you can possibly remember, every gift you gave him, every gift he gave you, details about anytime you stayed late for personal reasons, and anything, whatsoever, that might be used against you."

"It's all pretty much in the nursing notes," Alice says.

"The nursing notes are meaningless, at least for what we need. We need to know what's between the lines, not what's in those reports," Bill says.

"What do you mean?"

"I understand you taught him how to play chess," William chimes in.

"Yes, I did, so what?"

"That's not in your job description."

"No it isn't, but what difference does it make whether I taught him to play chess or not?"

"Playing chess with Clyde is one thing, playing chess with him on company time is another. The good news for you is Clyde left you a hell of a lot of money and two hundred acres of some of the most valuable land in the county. The bad news is when Bill Nason finds out about this, which will be two hours from now, he is going to go bonkers. He's going to accuse you of taking advantage of his brother," William says.

"I didn't."

"That doesn't matter, he will say you did."

"Well, I didn't."

"Think about what happened. Bill Nason takes care of his brother for five years. Without Bill's help, Clyde would have had to move to a residential care facility, no question. Yet Clyde leaves him nothing. Instead, he leaves most of his estate to a home health aide who visited him four hours a week, for less than three years. That doesn't make sense," William says.

"Do you think I took advantage of Clyde?"

"It doesn't matter what I think."

"Yes, it does matter, it matters a great deal to me. Do you think I took advantage of Clyde?"

"Probably not intentionally but you are a young woman and Clyde was a very lonely, old man."

"Clyde wasn't lonely or old."

"His brother will say he was lonely and that you took advantage of him," William says.

"I did not. How many times do I have to say that?"

"Alice, we're on your side," William says and hands a letter to her from Clyde. "Read this."

Alice pauses a moment before reading the letter. She closes her eyes, sighs and takes a deep breath. I did my job and I did it well, Clyde knew that. She looks down at the paper and begins to read.

'Dear Alice, I want you to have my property and my money. You deserve it. You treated me with respect. Don't worry about what Bill will say about you. He doesn't know what he's talking about. I know I was too fat, way too fat, Bill reminded me every day. I wonder what he'd look like if he had two legs that barely worked. He was embarrassed of me and that hurt me. He doesn't deserve a penny. And when you get the money, the first thing I want you to do is buy a new car. I can hear you coming two miles away. That car is a death trap.'

Alice smiles at the last line. "I suppose I could use the money, I really do need a new car. What do I do next?"

"We meet with Mike Dean and Bill Nason at eleven this morning. The most important thing for you to do at that meeting is to say nothing, absolutely nothing," William says.

Alice agrees.

William walks her out of the office to the main entrance. "Remember, say nothing."

Alice checks the time on her phone. It's nine-forty. She remembers the afternoon she found Clyde dead. Ella was standing on his back, barking at her. The dog's food and water dishes were empty. Ella had knocked the kitchen wastebasket over and had dragged garbage across the floor, to the living room. The smell of Clyde's dead body combined with the stench of the rotting garbage and the half dozen dog shits that were scattered across the living room rug was so strong she gagged and nearly vomited.

Her car groans and shakes violently but starts on the first try. I really do need a new car.

CHAPTER 16

BILL NASON

"WHY WOULD HE do it?" Bill Nason says to his wife Charlotte.

"I don't know Bill. Give it a rest. I'm sick of hearing about it. There's nothing you can do now."

"Oh, yes there is. If you think I won't contest this will, you're kidding yourself."

"On what grounds?"

"She seduced him."

"Who?"

"Alice Hammond, who do you think?"

"Get a grip. Alice Hammond didn't seduce your brother."

"He left her everything. Why would he do that unless he was in love with her? And why would he be in love with her unless she seduced him?"

"Have you read his will? He wasn't in love with her, he was pissed off at you."

"I did everything for him."

"Yes, you did, and you reminded him every day."

"I did not."

"That's how you see it?"

"Yes."

"You need new glasses."

Bill and Charlotte were married the same year Bill's parents died. The wedding had been set for June but was moved to October because of the unexpected deaths of his parents. The first time the two met was so contentious it surprised everyone they ended up together. Charlotte was driving the speed limit on Beckley Hill Road, thirty-five miles per hour, way too slow for Bill who had just left Clyde's house. He pulled his car so close to hers she couldn't see his front bumper in her rearview mirror. He banged his horn eight times. She checked her mirror. He waved to her, the way a cop waves when he wants you to pull over. She waved back as if they were friends. She drove around one of the switchbacks and stopped suddenly to avoid hitting two wild turkeys. Bill's car smashed into hers.

"What the hell were you doing stopping in the middle of the road?" he said.

"I was saving two turkeys."

"PETA would be proud. Next time, hit them."

"You were too close."

"I wasn't that close."

"Yes, you were, plus it doesn't matter, you hit me from the back, you're at fault."

"What are you a lawyer?"

"Yes, as a matter of fact, I am."

"Figures." He retrieved his insurance card and gave it to her.

"I see your front bumper is dented. Don't try to get that fixed on my dime," she said.

"Looking at your car, my guess is you don't have much more than a dime."

"Very funny."

They started dating three weeks later and were engaged by their second year together. The biggest hurdle for them was getting used to each other's family. The Nasons and Olsens couldn't have been more different if they had been two different species. The Olsens were quiet and reserved, thoughtful and polite. Charlotte's father Liam had a PhD in Greek literature and had published four books almost nobody read. Her mother Klara was the president of the Providence Garden Club. Their main job was to plant flowers in the green space between the North and South lanes of Main Street in downtown Providence. The club takes its job very seriously.

The Nasons were in-your-face loud. They laughed a lot, hugged a lot and touched each other constantly. None of them had much of a filter when commenting about other people. The first time Charlotte ate dinner at their house she got almost no food and no one noticed. At her house her father slowly served the main course to everyone. He served the oldest woman first, then the next oldest woman to the youngest girl, and then the oldest man at the table to the youngest boy. Everyone waited patiently and didn't start eating until they had all filled their plates. Depending on how many people were at the table, the serving could take ten minutes or more. By the time everyone got their food, it was often cold. Their conversations were thoughtful and no one interrupted anyone else.

Not so for the Nasons. The food was placed in the middle of the table and getting food was pretty much everyone for themselves. Everybody talked at once and no one actually listened to anyone else. It took Charlotte nearly eight months before she left a Nason meal without a splitting headache.

The first time Charlotte met Clyde, she laughed to herself, I think I am dating the wrong Nason. He had just returned from logging and his sweaty T-shirt was clinging to his body. When she heard about his death she was devastated even though she hadn't seen him in eight months. She did not let her husband see her cry. She cried hard and long.

Bill also wept in private. To anyone but Charlotte, Clyde's death seemed to have little impact on him. But she knew the truth. Clyde was Bill's hero. Before the logging accident, everything Clyde did was bigger and bolder than anything he could do.

When Bill was fourteen he was selected for a night watch vigil at his summer camp. He had to spend a night in the woods by himself. It was a great honor to be picked. The selections were revealed at a camp bonfire. He would not have been chosen if it hadn't been for Clyde. Clyde was one of sixteen camp counselors. Each week the counselors selected two or three campers out of the one hundred fifty boys at the camp for the honor. No one chose Bill. They said he would panic. Clyde convinced them Bill would be the perfect choice.

"Only the best of the best are picked for the night vigil," the camp's headmaster said to the boys. One of the counselors pulled Jack Delehanty from the line, toward the fire. "Jack Delehanty, you are one of the chosen few," the headmaster said. The counselors gave out a loud war whoop.

Another counselor grabbed Bill and pulled him toward the fire. "Bill Nason, you are one of the chosen few," the headmaster said.

The terrified look on Bill's face told Clyde he had made a mistake, Bill was not ready to spend a night in the woods alone. Clyde whispered into his ear, "Don't worry little brother, you'll be fine."

Clyde and another counselor guided the two boys from the campfire, through the woods, to the shore of the lake and across a bridge to a small island just a few yards from the shore. The island was a half-mile mile long and a quarter-mile wide. The other counselor pushed Delehanty to the left and walked him several hundred yards into the woods. Clyde pulled Bill to the right and guided him to the North end of the island where they could see the bonfire and the lights at the two bathrooms.

"All you have to do is sit here for seven hours. There is absolutely no one on the island, nothing bad can happen to you," Clyde said. He handed Bill a sleeping bag and a whistle. "If you can't do it, blow this and we'll come and get you."

Bill started to cry.

"I know you're scared but don't be, nothing will happen to you, you have my promise."

"What about bears?"

"There are no bears here, that's why they chose this island. And you can't get lost, there's nowhere to go. Just sit here, you'll be fine."

"What about raccoons?"

"The only thing you need to worry about is the skunk and he is usually on the other side of the island. The worst thing that could happen is you'll stink."

"Stay with me."

"I can't do that. I have to check in and tell everybody you're okay." Bill sat against a tree, pulled his knees to his chest, looked across to the camp and watched the flames of the bonfire. "I'll be back at six to get you. Just remember, nothing will happen to you."

"I can't do this, I'm too afraid."

"I tell you what, I'll tell everyone you're okay and then I'll sneak back here in an hour. Can you last an hour?"

"Yes." His voice trembled.

When Clyde returned, Bill was quietly crying.

"I'm back," Clyde said.

Bill hugged him. "I'll stay with you until five but then I've got to go back so I can come and get you. Okay?"

"Okay."

Clyde tucked Bill under his arm and sat with him. Bill fell asleep quickly. Clyde checked his watch every half-hour. When he left at five Bill was still asleep. When Clyde and Bill and the other boy and the other counselor returned to the main camp at six-thirty, the headmaster, the counselors and the other boys met them at the bridge with a loud, huzzah cheer. Bill squeezed Clyde's hand.

CHAPTER 17

HAROLD DOTY

ALICE PULLS HER car to the curb in front of Harold Doty's house. The three junk cars on the front yard are gone, the debris on the porch has been removed, the grass is mowed and there is a gray-haired man with no shirt scraping loose paint off the side of the building. The man is balding but has a long, gray ponytail that hangs nearly to his waist. His back and arms are covered with tattoos. The tattoo on his back is an eagle holding a dozen arrows in its claws with the words, *Don't Tread on Me* written under its talons. The eagle has big, bulging eyes and looks angry. The paint scraper has an unlit cigarette balanced on the top of his left ear and a lit cigarette in his mouth. The lit cigarette bobs up and down as he scrapes. Alice grabs her cellphone and calls her boss Susan Young.

"Yes, you have the right address. Harold Doty has not moved," Susan says.

Alice steps out of the car and grabs her work bag. The man scraping the paint glances at her. The screen door opens. Harold is sitting in a silver wheelchair with a black seat. A small, oxygen tank is attached to the back of the wheelchair. He is not wearing the nose tube. There is a new wheelchair ramp on the right side of the porch. He rolls his wheelchair down the ramp. He waves to her. "What do you think?"

"About what?" She walks toward him.

"About my place. Looks great, dozen it."

He waves his arms and beckons the paint scraper to join him and Alice.

"Looks great Mr. Doty," Alice says.

Harold points to his son, who has joined them. "Meet my son, Ron."

Ron's body is old but strong. He flicks his lit cigarette to the grass, grabs a blue T-shirt that was draped on the porch handrail, and puts it on. "Ron Doty."

"I'm Alice, Alice Hammond."

Ron is covered with paint chips and sweat. He wipes the sweat from his right hand on his pants. He steps to Alice, grabs her hand and shakes it. His grip is firm but not painful. "I bet you thought I was in prison for life. So did I. I'm out now, I'm almost a free man, never thought that would happen. Don't fear me, I'm harmless. Prison changes a man. I'm sure my father told you I was a violent, evil man. I was, but I'm not now."

"I'm not afraid of you," Alice says. Her body language tells him otherwise.

Ron steps away from her to give her space. Alice looks at Harold, nods her head toward the house, grabs the back of his wheelchair and helps him roll the chair up the ramp.

"It's nice meeting you, your father has said many good things about you," Alice says to Ron.

"My father wouldn't say good things about Mother Teresa." He smiles.

"You're probably right," she says and laughs. She pushes Harold's wheelchair through the front door to the living room. She drops her nursing bag on the coffee table in front of the couch, walks to the kitchen and washes and dries her hands. The house has been thoroughly cleaned. The newspaper piles are gone, the cats' litter box, which is clean, has been moved from the hallway to the kitchen floor, next to the refrigerator, and all the various boxes of junk are gone. The hallway is clear and smells like Pine Sol and all the windows have been washed. There is a flowerpot filled with daisies on the windowsill above the kitchen sink and a flowerpot on the counter, next to the microwave.

Alice fills a washbasin with warm water and carefully carries it to the living room. She grabs the remote from the top of the television and pushes the power button. Drew Carey is watching a woman wearing a sweatshirt that says, *Your Design Here* on the front, incorrectly guess the price of a jar of peanuts. Drew tells her, her guess is too high. She taps her forehead in dismay. "Better luck next time," Drew says.

Alice hands the remote to Harold, puts on a pair of latex gloves and kneels at his feet. He changes the channel to Law and Order. Jerry Orback is questioning a suspect who is chewing on a toothpick and staring at the ceiling, pretending he isn't listening. "You'd better listen, wise guy," Orback says.

Harold's left foot is gone. The stump is healed.

"Does it still hurt?" Alice says.

"No, hasn't for a while."

"Your leg looks fine. Your skin looks good. You're moving in the right direction."

"Looks good my ass."

"I know losing your foot is traumatic but."

Harold interrupts her mid-sentence. "But what? What do you know? You're twenty. You're healthy. You've got both your feet."

"Actually, I'm twenty-eight."

"Twenty, twenty-eight, what difference does it make? You're still a kid. I got fillings in my teeth older than you. You've got two feet, I've got one. You can run, I can't walk."

"You might walk again."

"When?"

"I don't know when, soon."

"I doubt that."

"Have you met with Phyllis Karin?" Alice asks.

"Who?"

"Phyllis Karin, your physical therapist."

Harold nods his head. "I met with her last week. She's a quiet bugger, that's for sure, she doesn't say boo."

"If anybody can get you back on your feet, she can."

"Back on my foot. I'll never get back on my feet. I have one foot now, not two. You can't walk with one foot."

"You'll walk Mr. Doty. You'll get a prosthetic foot."

"I don't want a fake foot. They look stupid."

"No, they don't. You'll look fine. You may have some balance problems, at least at first, and your legs will be weak, but you will walk and your legs will get stronger. One of my patients has two prosthetic legs and he walks just fine."

"I doubt that."

"His gait isn't smooth and sometimes he uses a walker but he gets around. You will too."

"Well, goody for him, a regular goddamn hero."

Alice washes and dries Harold's stump. She slides a tube sock onto his leg. "Have you talked to Aliyah?

"Who?"

"Aliyah Taylor, the social worker."

"Why do I need a social worker? I'm not a welfare loser."

"I didn't say you were. Aliyah has lots of experience helping people who've lost a limb."

"I didn't lose a limb, my foot got cut off." He bends forward and touches his leg. "Feel that, no foot. You can call me stumpy."

"I'm not going to call you stumpy."

"Why not? That's what my son calls me."

"I do not," Ron says. He is in the hall smoking a cigarette. "Don't believe a word he says."

"I usually don't," Alice says.

Ron smiles.

"I don't need a social worker, social workers are for losers. Read my lips, I don't need a goddamn social worker. I'm not a welfare cheat," Harold says.

"No one thinks you're a welfare cheat Mr. Doty, but it won't hurt you to talk to her. I'll make sure she comes here this week. Aliyah is very nice, you'll like her."

"She's not Black is she? I don't like those people."

"No, she's not a Black woman."

"Good." He grabs his oxygen hose, straps it over his head, and takes a deep breath. "You guys have too many goddamn staff. Every time I turn around somebody new is coming through the door. If she comes, I won't talk to her." He is panting hard and his face is flushed red.

"If you don't talk to her, that's your choice. You don't have to say anything."

"Jen said the same thing yesterday." He takes a second, deep breath of oxygen. His body shakes when he inhales.

Alice lightly touches his thigh. "If you get a throbbing sensation or pain in your leg, call the office, anytime, even at midnight."

"Just what Jen said."

"Brilliant minds think alike." She takes his blood pressure and pulse, notes the numbers on her laptop, packs her bag and carries the washbasin and towels to the kitchen. She throws the wet towels into the laundry basket on the kitchen table and washes and dries her hands. She returns to the living room, grabs both of the armrests of Harold's wheelchair and leans toward him. "I'll see you next week. Emily comes Friday."

"I don't like Emily."

Alice ignores his comment.

Ron follows her to the driveway. "So how's my father doing?"

"He's doing fine, or at least fine for someone with one foot, diabetes and chronic lung problems."

"What do you think, not gonna live too long?"

"Who knows?"

Ron opens her car door as if he were a valet at a high-end restaurant. "Please don't fear me. I really am harmless. Jail is a terrible place. It eats the core of your soul. Most of the men who come out are worse than when they went in. I think I'm a better man now, at least I hope I'm a better man."

"I hope you are too."

"I deserved what I got. I beat a man to death with a lamp. He was a good man. He had a wife and three kids. He didn't deserve to be beaten to death just because he couldn't keep his pecker in his pants. The only reason I'm out now is because they needed my bed, too many prisoners. I'm on parole for two more years. I can live in Vermont if I stay with my father, otherwise I got to live near Plattsburgh. My father, he's definitely a tough man to live with. Better than prison, though. When I'm totally free, I'm going to move to North Carolina. Maybe I'll take my father with me if he's still alive. We'll see."

"Sounds like a plan. And no, I'm not afraid of you. I was before but I am not now."

"Thank you."

Alice gets into her car and closes the door. Ron taps on the window. She rolls the window down. He leans toward her. "I know my father can be a racist, but he's harmless, really. He doesn't know any Blacks. He doesn't actually hate anybody. He just talks tough. Before prison, I was a racist too. If there is anything good I got out of prison it's that I'm not a racist now. Some of my best friends in prison were Black men. In fact, I'm gonna move to North Carolina to be near my friend Ben Jackson. We shared a cell for seven years. He's the kindest, smartest man I've ever known. He said he can get me a job in a plastics factory. Nobody here will hire me."

"Don't give up, somebody will hire you."

"I doubt it. I've tried everywhere I can think of but when I tell them I've spent twenty-five years in prison they say, 'Sorry we forgot, the position has just been filled.' How stupid do they think I am? I can't blame them really." He drums his fingers against her car door and walks back to the house.

Alice rolls up the front window, starts the car, turns on the radio to All Things Considered and checks her work assignments, nothing until one-thirty, Danny Myers and his vicious dog. *I don't know who I hate worse, the dog or Myers. He complains constantly about everything, especially about the other home care aides. It gets old.*

CHAPTER 18

CLYDE NASON

ALICE'S BACK IS pressed against the backboard of her bed. Her feet are flat on the mattress and her laptop is resting against her thighs. She is holding a bottle of Sprite between her feet and has a paper plate of Cheetos Puffs under her knees. Her finger tips, lips, chin and the bottom half of her white T-shirt are orange from the Cheetos. Ella is asleep on the pillow next to her. She is struggling to write what happened between her and Clyde Nason from the first time they met until she found him dead. She has been staring at her computer screen for a half hour. She has written only three sentences. "I can't do this," she says out loud.

Six weeks before Clyde died he got stuck in his bathtub. They both laughed at his predicament.

"How are we going to get my big, fat, wrinkly butt out of here?" he said.

"We, Kemosabe?"

"Yes, we." He shook and shimmered his body and she tugged on his left arm. Eventually he popped free.

"Good thing, you probably would have had to get a forklift in here and I don't think it would fit through the door," he said.

What she remembers most are the stories he told her about the woods behind his house. He'd hypnotize her with his humor and splendid details. Her favorite story was about a fox family that lived four miles directly east from his back porch, just a quarter mile west of the Providence National golf course. Every summer the foxes stole golf balls from the course, right off the fairway, and stored them in a pile next to their den. In the winter, Clyde would snowshoe to the den and steal the balls from the foxes and sell them back to the club for fifty cents each. One year he made thirty-two dollars. The foxes would watch him collect the balls. They never attacked him. One fall someone shot four of them, cut their tails off and left them dead on a pile of leaves. Clyde posted his land after that. Several hunters wrote nasty letters to the *Providence Herald* complaining that he had closed some of the best hunting land in the state.

"You probably didn't know this but foxes are the only dogs capable of retracting their claws like cats do," he said.

"I did not know that."

He sent an article and several pictures about the foxes to *The World of Foxes* magazine but they never printed it. He got a very nice letter thanking him for his article. It wasn't quite right for the magazine. He showed Alice the rejection letter and the carbon copy of the article he had submitted and the pictures. The article was written on a typewriter. Alice had never seen a carbon copy before. The story was much better than she had expected but was way too long, fifteen, single-spaced pages and the pictures weren't very good. He was too far away from the fox. It was hard to tell if the animal in the picture was a fox or some other animal.

Clyde started his logging business from the money he got following the death of his parents. When he was twenty-nine and Bill twenty-four, their parents died in a grisly car crash. Their car was T-boned by a drunk driver's pickup truck. The police said their father Charles was killed instantly when his head hit the steering wheel. The airbag on his side had not worked and he wasn't wearing a seatbelt. His mother Eileen was found unconscious but alive. She lived four more days. The drunk driver's blood alcohol level was twice the legal limit. It was his third DUI. At his sentencing hearing he cried and asked Bill and Clyde to forgive him. He pleaded with the judge to give him a light sentence. "I'm so sorry I didn't mean to kill them," he blubbered through his tears. The judge was not moved. She sentenced him to ten years in prison. It took three years to get the money from the insurance settlement. The brothers split six hundred seventy-five thousand dollars. Bill used his money to pay for law school and for a down payment on a house in Providence. Clyde used his money to buy the two hundred acres behind his house and for a new skidder and new tractor for his logging business.

One afternoon Clyde grabbed his canes and led Alice to the back of his garage to show her the skidder.

"I haven't operated the skidder in six years. I wonder if it still works?" He gave her the key and told her to climb into the cab and start it.

"You're not serious. I wouldn't know where to begin."

"It's simple, anybody can do it." He told her how to start the engine. She climbed into the cab. "If I get hurt, I'm going to sue you."

"You can't get blood out of a stone."

"Maybe not but I can get your property." She laughed. That was the day she learned he owned two hundred acres. "Wow, I had no idea," she said when he told her how much land he owned.

"I'm a regular land baron, like Weyerhaeuser."

"Who?"

"Frederick Weyerhaeuser. I think he owed half of Montana or maybe it was Idaho, can't remember. Me and Fred, timber kings."

"Should I call you King Nason?"

"No, I'd prefer King Clyde, it has a better ring to it."

"Okay, your majesty, but if I get hurt, your land is mine, all of it, all two hundred acres and you'll have to call me Queen Alice."

She turned the key. The skidder did not start. She tried several more times, also with no success.

Alice types the story about the foxes into her laptop. Soon after her doorbell rings. The ring startles her. The soda and Cheetos spill onto the sheets. She picks up the soda bottle and places it on the bedside table. The bell rings a second time. She is wearing underwear and the Cheetos-stained T-shirt. She grabs a pair of Jeans from the floor and pulls on a gray sweatshirt. The bell rings a third time. "I'm coming, I'm coming."

William Keough is at the door. He has a briefcase in one hand and a bottle of red wine in the other. "I thought I'd help you write your notes about Clyde."

"Do I need help?"

"A second set of eyes on your document definitely would help, four eyes are better than two."

"There is no document to review. I've written nothing. When is this due?"

"The sooner the better, tomorrow if you can. If we sit down together and work on your draft this evening, I bet we can get most of it done tonight."

"How did you know where I live?"

"Your father told me."

"Good old Dad. What's with the wine?" She points to the wine bottle.

"Nothing, I just thought wine might help loosen things up, get your thoughts rolling?"

"You're married, right?"

"No, I'm not. Well, technically I am still married but I've been separated for almost six months. Not to worry, this is just about work. The sooner we get your notes done the better. Bill Nason likely will be on the attack by the end of the week, if not before. What you and

I need to do is to put our noses to the grindstone and get this done."

"I've got a better idea, I'll put my nose to the grindstone tonight, and tomorrow I'll show you what I've written and we can work on it at your office, you and me and your secretary, three sets of eyes are better than two, wouldn't you agree?" She grabs the wine bottle from him. "Thanks, I love this kind. See you tomorrow." She pushes him into the hallway and shuts the door. She walks across her living room to the kitchen, opens the wine bottle, fills a Dixie cup and places the cup on the kitchen table.

She returns to her bedroom, removes the laptop and the empty paper plate from the bed and places them on the bedside table. She crumbles the Cheetos bag into a ball and tosses it across the room toward the wastebasket, next to the dresser. The bag bounces off the rim of the trashcan and drops to the floor. She pulls the wet sheets off the bed and throws them into a laundry basket in the clothes closet. She grabs the laptop, walks to the kitchen, sits at the table, and drinks all the wine in the cup in one gulp. *What the hell is it with middle-aged men and wine?* She erases the story about the foxes and starts over.

. . . .

CLYDE NASON WAS a good, kind and decent man. He was my friend, maybe my best friend. And he was really funny. He had a dry sense of humor. Unless you paid attention exactly to what he said, you didn't get it. One day he told me a farmer friend of his was out in the pasture with 196 cows. When he rounded them up he had 200. I didn't get it at first. I thought he was telling me a real story.

I worked with him for nearly three years, from August 1, 2016 to April 3, 2019, the day I found him dead. I was one of his home health aides. I think there were five or six of us over that time and Jennifer Mason his RN and maybe two or three other nurses and Sid Ryan his occupational therapist and Phyllis Karin his physical therapist. I helped him wash himself and bathe himself and wash his feet. I checked for sores on his skin and I did some light housework for him, mostly sweeping the floors and washing the dirty dishes. Occasionally I washed his clothes and some days I cooked him breakfast. I took his vital signs and checked his weight, at least until he got too heavy for the scale. We tried to exercise but as he got heavier that became very difficult. I gave him four gifts that I remember, a chess set, a DVD and two books. He never actually got the DVD or the second book because I had them with me the day I found him dead. The chess set cost me $50 maybe $60, I don't remember exactly how much. I got both books at the library book sale for a buck a piece.

I gave him the first book, Robert Frost poems, on his 54th birthday and had planned to give him the DVD and the second book on his 55th birthday. The DVD was $5.99. I think I must have left the second book and the DVD at his house because I don't have them now. I taught him how to play chess early on, the fifth or sixth month I worked with him, I don't remember exactly when. Maybe I shouldn't have done that but I did. We played for five to ten minutes after I was done with my tasks, probably after about half of the visits, maybe a little less than that.

He loved jazz and some days he'd play a jazz album. I hate jazz but I listened anyway and said good things about the music. After I told him about my father's record collection he gave me two vinyl albums. I told him I couldn't take the gifts from him but he insisted and shoved them into my nursing bag. I gave the records to my father. My father told me that one of the albums, *Thelonious Monk with John Coltrane*, is worth about $120, maybe a bit more. If I had known that I wouldn't have taken that album.

He also gave me a framed picture he took from his porch. It was a large picture, 16X20 inches, in a really nice, dark walnut frame. I told him I couldn't take it, I could get fired. If you don't take it, he said, he would tell my boss I was a lazy slob and I fell asleep on the job and that's why my home visits with him took so long. And then he laughed really hard. You worry too much, he said. The picture is of a sunset over Elmwood Mountain. It is very beautiful. What I didn't notice at first is in the bottom right-hand corner there is a moose watching him take the picture.

On my twenty-seventh birthday he gave me a photo album filled with pictures from his property. Most of the pictures he took when he was logging. Some are very beautiful.

For the first four months I worked with him, he barely talked to me. When I asked him questions he would just grunt yes or no and that was about it. I think the chess set changed that or maybe he would have changed anyway. By the second year he'd tell me long, involved stories. He could tell a story better than anyone I've ever known.

From what you said, you expect Bill Nason will say I took advantage of Clyde and I tricked him into leaving all his property to me. That is so ridiculous, I don't even know how to respond. Was he attracted to me? Probably not but who knows. Even if he was, what difference would that make? He was always a perfect gentleman with me, not sure if anyone uses that term anymore. We never, ever had a conversation that was inappropriate or sexually charged. NEVER! The closest he ever came to commenting about how I looked was one time he told me he liked my jacket. It was a winter jacket, hardly anything to lust over. Too bad more men aren't as respectful as he was.

I probably shouldn't have stayed with him so often after my home health tasks were done. Except for me and the others from the VNA, nobody visited him but his brother Bill. Apparently he had lots of visitors right after his accident. Each year fewer and fewer of his friends stopped by his house. He had no wife and no children nor any close friends that I know of. If staying late with a lonely patient is a crime, three quarters of the home care aides are criminals.

I have absolutely no idea why he left most of his estate to me and not to someone else. You'd have to ask him but of course you can't do that. I do know he and his brother Bill were in a rough patch. They bickered a lot, mostly over stupid things, Bill had bought the wrong cereal or Clyde had forgotten to pay a bill, stuff that really didn't matter one way or the other. When Bill was angry he let Clyde know it. One day, just a few weeks before Clyde died, when I was helping him with his bath, Bill came into the bathroom and yelled at him for not paying the electric bill. The bill was four months past due and the notice from the electric company said they would shut the electricity off in two weeks unless it was paid soon. Bill read the cancellation letter to Clyde, word for word, and then waved the letter in Clyde's face. Clyde wanted to get up and confront Bill but he couldn't get up without my help. Instead he just sat there in the tub, wet and cold, while his brother yelled at him. I told Bill to stop yelling and go home. He totally ignored me.

Bill felt really terrible about what he had done and he apologized to Clyde and me the next day. He left a message for me at my work to call him and I did. He said he had a very bad day at work and he took out his frustration on his brother and me and that wasn't fair to either of us, and he was very sorry.

Some days Bill was a total prick to Clyde and some days Clyde was a prick to Bill. Most of the time they got along pretty well. On the bad days he and Clyde said almost nothing to each other. Bill would do whatever he had to do at Clyde's house and Clyde would ignore him and treat him as if he was just hired help and not his brother. On the good days they laughed hard, usually about something stupid either I had done or one of the other home care staff had done. I actually fell for the left-handed monkey wrench business. When Clyde asked me to go get one in the garage I told him I didn't know what it looked like.

He and Bill got a big belly laugh about that.

I am honored that Clyde considered me his friend. I certainly was never inappropriate with him, and he was never inappropriate with me. I was a friend and caregiver, that's all, nothing more.

. . . .

SHE CLOSES HER laptop, fills a Dixie cup with wine, and drinks it in one gulp. Ella is sleeping on the floor next to her feet, snoring. She checks the time on the stove clock. It is eleven-fifteen. I can't believe that took so long to write. She refills the cup. She shakes her dog awake. "This is pretty tasty wine, Ella." Ella licks her hand.

CHAPTER 19

MICHAEL WAINWRIGHT

MONDAY IS THE one day of the week Alice must be on time, at least for her first visit. Every Monday morning she helps Michael Wainwright get to his work. She gets him out of bed, helps him clean, shave and dress himself, cleans his catheter bag and gets him a new one, fixes his breakfast and gets him to the work van by eight-thirty, not a second later. The van is never late. The driver, a tiny woman who would chain smoke in the van if she were allowed, does not wait for anyone. The six who take the van, five men and one woman, each with one disability or another, call her The Van Nazi.

Alice rarely sleeps well on Sunday nights. To make sure she is not late to Wainwright's apartment, she sets her phone alarm, the stove alarm and the alarm on a windup clock that loudly ticks all night long.

Wainwright broke his neck twelve years ago, seven weeks after his high school graduation. He lost control of his legs and has diminished use of his arms. He broke his neck on a dare from his best friend Derrick Adams. The dare was for him to dive off the twenty-foot cliff on the east bank of the Mercy River in Williamstown.

"It's now or never," Adams said to him as they stood at the top of the cliff.

Wainwright had never before summoned enough courage either to dive or jump off the cliff. He was a poor swimmer, he hated cold water, the Mercy River was always very cold, even in August, and he was terrified of heights over ten feet. And he was aware, as was everyone in town, that two men had died diving off the cliff since nineteen fifty and another four had been paralyzed. Wainwright did not want his name added to either list.

"Dive, you chickenshit," Adams told him. Both boys were leaving town in one week and they knew, even though they did not want to admit it, that they probably wouldn't see each other again or at least not in any meaningful way. Adams was set to join the army on Labor Day weekend and Wainwright would be a freshman at Boston College. Thirteen years together, ever since their first day in kindergarten at Sacred Heart School, so close that all their friends referred to them as Adams and Wainwright, as if they were one being in two bodies, would end and there wasn't anything either of them could do about it.

Adams had dived off the cliff five times, the first time when he was only fourteen. "It's no big deal," he told Wainwright, "don't be a wuss."

When Wainwright stood at the top of the cliff just before his dive, he remembered the day he met Adams. His teacher, Sister Mary Bartholomew, a woman whose ability to control twenty-five kindergarten children without any help, was legendary, gave an eight-pack of crayons to each child in the class. She asked the children to hold up their red crayons. Adams held his orange crayon over his head and waved it proudly. Several children laughed at him. "That's not appropriate," she said to them. Her voice was calm but stern and her eyes told them she was annoyed. The children who laughed looked to the floor in shame.

She asked the children to hold up their green crayons. Everyone did except one boy who was not paying attention. "Mr. McCormick in this class you will pay attention." The boy desperately wanted to hold back his tears but failed.

"Children, please hold up your black crayons."

Everyone did but Adams. "Mr. Adams, show me your black crayon." She pulled a black crayon from her box and held it up even with her right shoulder. "This is what a black crayon looks like."

Adams could not show her his black crayon because he had eaten it. He thought it was liquorice. At that moment Wainwright knew he and Adams would be best friends.

. . . .

ALICE TAPS LIGHTLY on Wainwright's apartment door. "Michael, it's me, Alice." There is no answer. She checks her phone. It is six-forty-five. He should be awake. She raps hard on his door. "Michael, it's me, Alice," she says again. Still no answer. She lifts the doormat, grabs the key and unlocks the door. She walks through the living room to his bedroom. He is asleep, snoring loudly. She clicks the ceiling light in his bedroom on and off four times.

He grabs a pillow and covers his head. "Stop that. Go away, I'm not going to work today."

"Are you sick?"

"No, I'm just not going to work."

"You are going to work today and tomorrow and the day after that," she says with intensity. "You use that line every day, it's getting old."

"How do you know what I say every day, you're here only on Mondays?"

"We compare notes."

"A bunch of evil witches." He rubs his eyes with his fingers. "By the way, did you sleep in your clothes? Ever use an iron? No time to brush your hair?" He smiles and waits for a reaction from her. She ignores him. "Buy your shirt at the Salvation Army? You wasted a buck. Nobody wears flannel but hicks."

"Good morning to you Mister Sunshine. You sure know how to

brighten up the day." She grabs his wheelchair next to the clothes bureau, pushes the power lever to on, guides it to the bedside, and locks the wheels. She grabs the bed's control, which is dangling off the side of the bed, and shifts the mattress to a sitting position. She pulls the bed covers off him, rolls them in a ball and tosses them to the foot of the bed. Wainwright closes his eyes. "My head hurts."

"Mine does too."

"I'm cold."

"You're not cold."

"Yes, I am."

"Too bad." She places one arm behind his shoulders and her other arm under his knees and turns him to face her. She drapes his legs over the side of the bed and lowers the bed so his feet are touching the floor. She places her knees on the outside of his left leg and her arms underneath his armpits. "On three," she says. He counts with her. She slides him into the wheelchair. He gives her as much support as he can. She checks to make sure his head and neck are properly supported. "Looks good," she says.

"I always look good, I'm a handsome devil."

"In your dreams." She guides him to the bathroom, helps him shave with an electric razor then removes his undershirt and underpants. She helps him wash his upper body, comb his hair, brush his teeth, and change into clean underwear. She takes the filled catheter bag from him, empties it in the toilet, washes the bag, hands him a new bag, and wipes him dry.

"I want aftershave."

"Aftershave, you never wear aftershave."

"I want to, today."

"Why?"

"I just do."

Dressing him takes much longer than usual, not because he is more difficult to dress today, but because he keeps changing his mind. Six different shirts and three pairs of pants before he selects what he wants.

"What's up?" Alice asks.

"Nothing's up."

"Something's up, you never care about what you wear."

"I do today."

"Why?"

"I just do."

"Tell me why or I won't get you to the van on time."

"That's extortion."

"Yes, it is."

"I work with Rita today, alone all day, just the two of us."

"Rita who?"

"Rita Ives."

"The cute redhead with the dimples."

"Yes, that Rita."

"Haven't you two been dating forever?"

"Not forever, four years next month."

"That's pretty much forever." She helps him guide his wheelchair to the kitchen. She checks the time on the wall clock. "You don't have time for a big breakfast, maybe toast and a cup of coffee, nothing more than that."

"We have plenty of time, The Van Nazi can wait. I'm starved. I want bacon and eggs, two eggs over light, don't overcook them like you did last time, and surprise me, no shells in the yoke. And I want four slices of bacon, crispy brown, that's crispy brown, not burnt cinders."

"We don't have time. She won't wait. She wouldn't wait for the pope."

"Probably not, she's a bitch."

Alice pulls a pair of argyle socks on his feet. "Are these shoes okay, Mr. Dapper or should I get a different pair?" She puts on his shoes and grabs a light jacket from his closet.

"Very funny."

He finishes his toast and coffee. Alice brushes the breadcrumbs off his face and wheels him out the front door, down the hall, to the elevator.

The Van Nazi is standing outside the van, leaning against the side door, tapping her wristwatch with her fingertips. "One more minute and I'm out of here," she says.

Alice and Michael just make the deadline. The driver opens the side doors and lowers the wheelchair lift. "You just made it," the driver says. She sniffs and rubs her nose with her left sleeve.

Inside the van one of the men mumbles, "The Van Nazi." The others laugh.

"I heard that," the driver says. She secures the wheelchair to the lift.

Alice leans over to Wainwright and whispers into his ear, "Next time, forget the aftershave."

"I smell good."

"No, you don't. Eau de grandpa." She shakes her head no. She returns to his apartment, makes his bed, cleans the kitchen, and washes a load of laundry. She checks her work schedule. Barbara Fermonte is next. She is one hundred next week. I won't live that long, no way. Not sure I want to.

CHAPTER 20

BARBARA FERMONTE

BARBARA FERMONTE IS staring out the window of her hospital room. She is fully dressed and ready to go home. She is wearing a blue sweater with six, black buttons and a blue, knit cap. In her lap she is holding a red, plastic pocketbook with a fake leather handle. The pocketbook's clasp is not latched and the plastic on the bottom is cracked. She has been ready to go home since nine this morning. She is waiting for her son Paul who had assured her he would be at the hospital by ten at the latest. It is twelve-fifteen. "That man will be late to his own funeral," she says to herself. She finds a roll of Tums in her pocketbook, peels a tablet from the roll and pops it into her mouth.

"You sure you don't want lunch" Lindley Miller asks her. Miller is the hospital aide whose main job is to deliver meals to the patients on the third floor of Providence Regional Medical Center. It is a simple but often unpleasant task because almost no one likes the food. One day, a very old man with ears and a nose so big it looked as though he had purchased them at a novelty store and glued them on his bald head, threw his tray at her and blamed her personally for what he said was food not fit for his dog. He missed her but she had to clean the mess.

Barbara entered the hospital four days ago when her visiting nurse, Jennifer Mason, found her half-conscious on the floor of her apartment, slumped against the chair that faces the television. Jennifer was afraid Barbara had a stroke. That is not what happened. Her problem was she was severely dehydrated. She often forgets to drink the amount of water she needs and, when asked by Jennifer or any of the other staff from the home care agency how much water she drinks, she lies to them.

Her four days at the hospital were awful. She couldn't sleep well, the bed was too hard, there was too much noise, even at midnight, and the room was never completely dark. Her doctor looked like a fifteen-year-old boy to her and he spoke with a slight accent, probably from India or Pakistan, which annoyed her. On the second day she asked him, "Where are you from?"

"Syracuse, New York," he said.

"No, I meant where are you really from?"

"Do you mean where are my parents really from?"

"Yes, where are your parents from?"

"My parents are from India. My family moved here in nineteen eighty-nine. I was born in New Delhi and moved here when I was three. I don't remember anything from before I moved to America. I've been to India four times and every time I go there I feel like I'm a stranger in a strange land. I was born in New Delhi but I consider myself from Syracuse, New York. I am an Orangeman through and through." He has told this story, pretty much word for word, many times before, usually to patients like Barbara, who remember a golden age when all the doctors were white men and all the nurses were white women wearing nurses' caps.

"Why aren't there any white doctors here?"

"There are plenty of white doctors here, just not me. Don't worry, I studied at Harvard or as we like to call it, ha vad." He uses the ha vad line frequently. She laughed. Most of his patients laugh when he says ha vad.

Barbara checks the time on her phone. It is twelve-twenty. She is annoyed. Her ha vad doctor walks into the hospital room with her son Paul at his right side. A woman, holding a briefcase in her left hand and wearing a dark blue, polo shirt with a logo above her left breast that says 'Pleasant Valley Senior Living' is one step behind them.

"Good morning Mrs. Fermonte, it's me, doctor Navin Chadha, your ha vad man."

"What, I can't hear you," she says.

"Good morning Mrs. Fermonte," he says again, this time at a volume so loud everyone in the hallway hears him.

"It's afternoon." She points to the clock on the wall. It is a very large clock with very large numbers. "Twenty after twelve to be exact, two hours and twenty minutes late."

"Then good afternoon to you. I was wrong." He bows slightly. "It's me, doctor Chadha."

"I know who you are, I've seen you every day for the past week."

"Actually, it's been only four days Mrs. Fermonte, it may seem like a week, but it's been just four days."

"I've been here too damn long."

"I have a few minor things to discuss and then you'll be on your way." He scans his clipboard and says "hmm, hmm, hmm" to himself. "As you know from our discussion yesterday, you did not have a stroke or a heart attack, that's the good news. The bad news is you were severely dehydrated. I believe this is the fourth time in the past nine months that you've been here in the hospital because you were dehydrated."

"Just three times."

"My chart says four times."

"What?" She cups her ears with her hands.

"My chart says four times, Mrs. Fermonte." He speaks so loudly a nurse walking by the room looks inside to make sure nothing is wrong.

"Just three times overnight. The first time I went home after nine wasted hours."

"Three or four, either is too many." He checks his chart again. "How much water do you drink each day?"

"Eight glasses, just like I'm supposed to."

"Oh Ma, please," Paul says. He is sitting on the radiator under the window. "You're lucky if you drink a full glass a day."

"How do you know what I drink, you don't live with me, you're never at my apartment?"

"Mother, who are you kidding? If I were there any more I'd have to pay rent."

She waves him away to let him know he is talking nonsense.

Chadha directs the woman wearing the Pleasant Valley shirt to join him. She was standing at the doorway. "Do you know Theresa Cioffi?"

"No and I don't want to," Barbara says.

Paul jumps off the radiator and joins Chadha and Cioffi at the bedside. "Ma, we had a meeting this morning, that's why we were late. We think it's best for you to move to Pleasant Valley Senior Living. You can't live by yourself anymore. It's not safe. It's a fantastic facility. You'll have a single room, you won't have to share your room with anyone. It's a great place, you'll love it."

"If it's so great, you live there."

Theresa pulls several brochures from her briefcase and gives them to Barbara. Barbara grabs them and looks them over. All three brochures feature healthy, active, very attractive seniors, all of them much younger than she is and all of them so fit you wonder why they would live in a nursing home. One picture shows two couples playing tennis and a second shows several women in a water aerobics class. The only frail senior featured is a handsome, well-dressed man in a wheelchair with an oxygen tube in his nose. Despite the oxygen tube, he looks totally healthy and he is smiling at a very attractive, young nurse who is pushing his wheelchair.

"Everybody is having such a great time, what a wonderful place, you're right Paul, I should live there." She throws the brochures to the floor. She looks at Cioffi. "Your name Theresa?"

"Yes."

"Theresa, tell my son to go fuck himself. I'm not moving anywhere."

"Mother, you can't stay in your apartment, it's not safe. You've fainted four times in nine months. One of these days no one is going to find you until it's too late."

"I'll be dead soon enough anyway, I'm a hundred years old, how much longer do you think I'm going to live." She takes her wool cap off, sticks it into her pocketbook and looks at Cioffi. "Theresa, tell my son to go fuck himself."

"I can't do that Mrs. Fermonte."

"Doctor Chadha, tell my son to go fuck himself."

"I think you just did."

Cioffi grabs the brochures from the floor and stuffs them back into her briefcase. "Maybe this was a bit premature," she says quietly to Paul and turns to Barbara. "It's been nice meeting you Mrs. Fermonte."

"Not much more I can do here," Chadha says to Paul. "The most important thing, your mother needs to drink lots of water, five, six glasses a day, minimum, whether she wants to or not, otherwise she's pretty healthy for someone who is one hundred."

Barbara tries to hear him but cannot. "What, what did you say?"

"I said you need to drink more water." He tucks his clipboard to his side and leans toward Barbara, his face just inches from hers. "Mrs. Fermonte, I am going to have a home health nurse check on you first thing tomorrow morning. In the meantime, think about what your son said about moving to Pleasant Valley. It's for your own good."

Barbara looks away from him to her son Paul. "Paul, tell doctor Chadha to mind his own damn business."

"All right mother, you win, I'll take you home."

"Not yet, I'm hungry. I want to eat my lunch first. Go find the girl with the lunch cart."

Paul shakes his head. "Mother you are a piece of work, that is for sure."

CHAPTER 21

MICHAEL WAINWRIGHT

MICHAEL WAINWRIGHT TELLS Alice to enter his apartment before she knocks on his door.

"Come in, it's not locked," he yells just as she is set to rap on the door and slip the key into the lock. He had heard her distinctive walk down the hallway. She thumps across the floor like a toddler. When she hears him beckon her, she replaces the key under the doormat and opens the door. She turns on the living room and bedroom lights. He is reading the *Providence Herald* on his I-Pad. "Have you seen today's newspaper?"

"No, should I?"

"Absolutely." He reads a headline. "Nason alleges home health aide took advantage of brother." The headline is from the lead story on the bottom half of the front page. On the printed copy it would be just under the fold.

"Not surprised, the reporter called me last night. He was very annoying."

"You're pretty evil, I always knew that." He reads the opening paragraph. "Providence resident Bill Nason, brother of Clyde Nason, who died in his home on April first, is threatening legal action against the Providence Visiting Nurses Association and home health aide Alice Hammond. Nason alleges Hammond took advantage of his brother Clyde and convinced him to leave the bulk of his estate to her, two hundred acres on Beckley Hill and one hundred twenty-five thousand dollars, and the agency had known for nearly three years that Hammond's behavior toward Clyde was inappropriate." He hands Alice his I-Pad. "Don't bother trying to take advantage of me, I'm too smart and I've got nothing to give you except for my Stars Wars action figures and you're not getting them."

"They're dolls, not action figures, dolls, short Barbies with light sabers. But you are absolutely correct, I am an evil, wicked woman, even worse than you know, way worse. I kidnapped the Lindbergh baby, I shot Kennedy from the grassy knoll, I gave Elvis his cape and his white, bell bottom stretch pants, and I deflated footballs for Tom Brady, not just the one time he was caught but fifteen times in all, including all six of his super bowl wins."

"You're right, you are way worse than I thought, especially the bell bottoms for Elvis, that's real evil, ninth circle of hell evil."

"If you google wicked women, I'm the third listing down on the first page just under Lady Macbeth and Mata Hari," Alice says

"No, you must be the fourth listing, my aunt Emily is worse than you are, by far."

Alice gets the joke, Emily is a clueless, old school boomer. Most of her conversations with Michael start with, In my day.

He grabs the I-Pad from her and points to the screen. "Why didn't you say something?" Before she responds he reads two more lines from the story. "Hammond had no comment. Agency director Charles Connor also had no comment." He shakes his head. "You should have said something. Connor sure as hell should have said something, she's a valued employee or she works really hard, her client's love her."

"My lawyer told me not to say anything."

"No comment makes you sound guilty. And no comment from Connor makes you sound even more guilty. Is he a putz?"

"No, he's not a putz or at least I don't think he's a putz. I don't know him from Adam and no, I am not guilty of anything."

"I didn't think you were. Don't listen to that asshole, he's an ambulance chasing shyster. Have you seen his commercials?" He changes his voice and word cadence to mimic Nason's serious tone and fast delivery. "I will get you acquitted of the charges against you, my personal guarantee, or my name isn't Bill Nason."

"I'm glad you can laugh about it," Alice says.

He gives the tablet to her. She tosses it on the bed.

"So what are you going to do with all that money? You should go on a round-the-world cruise. Maybe you'll meet the man of your dreams or any man for that matter."

"How do you know I want a man, maybe I want the woman of my dreams?"

"Maybe you'll meet the woman of your dreams. Either way, you're not getting any younger."

"I'm twenty-eight, hardly old. I don't want to meet the man of my dreams or the woman of my dreams, at least not now. I'm happy alone."

"Sure you are."

"I am."

"Nobody's happy alone. You need a partner, you just don't know it yet."

"I know what I need and a partner isn't it."

"If you say so."

"Enough of this nonsense, we've got to get you ready for work." She clicks on the power switch on his wheelchair and guides it to the bedside.

"Okay Mom. But first I need to show you something." He points to the clothes bureau across the room. "Open the first drawer and take out the blue, ring box."

Alice opens the drawer, grabs the box and opens the lid with her thumbnail. Inside there is a diamond engagement ring. "Back up Romeo, who is this for? Rita?"

"Yes, Rita, who else?"

"The redhead?"

"Yes."

"You've got to be kidding me." She helps him transfer from the bed to the wheelchair. She removes his catheter bag and empties it into the toilet.

"So what do you think?"

"About what, about the ring or about you getting engaged?"

"About both?"

"About the ring, very classy. I'm surprised, I figured you for a too big, totally cheesy diamond man, the kinda guy who'd buy a low quality diamond the size of the lollipop."

"My mother helped me. What about the engagement? What do you think?"

"Took you long enough."

"That's what Rita said."

"Good men are always clueless."

"Are you saying I'm one of the good ones?"

"Maybe."

"I have a question for you and I want you to say yes."

"Depends on the question."

"I want you to be my best man."

"Hate to break it to you, Michael, but I'm a woman."

"Then be my best woman, my best person, whatever."

"Why me?"

"Why not you?"

"I thought you hated me."

"I do hate you." He laughs. "But you're the person I hate the least."

"I'm honored to be the person you hate the least. For my grooms person's gift you should get me a plaque that says, Alice Hammond, the person I hate the least. I'll hang it in my living room, just under the most improved award I got in fifth grade soccer. I sucked." She points to the plate of scrambled eggs. "Eat."

"So, that's a yes?"

"Yes, why not, what the hell else do I have to do." She pulls the ring box from her pocket, takes a second look at the ring, closes the lid and places the box on the kitchen counter. "You're not going to make me wear a monkey suit are you?"

"Yes, powder blue with black trim and a black cummerbund. The same suite my father wore in nineteen seventy-four. Retro ugly is in. I'll grow my hair shoulder length and wear a leather headband with the word peace etched into the leather."

"Good idea. So when's the big day?"

"Saturday, October fifth."

The transport van peeps its horn.

"Damn," Alice says. She runs through the kitchen and the living room to the front door, out the door, bounds down the steps to the first floor, runs to the building's entrance, out that door, down the four steps to the sidewalk, and across the wet grass to the van. She waves to the van driver as she runs. "Wait," she screams. When she gets to the van she pounds on the hood. "Can you wait five minutes?"

"No can do missy," the driver says. She waves to Alice as she drives off.

Alice tells Michael he has missed the van.

"No big deal, you can take me," he says.

I can't take you, the agency doesn't allow patient transports."

"Just this once, who's going to know?"

"You read the paper today. I'm on thin ice as it is. Even if I could take you, I couldn't fit your wheelchair in my car."

"It'll fit in the trunk."

"I can't lift it, it weighs a ton."

"Good point. No problem, I can always work from home." He grabs his cell phone on the kitchen table and calls his work. "So, you are going to be my best person, right?"

"Okay, but no freakin monkey suit." Alice washes the dishes, sweeps the floor, makes his bed and puts a load of laundry into the washing machine. "I think I'm done here."

You haven't vacuumed the living room rug." He laughs.

"It's fine."

"I'll file a complaint."

"Go for it."

"I would but the complaint line for you is too long, it would take all day."

. . . .

SHE DRIVES FOUR miles to the Quick Stop gas station, fills her tank and buys a copy of the *Providence Herald*.

"Hey, it's you," the clerk says, pointing to her. He is wearing a New England Patriots' shirt and a matching hat. He is as thin as a cardboard figure.

"What?" Alice says.

"It's you, you're the home health aide who got all that money."

She shakes her head and walks to her car. There is a picture of her in the paper she hadn't noticed on the I-Pad. The reporter must have lifted the picture from the internet. She is holding a Bud Light blue can in her right hand. It is obvious from her eyes she had been drinking. She remembers when the picture was taken, the night before she graduated from the University of Vermont. She had gotten so drunk she passed out. She checks the messages on her phone. There are twelve messages from her mother. She deletes all twelve without listening to any of them. She checks her work schedule. Tim Rogers is next. It's foxtrot day today, one, two, three four. She taps her fingers on the dashboard to a four count beat.

CHAPTER 22

TIM ROGERS

TIM ROGERS IS wearing boxer shorts, an undershirt, and slippers. His shirt is ripped at the right shoulder and the neckline is frayed. His apartment is broiling hot. He awoke at three-thirty drenched with sweat and could not get back to sleep. He has no control over the thermostat. Some days his apartment is so cold he wears a sweater, coat, hat, and gloves, and some days it is so hot he wears just underwear. He has complained many times to the building supervisor but nothing is ever done.

The room is dark except for the light from the four street lamps across the road from his apartment building. The green power light on his CD player is blinking. Doris Day is singing 'The Street Where You Live.' Tim had set the volume to the lowest setting so the music wouldn't bother his neighbors. He can barely hear the music.

He is slowly shuffling across the floor whispering: "One, two, three, four; one, two, three, four," as he dances. His hands are placed in front of his body as if he were holding a dance partner. His wife Beatrice died sixteen years ago tomorrow. The day she died she said, "Don't ever stop dancing." He promised her he wouldn't stop but he did.

By the time Alice gets to Tim's apartment, the temperature in the rooms has cooled to a more reasonable level. He had opened the living room window and had gone back to sleep. She knocks several times on his door but he doesn't hear her. "Mr. Rogers, it's me, Alice. Time to get up."

"What, what time is it. Is it night or is it day?" He rubs his eyes.

"It's the crack of midday, time to dance. You promised to teach me how to foxtrot. One, two, three, four," she says as she dances across the living room.

"I'd love to but I danced last night. I'm too sore and too tired today, maybe next time."

"No problem. You owe me a foxtrot lesson."

"Next time for sure."

She takes his temperature, blood pressure and pulse. She checks his legs and feet for sores. "Looks good, looks like you'll live another day. Don't forget, foxtrot teaching day next Thursday, and no dancing the night before."

"Got it, foxtrot day, next Thursday, one, two, three, four."

"It's a plan."

The sound from the television in the apartment on the other side of the living room wall is heard clearly in Tim's apartment. Rachel Ray is adding cheese to something. The audience is clapping. "They always clap for cheese," Tim says.

"I do too. Don't forget, foxtrot next Thursday. What exactly is a foxtrot?" Alice says.

Tim smiles. Three years before his wife's death, he and Beatrice danced their last waltz in the living room of their Prospect Street house. It was their last day in their ten-room house. They had sold the house and were moving to a two bedroom ranch in West Providence. The movers were coming at nine o'clock. The furniture that wouldn't fit in their new house was either sold or given to their three daughters. Most of it was sold. Tim was surprised and disappointed that his daughters wanted so few pieces. He thought the furniture meant more to them than it did. Everything else he and Beatrice owned was in boxes.

It didn't bother Tim that the new house was so much smaller than the Prospect Street house because that house was simply too big and it was getting increasingly difficult for him to climb the stairs to the second floor bedroom. What he didn't like about the new house were the low ceilings. The ceilings in the Prospect Street house were ten feet high on both floors, high enough for a huge Christmas tree every year, trees so big he could barely drag them into the house. The ceilings in their new house supposedly were eight feet from the floor. When he measured, the actual height was only seven feet, ten inches. In her sales pitch, the real estate saleswoman told him the ceilings were eight feet high. He corrected her. "Duly noted," she said.

They had lived in the Prospect Street house for thirty-three years. Their daughter Anne was six when they moved in, Beth was four, and Kara was an eight-month-old toddler.

The house was in serious need of repairs, not really fit for a family with small children but it was the only large house they could afford. The previous owner had neglected routine maintenance. Beatrice's parents were dismayed when she and Tim bought the house. The ad in the newspaper said the building was a handyman's dream. For Tim it was as much a nightmare as it was a dream, at least in the beginning. He spent most of his free time the first five years rebuilding the house. He replaced all thirty windows, repaired the chimney, tore down the walls, one room at a time, insulated each room, replaced the horsehair plaster walls with wallboard and painted or wallpapered each room.

He ripped up the worn out, stained, wall-to-wall carpets that were in every room except for the kitchen and bathroom and discovered beautiful hardwood floors under the rugs. He sanded the floors and covered them with three coats of polyurethane. He was disappointed with the first floor he sanded because, in certain light, he could see all the sanding mistakes he had made and every spot where the polyurethane had bubbled. His floor sanding skills improved with each room and by the fourth room he was nearly as good as a professional.

He painted the outside of the house three times over the thirty-three years, one small section each summer. He divided the house into ten sections and painted each section once every ten years. To his neighbors it seemed as though he was always painting the house. They joked it wasn't officially summer until Tim took out his ladder and paint cans.

Four years before he and Beatrice moved to the ranch house in West Providence, his daughters chipped in and hired a painter to paint the whole house, not just one of his ten sections. Tim was set to paint the highest section in the back, the most difficult section to paint. The top peak was thirty-two feet from the ground. Hiring the painter was a Father's Day gift to him. When his daughters gave him the gift certificate he told them he didn't want it, why would they waste their money on something he could do himself for free.

"You're too old and you're going to get hurt," his daughter Kara told him.

"I'm not too old." He stormed out of the room. What he didn't know was Beatrice had asked them to hire the painter and had paid half the cost. She was afraid he would fall off the ladder. His balance and strength were not what they once were. She was pretty certain he would get hurt.

Tim bitched for weeks about the cost to hire the painter. Secretly he was glad because he wasn't confident he could climb the ladder anymore without getting hurt and he knew his strength had dropped so badly he could no longer raise and lower the ladder without help.

Tim and Beatrice lived in the West Providence ranch house for just two years when she got cancer. The cancer spread very fast. She was dead ten months after her diagnosis. It isn't fair, he told his three daughters, I was supposed to go first. How can I live without her?

He lived in the ranch house by himself for six more years after his wife's death and moved to his downtown apartment in 2009 because he needed money from the sale of the house. The 2008 stock market crash had wiped out his investments and had left him unable to pay his bills.

On their last morning in their Prospect Street house, Tim opened a bottle of Brut champagne and filled two plastic cups.

"It's been a long, strange trip," he said to Beatrice.

"It has been, indeed."

They tipped their cups together and drank the champagne. He opened the disk insert door on the CD player and checked to see if a CD was in the slot. There was a CD entitled Waltz Music. The first track was 'The Blue Danube.' Tim grabbed his wife's right arm and walked her from the couch to the middle of the living room. "Do you come here often?" he said pretending they were strangers in a bar, a game they had played many times before."

"More than you'd like to know," she said.

Tim hugged her and they both laughed. They waltzed across the living room through that waltz and two others. When the third waltz ended, 'The Waltz of the Flowers' from *The Nutcracker*, Tim sat down on the couch, grabbed his side and caught his breath.

"I'm so sorry, I'm not as young as I once was."

"You're young to me," she said. She kissed his forehead.

"How many times do you think we've danced in this living room?" he said.

"I don't know, two thousand times, maybe more, I have no idea."

When their three daughters were young girls they would dance with them, sometimes all five of them holding hands in a big circle as they waltzed across the room. Once the girls were teenagers they were embarrassed with the living room dancing, especially when the curtain to the living room window was open and the lights were on.

A waltz from *Swan Lake* played on the CD player. "God, I love that piece," Tim said. He reminded her that was the music they danced to the night they won the bronze medal at the New England championship. "Do you remember that night?" he said.

"I do. How could I forget?" she said.

Tim heard the backup bell from the moving van. "They're here."

"I guess so, I guess this is the end, our last day in this wonderful house," she said.

"There's one more thing I need to do," he said. He walked slowly up the stairs to the second floor. As he climbed the stairs he grabbed the banister with his left hand and pushed against his right knee to help him with the ascent. On the second level he walked through the attic door and painfully climbed the twelve steps to the top. The steps were very steep, almost too steep for him to manage. The attic was empty except for three cardboard boxes that were at the far end, near the roof vent. The boxes were filled with pictures and notes from every family who had ever lived in the house.

The first owners had the house built in nineteen fifteen. In the box with the oldest pictures there was a picture of the first parents and their son and two daughters with a message on the back of the picture that says, 'Easter 1918.' The girls and their mother were wearing fancy Easter hats and the father was in a suit. The girls were teenagers, possibly younger. The boy was nineteen. Tim knew that because the boy's age was written on the back of the picture. The boy was wearing an Army uniform. The sun was shining through his generous ears. He was in the middle of the picture, his mother was on his right, his father on his left, his younger sister was next to the father and the older daughter was standing next to their mother. On the back of the picture someone, probably the mother, wrote: 'Our beloved son Robert died May 28, 1918, at the Battle of Cantigny, he was 19. We miss him very much.'

The second owners lived in the house from nineteen thirty-six until nineteen forty-five. There were seven children in all, six girls and one boy. Tim wondered where they all slept and how anybody could survive six daughters.

The third owners, the family who lived in the house just before Tim and his family moved in, lost the house in a bank foreclosure in nineteen sixty-five. There were five children, two boys and three girls. One of the boys was in a wheelchair. In his note, the previous owner, whose name was Tod Smith, included a three-page rambling letter apologizing for not maintaining the house the way it should have been maintained. He said in his note he was injured on his job when he walked under a ladder and a hammer slipped from a workman's hand and hit his head. He wasn't wearing a hardhat. He was lucky he lived, he wrote. He was in a coma for four days. The man who dropped the hammer visited him in the hospital and cried. Smith returned to work a month later but he got too many dizzy spells and had to quit. The disability checks weren't enough to repair what needed to be repaired at the house. He was sorry, he wrote. His wife Sally wrote they did their best.

Tim opened the newest box of pictures and flipped through the pictures he and Beatrice had added to the collection. There was a picture of the five of them standing on the front porch on the first day they moved in. The note on the back of the picture read, 'July 14, 1966 - OUR FIRST DAY IN OUR NEW HOME.' There was a picture of them at a beach on Cape Cod in nineteen seventy-two. Tim considered removing the picture from the box because Anne, who was fourteen, was wearing a skimpy, two-piece bathing suit, not a bikini but small, nevertheless. He looked at the picture, hesitated for a few seconds and tossed it back into the box. There were several pictures of them at Disney World in nineteen seventy-one. In one picture, all three daughters were wearing huge sombreros with brims at least three feet wide, so big and heavy the girls were having trouble keeping the hats on their heads.

Tim grabbed the letter he wrote to the next owners and read it aloud. He told them about all the repairs he had made and warned them there is always something that needs to be fixed in a big house. It's a lot of work, but it's worth it, he wrote. He told them that his three daughters had all moved far away, the two oldest to Denver, Colorado and his youngest to Seattle. He wished they lived closer. He grabbed a ballpoint pen from his shirt pocket and added a sentence to his note. This is a great house, I hope you love it as much as we did.

He reached into his back pocket and took out a picture of him and Beatrice standing on the front porch, the same place where they had stood with their three daughters on day one. He had taken the picture three weeks before. On the back he wrote, Our last day in our house, August 3, 1999. It was a wonderful house, we will miss it. He signed his name and Beatrice's name. He tossed the picture into the box and closed the top. "That should do it," he said.

CHAPTER 23

MARIA GALLO

MARIA GALLO'S BREATHING is labored, and there is a gurgling sound at the back of her throat. Her eyes are open but they are not focused on anything. There is a thin crust of discharge in the corner of her right eye. Alice wipes the eye clean with a damp towel and dries the skin with a second towel. She washes and dries Maria's left eyelid, cleans her ears and face, and lightly brushes her hair.

"Is she choking? I don't want her to choke. Is this the end?" Tony says.

"I don't know, it's hard to tell."

Alice grabs Maria's left wrist. Her pulse is very faint and her skin is cold. She lowers her nose to Maria's mouth to smell her breath.

"Is she going to die today?"

"I don't know."

"You should know. You went to medical school."

"Yes, I did, but right now I'm a home health aide. My job is to observe and pass on what I know to the nurses. Jen Mason will know more than I do. She's been a hospice nurse for fifteen years. I don't know what's going to happen next, I wish I did but I don't. It is impossible to predict. She could hover between life and death for a few hours or a few days, or even longer." She steps away from the bedside and retrieves her phone from her shoulder bag. "I'm going to call Jen, she'll be here soon."

Tony sprints to the kitchen and tries to open the broom closet door. In his rush he forgets to turn the knob a full rotation. He pulls on the door. It does not open. He kicks it hard. The wood splits at the bottom of the door. He jams his big toe. "Stupid goddamn door," he says. He turns the knob fully on the second try and roughly opens the door. He grabs a shoebox from the top shelf and checks the contents. It is filled with four Kiwi shoe polish tins and several dirty rags covered with brown shoe polish. He throws the box to the floor and grabs a second shoebox. Inside that box is a can of three-in-one oil, four brown plastic jars of hydrogen peroxide, a tube of wood glue, several ping-pong balls and an empty Kleenex box. He throws the box to the floor. The ping-pong balls bounce across the room. One of the hydrogen peroxide containers cracks and the liquid oozes out of the bottle. He grabs the broom, mop and dustpan and throws them across the kitchen. The dustpan slides across the floor, to the opposite wall. "Dammit, you can't find anything in this goddamn house." He punches the door and cuts the knuckle on his right index finger.

"What are you looking for Dad?" Celeste says. Her words startle him. She is standing next to him.

"Candles."

"Why?"

"We need to lower the lights. We need to keep bright light away from Mom's face. We need to make her comfortable. No sunlight, sunlight is bad, we need to keep sunlight away from her eyes." He sprints back to the living room, closes the curtains and quickly returns to the broom closet. "We need to play soothing music. I can read her favorite poem." He sprints back to the living room, checks the bookshelf, grabs a book of poems and sprints back to the kitchen. He drops the book into a mop bucket. He pulls the book out of the bucket and throws the bucket across the room. The bucket bounces three times. He jerks the vacuum cleaner out of the closet and kicks it across the floor. It smashes into the kitchen table. "Where are the goddamn candles?" He punches the door.

"Right here Daddy, right here in plain sight." Celeste points to five red candles in a third shoebox. The fat ends of candles are sticking out over the top of the box.

Tony grabs the box from the shelf. "Where are the matches? Where are the goddamn matches?"

"Right there in the box next to the candles. We found them yesterday, remember." She rolls her eyes. "Get a grip, Dad."

He sprints back to the living room. He is holding the shoebox with the candles and candle holders, the matches and a flashlight, in his left hand, and the book of poetry in his right hand. One of the flashlights falls out of the box and tumbles to the floor. He kicks it to the wall. He turns off the ceiling light in the living room, lights the candles and places them and the book on the table that holds the television. He looks at Alice. She is tucking her phone into her nursing bag.

"We've got to create a peaceful, soothing atmosphere. That's what the internet says, create a peaceful, soothing atmosphere, the more soothing the better. We've got to make her last hours the best, the best ever, the most peaceful ever. We can do that. I'm sure we can do that. I've run this moment in my head a hundred times. I know just what to do. I'll play Mom's favorite songs. I'll read to her. I'll read her favorite poem. No, wait, I'll read something from the Bible. She likes the verse about love, love is simple, love is love," he says.

"Love is patient, love is kind," Alice says.

"What?" Tony says.

"Love is patient, love is kind. I'm pretty sure that's what the Bible says, not love is simple."

"Are you sure?"

"Pretty sure."

He sprints to the bookshelf, grabs a Bible from the bottom shelf and tosses it to Alice. "Find it."

"I don't know where it is, in Corinthians I think, but I don't know which verse."

"Here, use my phone." He tosses Alice his cell phone. She types 'love is patient' into the Google search box. She checks the first link on the page. "I have it."

"Give me the phone." He grabs the phone from her, steps back to the bed, kneels next to his wife and gently strokes her hair. He reads so quickly each word blurs into the next. Celeste and Alice miss most of what he said. He drops the phone to the floor. "It's useless, she can't hear me."

"No, it is not useless, she can hear you," Alice says.

"No, she can't."

"Yes, she can. Read it again, slower this time. You read too fast, I could barely understand what you said."

Tony grabs the phone from the floor and gives it to Celeste. "You read it Celeste, Mom would love that."

Celeste reads the passage slowly and clearly as if she were auditioning for a play. "Love is patient, love is kind. It does not envy, it does not boast, it is not proud. It does not dishonor others, it is not self-seeking, it is not easily angered, it keeps no record of wrongs. Love does not delight in evil but rejoices with the truth. It always protects, always trusts, always hopes, always perseveres. Love never fails."

"That was beautiful," Alice says. She gently squeezes Celeste's right shoulder.

Maria's body stirs and her left arm flaps twice. She draws in air and exhales and shakes her head as if she had noticed something on the other side of the room. She cries out. The sound is more noise than words.

"What did she say?" Celeste says.

"She's angry," Tony says.

"No Dad, she's not angry, she's dying."

Tony gently strokes Maria's hair. Celeste grabs her mother's right hand and cradles it in her hands. Maria's breaths are labored. Alice drops her right ear to Maria's chest and listens for breathing and for a heartbeat.

"Is she gone?" Tony says.

"No, she is still with us," Alice says.

"Daddy, I have to tell Mom something in private," Celeste says. She points to the door to let him know she wants him to leave the room.

Tony doesn't move.

"You need to go away. It's just between Mom and me."

"Okay. I can take a hint."

He and Alice start to leave the room. "You can stay," Celeste says. She points to Alice.

"That's not private. I thought you said it's between you and Mom," Tony says.

"It's girl stuff, nothing you'd understand."

"Sure I would."

"No, you wouldn't."

Tony walks to the kitchen.

"That's too close, you need to go upstairs or go outside," Celeste says.

"I know when I'm not wanted. Good thing I've got work I need to do in the garage."

Once his footsteps are out of earshot, Celeste grabs her mother's hand and Alice's hand. "Mom, I've got a boyfriend. His name is Tim, Tim O'Connor. He's very nice. He's in eighth-grade. He's not too old, it's only one grade difference. He's not like the other boys. He doesn't make fart sounds with his armpits and he listens to me, he really listens to me. He doesn't fake listen like most boys do. I know you think I'm too young to have a boyfriend but I'm not. Most of my friends have already kissed a boy. I haven't kissed a boy yet but I want to, I want to kiss Tim. I've come close. His breath smells like spearmint gum. I want you to be the first person I tell when I kiss a boy. I will kiss Tim today and I'll tell you about it tonight." She looks at Alice. "Do you think I'm too young to have a boyfriend?"

"I can't say, I'm not your mother," Alice says.

Celeste brushes Maria's hair with her right hand. "Mom, I'm going to miss you so, so much. Who's going to help me braid my hair? Daddy can't do it, he has no idea what to do."

"I can teach him, it's not that hard," Alice says.

"What about washing my clothes, I don't want him touching my underwear, gross. He'll mix the colors, all men do that. All my clothes will be ruined."

"He can be trained."

"I'm not so sure. What about my period? I can't ask him about it, that would be awful. I suppose I could ask Aunt Connie for help. I don't want to ask her. She's always correcting my grammar and telling me to stand up straight. That gets old." She looks back at Alice. "When I get my period, can I call you?"

"Definitely."

"Well, Mom, I don't have much more to say. I wish you could meet Tim, you'd like him a lot, he's very funny. His Trump voice is so, so funny. You'd laugh, I know you would. 'It's fake news, fake news,' he says. So funny." She lightly rubs her mother's forehead.

"I love you Mom." She cradles her mother's head in her arms. She looks at Alice. "You can go get my father now."

Tony is on the porch. When he hears the words, 'you can get my father,' he jumps off the porch and runs into the garage. Alice finds him sharpening a saw blade. "You can come back in the house now. I hope you didn't hurt your ankle when you jumped off the porch," she says.

"You saw me?"

"Yes, I did, in fact I saw you peeking through the door."

"Please don't tell Celeste."

"I won't."

"Will you come when Celeste needs you?"

"Yes, of course, call me whenever you need me."

Alice puts her right arm across Tony's back and guides him back to the living room.

Celeste is whisper-singing the words to 'Five Hundred Miles Away From Home' to her mother. Her face is nearly touching Maria's face. Maria's breaths are irregular and much louder than when Alice entered the room two hours ago. The time between each breath is nearly a minute. The gurgling sound is constant. Tony cups his ears to muffle the sound. "I don't know if I can do this," he says.

"Yes, you can, Dad."

Alice pats dry the secretions on Maria's lips and chin with a towel.

"Let me do that," Tony says. He grabs the towel from Alice and dries the moisture on Maria's face. Maria's breathing stops. Alice checks her watch and waits five minutes. She lowers her head to Maria's chest.

"Is she gone?" Tony says.

"I think so."

"No, no, no" he cries out.

"Dad, we're here, we were here at the end." Celeste lightly touches her mother's face and hugs her father hard. "We were here, that's what matters."

There is a knock at the front door. "Hey, it's me, Jen Mason," Jennifer says as she opens the door.

"We forgot to play soothing music, we should have played soothing music. Mom would have loved soothing music. It's too late now, damn, damn, damn, it's too late now," Tony says.

No, it's not too late, her spirit will hear the music," Celeste says.

Tony selects 'Saturday Night Waltz' on the I-Pod attached to the stereo. "This is her favorite music by far. She told me to play it at her funeral. She said no sermon, just play 'Saturday Night Waltz.' It's beautiful."

"Yes, it is," Jennifer says. She walks to Maria and checks the carotid artery for a pulse. There is none. She listens for a heartbeat with her stethoscope. She checks Maria's pupils with a light. She pulls the sheet and blanket up to Maria's shoulders. She places her stethoscope and flashlight in her nurse's bag and zips the bag shut. "As I'm sure you know, Mr. Gallo, your wife has passed."

"She didn't pass anything, you pass a test, she died," Tony says.

"Sorry, Mr. Gallo, your wife has died."

"What do I do now?" Tony asks, his voice cracks.

"Nothing, just pray, we'll handle everything from here," Jenifer says. She leaves a message with Maria's doctor and calls the funeral home.

"Everything's all set. The ambulance will be here in about twenty minutes."

"Thank you," Tony says.

He hugs Celeste. "She was the best mom ever."

"She was," Celeste says.

Alice hugs Celeste and hugs Tony. "If you need me, I'll be here."

"We will, that's for sure." Tony says. He hugs Celeste and rubs her hair with his fingers.

Alice grabs her bag and walks to the front door. "I'm glad I was here, thank you," she says to Tony. She looks at Jen Mason. "Let me know if there is anything you need me to do."

Jen nods yes.

Celeste follows Alice to her car. "You won't tell my father about Tim? Please don't tell him about Tim."

"Tim who?"

They both laugh.

Alice drives five blocks to the McDonalds parking lot, bangs the steering wheel with both of her fists and sobs. A teenage boy riding a skateboard stops at her car and taps on the glass. "You okay ma'am?"

"I'm fine," Alice says. I must be getting old, no one has ever called me ma'am before. I don't think I like it.

CHAPTER 24

ALICE HAMMOND

ALICE IS SITTING in her car in her parents' driveway listening to the radio. A commentator for BBC is talking about forest fires in California. She is trying to pay attention but has missed most of what was said. There is a rap on the driver's side window.

"Alice, what are you doing? You've been sitting here for half an hour," her father Dan says. He is wearing slippers and a bathrobe.

"Nothing, just listening to the news."

"Are you okay?"

"I'm fine."

"You're not fine, you've been crying."

"I have not."

"Yes, you have. What's wrong?"

"Nothing's wrong, Dad."

He opens the passenger's side door and sits next to her. "Alice, what's wrong?"

"One of my patients died today. She was so kind. She was my tenth grade math teacher. I loved her. She was one of my favorite teachers."

"Take the time to grieve but you need to move on. Patients die every day."

"This one was different. She was only thirty-eight. She had a thirteen-year-old daughter. Her daughter is devastated."

"Time will heal."

"I'm not so sure."

"It will. It usually does."

"How do you deal with death? I know it happens every day. Thirty-eight, that doesn't make sense."

"Death often doesn't make sense, it's cruel."

"Your patients die?" Alice asks.

"Everybody dies."

"You know what I mean. They die on the operating table. They die too young."

"Some do, not many, but some. I am a heart surgeon, death goes with the job."

"How do you face the families, especially with the death of a young mom or a child?"

He grabs her right hand and squeezes it. "Let me tell you a story from when I was a medical student that I will never forget. I think about it before every surgery. I was just about your age. I was twenty-seven, in my first year residency in Boston. I was scheduled to observe the heart surgery of a young boy, he was only ten. This was his fourth surgery. He had one when he was three, another when he was four, and his third heart operation when he was seven.

"He was so tiny. He looked like a six-year-old. He showed me a rookie baseball card of Tom Seaver. He was very proud. 'This is worth a lot of money,' he said. I grabbed it from him and said, 'Tom Seaver, why Tom Seaver, you're a Boston boy, what about Jim Rice or Dennis Eckersley?' He laughed. 'Because Tom Seaver's the best,' he said.

"Under his pillow he had a brand new baseball glove he had gotten for Christmas. It was a Tom Seaver glove. It smelled like mink oil. The pillowcase was grease stained. He told me he was going to play little league baseball in the spring. He had never played little league before. He was very excited.

"The operation was long, over five hours. I was exhausted just watching. I could tell from the surgeon's body language and the tone of his voice things weren't going well. The boy died at eleven-twelve. I remember the time because the surgeon looked at the clock on the wall and said, 'The time of death, eleven-twelve.' I can still hear his voice.

"The boy's mother wailed when she was told. The surgeon was very kind. He hugged her and hugged her husband and told them their son was just too weak to live. 'I know,' the father said, 'we didn't think Eric would live this time.'

"We left them and went to the cafeteria for lunch. On our way there, several doctors and nurses told the surgeon they had heard the news and were very sorry. He shook his head in dismay each time and thanked them for their concern. At lunch he said he was going to the gym for a quick workout before his next surgery. He asked me if I wanted to join him. 'Are you crazy, you just lost a ten year-old-boy, how can you go to the gym? Don't you have a heart?' I said. I was so angry I wanted to punch him in the face.

"He laughed and tapped my shoulder. 'Hammond, you're young, you're very young,' he said. 'I have another surgery at two o'clock this afternoon. I must have my head totally clear by then. My workout helps me focus. Eric was a beautiful, young boy. His death is awfully sad. He isn't the first child who died in my surgery and he won't be the last. My patient for the two o'clock surgery needs my full attention. Her surgery is just as complicated as Tim's, maybe more. She deserves my best. Death is terrible, especially when it happens to a child. I'm a surgeon, I have to move on and sometimes I have to move on quickly.'

"I've never forgotten what he said. At the time I thought he was a cruel bastard but I learned the hard way he was right." Dan hugs his daughter. "Death of your patients, especially if they're young, is never easy."

Alice's mother Lesley is watching them from the living room window.

"You better come inside or your mother will worry herself to death," Dan says. He pulls Alice to him as they walk toward the house. "Everything will be fine, it really will."

"I hope so Dad."

CHAPTER 25

ALICE HAMMOND

A MESSAGE PING from her cellphone wakes Alice from a frightful dream. In her dream she was pushing Michael Wainwright in his wheelchair down the center aisle of the church for his wedding. The church floor was steeply sloped, as steep as a painter's ladder leaning against a house. She lost her grip and the wheelchair rolled fast down the aisle toward Michael's future wife. All the people in the pews watched in horror as the wheelchair streaked, jet fast, toward the altar. Alice awoke just seconds before Michael and his wheelchair were set to crush his fiancée, her parents, and the minister.

Alice checks the time. It is one o'clock. She grabs her phone under the pillow. There are four messages, all from her mother. Oh mother please go back to sleep, it's Saturday.

Alice's mother frequently can't sleep. When she can't sleep she frets about everything imaginable and sends text messages to her children.

The first three texts plead with Alice not to be late for her father's sixty-fifth birthday party, which is today. The fourth message includes a link to a story from *Atlantic* magazine about several students who had dropped out of medical school and had returned and were the best students in their class. The time off helped them better understand why they were in medical school. 'You should read this, you're not alone,' her mother's message says.

Alice shakes her head. "Give it a rest mother," she says as if she were talking directly to her. She tries to go back to sleep but fails, too many thoughts in her head.

Yesterday, she was deposed by Raymond Hebert, the lawyer for Bill Nason. Hebert looked like a lawyer in a TV western. He wore a brown wool suit with a vest, a red bowtie, a stiff collared, white shirt and a gold pocket watch with a gold chain. At the start of the meeting he flipped open the watch cover to check the time. Is it high noon yet marshal? Alice considered asking him but decided to say nothing. Hebert asked her if she had given gifts to Clyde. She told him that she gave Clyde a chess set, two books and a DVD.

"Do you think it was appropriate for you to buy Clyde Nason gifts, isn't that specifically prohibited by company policy?" He grabbed a document from a file on the table and held it up to Alice. He smiled as if he had just won an I-told-you-so bet. He took off his glasses, scratched his right ear with one of the stems and put them back on.

"Did you give Mr. Nason any other gifts besides the chess set, the books, and DVD?" He scratched his ear again, this time with his index finger.

"I don't think so."

"How about this scarf?" He pulled a gray, wool scarf from his briefcase and handed it to her.

"I totally forgot about that."

"Any other gifts you totally forget about?"

"I don't think so."

Hebert pulled a snow globe of Niagara Falls from his briefcase.

"What about this?"

"I guess I also forgot about that. Yes, I did give him the snow globe. I told him I was going to Niagara Falls. He asked me to pick one up for him. He said he always wanted to visit Niagara Falls but he never got there and this was as close as he would ever get."

Hebert pauses for a few seconds and looks out the window. "Mzzz Hammond, how long, on average, are your visits with your patients?"

"An hour-and-a-half or so, sometimes a little more, sometimes a little less, depending on what I have to do."

"How about your time with Clyde Nason, how long were your visits with him?"

"About the same, maybe a bit longer."

"Your supervisor, Susan Young, said your visits to Mr. Nason were much longer. She said you averaged nearly two-and-a-half hours with him, much longer than your visits to your other patients."

"I don't think that is true."

"Oh, it is true Mzzz Hammond, definitely true." Hebert shuffled through some papers that were on the table, grabbed one, scanned it and placed it back on the table.

Two-and-a-half hours, that's a long time to bathe a man, don't you think? Were your visits to mister Nason longer because you stayed after your job was done to play chess with him?"

"No, they were longer because Clyde was a very heavy man. Helping him get in and out of the tub was very difficult and time consuming plus he lived way out in the boonies, at the far end of Beckley Hill Road. It took me a half-hour to get to his house in good weather. When the road was muddy or covered with snow it took a lot longer, sometimes an hour one way. The two-and-a-half hours includes travel time."

"So you never played chess with Mr. Nason?"

"I didn't say that."

"Is playing chess in your job description?"

"No."

Hebert drank a big, loud gulp of water, cleared his throat and refilled his glass. The glass left a water ring on the table. He rubbed it dry with the palm of his right hand and dried his lips with a napkin.

"Did Mr. Nason have a crush on you?"

"No, that's ridiculous."

"A crush on her? Was that a serious question?" Bill Keough said. His thick, white eyebrows wagged up and down when he spoke. Alice noticed a long, gray nose hair sticking out of his left nostril that should have been trimmed.

"Yes, it is a very serious question. Let me repeat, Mzzz Hammond, was mister Clyde Nason sexually attracted to you?"

"No, absolutely not."

"Absolutely not. Are you sure, you're a young woman, Mzzz Hammond, why wouldn't Clyde Nason be attracted to you? He was a lonely, old man."

"He wasn't lonely and he wasn't old," Alice said.

"Mzzz Hammond, did you flirt with Mr. Nason?"

"No, never." She stood up from her chair and walked toward the door.

"Where are you going, Mzzz Hammond, we're not done?"

"I object to this line of questions," Bill Keough said.

Hebert ignored his comment. "Why would Clyde Nason leave you two million dollars in property and one hundred twenty-five thousand dollars in cash? That makes no sense, unless he was in love with you? Can you explain that to me, Mzzz Hammond?"

"You don't know if he was or wasn't in love with her, and even if he was, so what. If you're suggesting Alice acted inappropriately and tricked him in to falling in love with her, you better damn well have proof," Keough said.

There was a light rap on the office door. "Knock, knock, knock it's me," William Keough said as he entered the office. "Sorry I'm late."

"Got here just as things are getting interesting," Bill said.

Hebert took a second drink of water, wiped his chin dry with his shirtsleeve and handed a glass of water to William.

"Mzzz Hammond, was mister Nason in love with you?"

Before she answered, William placed his left hand on her right shoulder. "She won't be answering that question or any similar, inappropriate questions."

"It's a legitimate question that needs to be answered."

"We'll let a judge decide that," William said. "Any further, appropriate questions, otherwise we're out of here."

"Yes, I do. Mzzz Hammond, did you ever drink alcohol with mister Nason?"

"No."

"What about New Year's Day, two years ago?"

"Clyde had a bottle of champagne. He opened it and asked me to toast in the new year with him."

"So you toasted in the new year with Mr. Nason. With champagne, Mzzz Hammond? Isn't that against agency policy?"

"Yes."

"Alice, how much did you drink?" Herbert asks.

"About a half a cup."

"I get more alcohol in my mouthwash." Bill Keough said. He stood up, walked across the room, returned to his chair and blew his nose. The rogue nose hair was now stuck to the skin on the peak of his nose.

"Alice, I must ask you again, was Clyde Nason in love with you?" Herbert said.

"No."

"Alice, you don't need to answer that question," William said. He pointed to Hebert. "We're done here. Any more questions, send them to me in writing." He stood up, looked at his father and Alice. "Let's go." At her car William asked Alice if Clyde Nason was attracted to her.

"No. Absolutely not."

"Are you sure?"

"Yes, I'm sure. You're as bad as Hebert."

"I'm just playing the devil's advocate here. Remember, I'm on your side."

"You don't sound like it."

"I have to ask you one more time, was Clyde Nason in love with you?" William asked. He said the words 'In love with you,' very slowly.

"You don't get it. He wasn't in love with me, I loved being with him."

"Were you in love with him?"

"No, I loved being with him, that's different. He was kind. He treated me with respect. His stories were wonderful. I felt safe with him. Some days he'd say, 'Alice, don't you have another appointment, don't you have to leave?'"

"Best to keep that to yourself," Bill said. He checked his watch. "Don't worry, he's got nothing on you, nothing but hot air. He's just trying to bully you."

"It's working."

"Don't let him," Bill said.

"Easy for you to say."

CHAPTER 26

BARBARA FERMONTE

ON HER WAY to Barbara Fermonte's apartment, Alice stops at the rec. room on the first floor of Pine Manor Senior Living Center to look at the decorations. Martha Giroux, the secretary at the admissions desk, is getting the room ready for Barbara's one hundredth birthday party set for later today. Several dozen helium balloons have drifted to the ceiling and another dozen are bound together with red and blue ribbons and tied to a kitchen chair. The chair, painted with glossy silver paint, will serve as Barbara's ceremonial throne. There are paper hats and festive party horns on each table. Red, gold and silver glitter stars are scattered on the table tops.

Giroux is standing on an aluminum stepladder taping green crepe paper to the lights. At the back of the room, tacked to the wall above the fake log fireplace, is a banner that says, 'Happy 100th Birthday'. It is faded and cracked in several places. A news reporter and a photographer from the *Providence Herald* and the good news team from the local television station are scheduled to attend. The mayor has a key to the city for Barbara and the governor has sent a letter of congratulations.

Alice steps into the rec. room, walks to the first table, grabs a party horn and blows on it. The paper crackles as the roll unfolds and the horn blares. Giroux turns to look at Alice.

"Looking good," Alice says.

"Thank you."

"You realize she is going to hate this."

"Yes, I do. Not my call."

Alice stuffs the party horn and a party hat into her nursing bag. At Barbara's door she says, "Knock, knock, knock, it's me, Alice." She opens the door. Barbara is leaning on her walker. She is wearing a spring coat and a hat and is holding her pocketbook. "Looks like you're all dressed and ready to go. What about your bath?" Alice says.

"I don't care about my bath. I need you to take me out of here."

"I can't do that Mrs. Fermonte."

"Why not?"

"I just can't."

"Yes, you can, you promised."

"No, I never promised. I said I'd talk to your son Paul. I did. He wants the party. I couldn't talk him out of it."

"He can go to hell. We'll go to McDonalds. I'll have a Big Mac and apple pie and french fries. I haven't had a Big Mac in fifteen years. You can stick a birthday candle in the apple pie. I've got a box of candles in the cupboard. That's what I want for my birthday, just you and me and a Big Mac and an apple pie and french fries and a vanilla milkshake. Forget that, I'll have two vanilla milkshakes, it's my one hundredth birthday, I can do what I want."

"I can't do that."

"What?" Barbara says. She does not hear Alice.

Alice leans closer to her. "I can't do that Mrs. Fermonte, I wish I could but I can't."

"Why not, I don't want to be here." Her voice cracks. "They'll sit me in that stupid silver chair, it's really a death chair, nobody lives another three months after they sit in it, and they'll put a tiara on my head and everybody will clap and say how sweet I am, and believe me, no one-hundred-year-old is sweet, and the girl scouts will sing happy birthday and the newspaper photographer will take my picture. I'll look dead in it and my son Paul will stick his head in the picture and he'll grin like a fool."

"It won't be that bad."

"Yes, it will. You've got to get me out of here."

"I can't, it's against company policy."

"Screw company policy."

"Believe me, if I could take you out of here I would but I'd get fired for sure. I'm on thin ice as it is."

"Thin ice. Are you talking about that Billy Nason nonsense? Ignore him. Clyde was such a nice boy. So quiet and so strong. Not the brightest candle on the cake but such a good boy. Billy, he's another story. He was a weasel from the get go. He was our paperboy. He was always late, day after day. He'd walk down the middle of the street reading the paper. Drove my husband nuts."

"If I take you to McDonalds, I'd get fired. I need this job."

"You won't get fired. I'll say it was my idea. Remember, the customer is always right."

"Not this time. I can't take you to McDonalds, your son Paul would kill me."

"He's an asshole."

Alice slowly guides Barbara to the couch. "I still need to take your vitals."

Barbara does not hear her.

"I still need to take your vital signs," she says again, this time much louder.

"Why bother, I'm a hundred years old, what difference does it make what my blood pressure is?"

"You're probably right but I've got to do it anyway, that's my job."

Barbara does not hear her. Alice straps the blood pressure cuff around Barbara's left arm. Her arm is so thin Alice uses a cuff made for a child.

"You don't know this Alice but I wasn't always Barbara. My name was Bellezza Assumpta Campagna. On my first day at school the nun changed my name to Barbara. I didn't speak good English so the night before my first day I practiced saying my name. I laid in bed and said, 'Hello, my name is Bellezza Assumpta Campagna, I am happy to be at this school.' I said that over and over until I fell asleep. I made sure I said the English words correct. When I told the nun my name she kept telling me my name was Barbara. Every time I said, Bellezza, she said Barbara. I wanted to cry but I was too scared. From then on I was Barbara at school and Bellezza at home. Eventually, I became Barbara both at school and at home, except for my father, he always called me Bellezza. When he was in the hospital just before he died, I was fifty-eight, he said, I will miss you Bellezza Assumpta. That made me cry."

Alice pulls the blood pressure cuff off Barbara's arm. "Everything looks good."

"Everything looks good for a hundred-year-old."

"Yes, everything looks good for a hundred-year-old woman, especially good for an ornery, one-hundred-year-old woman." She stuffs the blood pressure cuff and the stethoscope into her nursing bag. She helps Barbara step on the scale. "Eighty-six pounds Mrs. Fermonte, same as last week."

"A regular heavy weight. Look out Mohammad Ali, I'm coming for you."

"I think he's dead."

"Look out Mohammad Ali, I'm coming for ya." She posts her fists in a punching position.

"My parents came to Vermont in nineteen seventeen. My father came here first, in nineteen ten. He went back to Italy to find a wife. Apparently, no one here was good enough for him. He came to

Vermont to be a lumberjack. Can you believe that? He was five foot five, one hundred forty pounds wet. When he went to the job site the foreman laughed at him and said, 'Go away you puny dago.' My father never forgot that.

"He was a good man but he couldn't keep a job. He'd start off each job okay but eventually he'd get in to a fight with his boss and he'd get fired. His problem was he always knew more about the job than any of his bosses did or any of the owners for that matter. Just when he'd get comfortable, he'd tell his boss exactly what the company was doing wrong. It never went over well. Each time he got fired he'd promise my mother he'd never do it again but he always did.

"When I was a kid, everybody who wasn't Italian called us guineas and wops. We even used those words ourselves. Have you heard the joke why don't Italians like helicopters?"

"No, I haven't heard that one," Alice says.

"Because the big blade goes wop, wop, wop and the small blade on the back goes, guinea, guinea, guinea."

Alice smiles and shakes her head.

"There were dozens of names for us, ginzos, greaseballs, greasers, guidos, dagos. Tony was the first Italian man allowed to join the Providence Country Club. Italians run the club now but they weren't allowed in until nineteen thirty-six. Twenty years later Tony was the first Italian president of the club. When he was sworn in, my father was there and he yelled out, 'Puny dago wins.' That embarrassed Tony but years later he liked telling that story."

Alice removes Barbara's shoes and socks and checks her feet. "Looks pretty good. I think I'll put some cream on your heels, they're very dry."

She walks to the kitchen, fills a washbasin with warm water, grabs a jar of soap and several towels from the kitchen closet and returns slowly and carefully to the living room. She washes and dries Barbara's feet.

"Do you have a boyfriend Alice?"

"No."

"Girlfriend?"

"No."

"Do you have any friends?"

"You're my friend Mrs. Fermonte."

"I got married when I was only eighteen. I was mending clothes for Mario Muzullo. He made men's suits by hand. Nobody does that anymore. I was waiting for Angelo to finish high school. I left school after eighth grade. My sisters did too. My brothers, they got to finish high school. Tony, he went to college. Things were different then, boys finished school, girls got jobs, at least in our family. I was married to Angelo for fifty-five years. Can you believe that? He was the only man I ever had sex with, that's even more unbelievable. At first he was terrible but he got better."

"That's way too much information Mrs. Fermonte, way too much information," Alice says.

"Oh nonsense you can handle it."

Alice rubs lotion onto Barbara heels. Her skin is cracked. Alice uses her thumb to massage the cream into the cracks.

"Angelo was a good man, a very good man, I couldn't have asked for a better man. He was kind and he never lost his temper, which is pretty unusual for an Italian man, and he treated everyone with respect. But just between you and me, and don't you dare tell anyone, he was pretty dull."

"Who would I tell?"

"His idea of a good time was to sit on the couch with a food tray in front of him and watch Bonanza. He thought it was wild we had waited til nine to eat. That was as wild as he got. He fantasized he was Pa Cartwright. He even bought the same leather vest and cowboy hat Pa Cartwright wore. He looked ridiculous in Providence, Vermont.

One year he bought leather cowboy boots. They were too hot in the summer and useless in the winter. He kept falling on his ass on the ice, it was pretty funny."

"I've got a pair of cowboy boots I don't wear. They were okay when I was in Baltimore but ridiculous here," Alice says. She returns the foot lotion and scale to the bathroom and the washbasin to the kitchen.

Barbara tries to pull on her socks. Bending over winds her too much.

"Let me do that for you Mrs. Fermonte," Alice says.

"I miss every dull minute with him. He's been gone now for twenty-seven years. I never considered anyone else. He was so rigid he drove me nuts. He ate cereal for breakfast every single morning, three hundred sixty-five days a year, never anything else. He'd rotate the cereals in the same order every week, Monday was Wheaties; Tuesday, Shredded Wheat; Wednesday, Grape Nuts; Thursday, Corn Flakes; Friday, Total; and hot cereal on the weekends, Cream of Wheat on Saturday and oatmeal on Sunday, every damn week for fifty-five years. He said he had to do that to keep the cereals from getting stale. When the kids were teenagers they'd hide the cereal scheduled for that day. He never found that funny." She scratches a scab on her head, pulls off a tab of skin, looks at it, and the flicks it off her hand. "Have you ever been pregnant?"

"No."

"I was pregnant just about every other year for twenty years. I ended it when I was thirty-eight. Angelo was furious. He was sure I'd go to hell. Who knows, maybe I will, I'll know soon enough." She scratches her right ear and rubs her eyes dry with her left sleeve.

"What is your father like?"

"He's okay."

"My father was the only person I know of who got arrested for driving a bicycle drunk. He had gotten really drunk at the Italian American Club. On his way home he crashed into the Italian ice stand at the end of our road. He knocked over all the lemon ice buckets. Me and my sisters and my brothers, we were totally mortified. We didn't want to go to school because we were knew our friends would tease us about what a loser he was. My best friend Tina asked me if I liked lemon ice as much as my father did. I cried. She felt bad and she apologized and we hugged."

Alice checks Barbara's pulse.

"How am I doing?"

"You're looking good."

"Yes, she is," Barbara's son Paul says. He had entered the room halfway through the lemon ice story. "She's looking very good. I should look so good when I'm one hundred. I won't live that long, but if I do, I hope I look as good she does."

"We all hope that," Alice says.

"Is that the first time you've heard the lemon ice story? It never gets old." He leans toward Alice and speaks softly so his mother won't hear him. "Stay for the birthday party, it'll be fun."

"I would if I could but I've got another visit in a half hour."

Paul taps Barbara's right shoulder. "Ready for your big day, Mom?"

"Happy birthday Mrs. Fermonte," Alice says.

CHAPTER 27

HAROLD DOTY

HAROLD DOTY IS sitting in a wheelchair, smoking a cigarette. His shoulders are wrapped in a red, wool blanket and he is wearing a black watch cap. His son Ron is standing behind him, smoking. Ron is blowing smoke rings into the air and punching them apart with his left fist.

"She'll be here soon enough, she's always late," Ron says.

Harold checks his watch. "Not this late." Harold swats his son's right thigh with a rolled up newspaper. "Take me inside."

Ron spins the wheelchair one hundred eighty degrees. He pushes it up the ramp to the porch. Just as the two men are about to enter the house, Alice drives her car into the driveway. Black smoke belches from the tailpipe. "Sorry I'm so late, I had a flat tire," she says.

"Where the hell you been?" Harold says when she gets to the porch. She repeats her story but with greater detail.

"You need a new car. I told your father that a month ago." He unrolls the newspaper and holds it so she can read it. "What is this nonsense? Home health aide refuses to answer questions. What questions?"

"No questions. It's nothing, less than nothing."

"If I had two good legs, I'd beat the crap out of that little piece of shit. Maybe I'll sic Ron on him, he'll beat him senseless."

"I'm not going to beat anybody up," Ron says. He holds the front door open with his right hand and pushes the wheelchair into the house with his left hand and left hip.

"So what's this all about?" Harold says.

"It's nothing. My lawyer says I'm not supposed to talk to anyone, not even to you, Mr. Doty."

"I'm not just anybody."

"True, but I can't say anything." Alice wheels him into the living room, turns on the television and removes the sock from his left leg. She cleans and dries Harold's leg and replaces the tube sock. She removes his shoe and sock from his right foot and washes and dries it.

"Won't be long before you get a new foot," Alice says.

"I'll be the Bionic Man."

"Who?"

"Steve Anderson, the Six Million Dollar Man, the Bionic Man."

"Steve who?"

"Steve Anderson, the Six Million Dollar Man. Lee Majors, how do you not know this?"

"No clue, never heard of him."

Harold shakes his head in dismay.

Alice smiles and helps him with range of motion exercises for both his legs and his arms. He complains about the pain.

"No pain, no gain," she says.

Easy for you to say." She checks his vital signs and examines his scalp and ears.

"So, what's this nonsense with Billy Nason?"

"I already told you, nothing, less than nothing."

"If you need a character witness, I'll testify."

"Thanks but I don't think I'll need you. I doubt this will go to court."

"If it does, I'll be there. But if they ask me if you show up on time, I'm not gonna lie, you're freaking late every day."

"I got a flat tire. I couldn't help it."

"What about last week? You were a half-hour late last week."

"My car wouldn't start."

"Get a new car."

"I can't afford a new car."

"Your father will pay, he's a millionaire."

"No, he won't and he's not a millionaire, not by a long shot."

"Right, and the pope's not eye talyen."

"You are correct, the pope is not Italian but wrong about my father, he is not a millionaire."

"Sure and I got two good feet."

Harold wheels his chair across the room to the television table and grabs an envelope from the table. "I need to show you something." He grabs a news clipping from the *Arizona Daily Star* and holds it above his head. "Read this."

"What is it?"

"It's my wife's obituary. She died last week. My son Stephen sent it to me. He shoulda called me but he didn't."

Alice reads the article. Donna Doty was eighty-two when she died. She had fought a courageous battle with lung cancer. She was born in Tucson and lived in Vermont for thirty-six years. She is survived by her husband Howard and her three children. She was active in the First Baptist Church of Tucson. She was kind and was loved by everyone.

"Who the fuck is Howard? We never got a divorce. I didn't know she got remarried."

"She didn't get married Dad. It's a typo. I've told you that ten times already. You never listen. They meant Harold not Howard, it's just a goddamn typo, how many times do I have to tell you before it sinks into that thick skull of yours," Ron says from the kitchen.

"You don't know that."

"Yes, I do. I talked to her five days before she died. She'd been sick for a long time. She was in great pain and was hoping to die," Ron says.

"Why didn't you tell me?" Harold asks.

"Because you never asked."

Harold grabs the news clipping from Alice, folds it and places it back in the envelope.

"I never stopped loving her ya know."

"I'm sure you didn't," Alice says.

"I was with a lot of women before I met Donna but she's the only woman I ever loved, no one before her and no one after her. We went through everything together, to hell and back a half dozen times. I was a mean son of a bitch. How she stayed with me so long, I'll never know."

"Tell me about it," Ron says. He walks through the living room to the porch. "If you need me, I'll be in the garage."

He steps off the porch, grabs a cigarette from the top of his right ear, lights it, inhales deeply, blows a cloud of smoke into the air above his head and walks through the smoke cloud.

"My son's having a hard time. He doesn't know what to do with himself. He doesn't have any friends, not one. The guys he went to high school with, or at least the few who are still here, are not interested in being his friend. They're a bunch of goddamn assholes, always were."

"Things will get better."

"I don't think so, at least not here in Providence. He's done his time, he's a different man than he was thirty years ago. That doesn't matter, not here anyway. Nobody will hire him, not even Walmart. They'll hire mouth breathers but not my son. He's got a college degree, he got it in prison. In this town he's a killer and he'll always be a killer. Whatever happened to Christian forgiveness? Doesn't exist. Two more years on probation and he gets to leave. I'd like to go with him but I don't think he wants me to. I'll probably be dead by then anyway."

"You'll have had two good years together, that's not too bad."

"I suppose you're right."

He pulls the clipping from the envelope and scans the text. "Maybe I should change my name to Howard." He laughs at his joke.

"I remember the night Ron was born, Monday night, January 9th, nineteen sixty-four, five-thirty in the morning. Donna had been in labor for fourteen hours. It was awful. I felt useless. She was in terrible pain and there was nothing I could do to help her. I told her to breathe slowly. She told me to go to hell. I bought a plate of ravioli from the hospital kitchen. The smell made her throw up. 'Take that away,' she said. When Ron was born she grabbed my arm and bit me. It hurt like hell. She drew blood.

"Ron was so small he scared me. The nurse said, 'Relax, he's fine, all babies are tiny.' 'But not that tiny,' I said. She just smiled. She tried to hand him to me but I refused to take him. I was sure I would drop him. He was small but he sure could cry. He cried nonstop for months. I was so tired half the time I didn't know if it was day or night.

"When I got home from the hospital the pipes were totally frozen. It was twenty-six degrees below zero. We were living in a trailer in East Providence, a double-wide. The place was a total dump. I was supposed to leave the kitchen sink dripping water to keep the pipes from freezing but I forgot. I had to crawl under the trailer with a blowtorch. It took me nearly an hour to thaw the pipes. By the time I was done my fingers were so cold I could barely hold the torch. I was lucky I didn't burn the whole goddamn place down.

"Four months after we moved in to this house, the pump for the septic failed and we had shit in the cellar floating in a sea of piss. Some of the pipes had to be replaced. That cost us four thousand dollars. We didn't have the money, we were too far in debt with the mortgage. I asked my parents for a loan. They said no. Donna's parents gave us the money. I heard her father tell her, 'What do you expect, you married poor white trash.' She didn't know I heard him. She never said nothing and I never did neither.

"Five months later the pump for the well stopped working and we didn't have the money to fix it. For nearly three months we had to fill water jugs from the stream in the field behind the garage. Donna begged me to call her parents to get money to fix it but I said, no. She said I was a stubborn mule, I'd bite off my nose to spite my face. She threatened to leave me and go back to Arizona with Ron and Betty. He was only three and Betty was just a few months old. If they had been older she probably would a gone. She was right, I was a stubborn fuck but I wasn't gonna accept any more money from those assholes."

"Sounds awful," Alice says. She picks the washbasin and towels up from the floor, walks to the kitchen, dumps the water into the sink and throws the towels into the laundry basket on the kitchen table.

"It was awful but it was misery we both shared. Shared misery is somehow bearable. You get married for better or worse. You don't realize when your twenty-six how much worse there's gonna be." He pulls the envelope from his pocket and pulls out a letter from Donna. "Read this."

She grabs the letter from him and reads it to herself.

"No, read it out loud."

"Dear Harold, I should have never left you. I don't know why I did. It wasn't the weather. I even miss winter, sometimes anyway. I don't miss thirty below zero but I do miss the first snowfall of the year and I miss snow on Christmas. A brown Christmas just isn't the same. I think of you every day. When you came to Tucson that time we met at the airport, I don't know what happened. I should have gone back to Vermont with you. I don't know why I didn't. The summers here are too hot, like sticking your head in an oven. I've been sick for a long time. By the time you get this letter I'll probably be dead. Don't cry for me. Ha ha, that's a song from *Evita*, don't cry for me Argentina.

"Last week I coughed up blood. I've talked to Ron almost every week since he got out of prison. He sounds like a good man. He was a difficult kid, so angry, even as a little boy. When he killed that man in Plattsburgh I wasn't surprised. I was surprised he hadn't killed someone before then. I'm glad that's behind him now. He's in a good place. He said when he gets off probation he'll come and visit me. I'll be dead by then so that won't happen. He told me about your leg. Sounds painful. Hope you're okay now. Stephen has been great to me. He and his kids visit almost every day. You'd be real proud of him. He's the night manager at Target. Betty's another story. She thinks she's too good for me.

"I can't think of anything else to say. I love you. I always have. If I could rollback time, I would, I'd be with you in Vermont. Love Donna."

Harold grabs the letter from Alice, folds it and puts it back in the envelope. "So, what da ya think?"

"I don't know what to think Mr. Doty."

"What I think is if you love someone, don't give up on them, even when things go bad."

"I'll remember that," Alice says. She packs her nursing bag.

"Same time next week?"

"No, on time next week, surprise me."

"Okay, same time next week but on time." She grabs the newspaper off the floor, rolls it into a tube and swats his head. "On time next week, that's a promise."

"I'll believe it when I see it."

"Next week for sure, I guarantee it," Alice says.

Harold just shakes his head to let her know she is wrong, she won't be on time next week.

CHAPTER 28

TIM ROGERS

TIM ROGERS' THREE daughters are driving him crazy. They are telling him he isn't eating well, his clothes are too old and worn out, he watches too much television, his apartment is too dark, he is too fat, his hair is too long, and he needs to shave.

"Leave me alone, I'm happy," he tells them.

He hasn't seen all three of them together in four years since his sister Arlene's funeral. The only time he sees them together now is at funerals. Anne and Beth live in Denver and Kara lives in Seattle, too far for frequent visits. The three of them and their husbands are here now. Today is Tim's ninetieth birthday.

His daughters have planned a birthday party for him at the Elks Lodge and the Providence Ballroom Dance Club is honoring him with a lifetime achievement award. In its heyday, the years Tim and Beatrice dominated the dance competitions, there were nearly three hundred members. There are fifty-five members now. Tim was president twice and Beatrice four times.

A week ago the club's president, Bob Barrett, and vice president, Sarah Morrison, came to his apartment to tell him about the award and the ceremony and to record his oral history about the club.

"What's an oral history?" he asked her.

"Just tell us what you know," Sarah said. She recorded him on her iPhone and took detailed notes.

"This is wonderful," she kept mumbling as he spoke.

"I joined the club in nineteen fifty-six. My sister Arlene wanted to join but she didn't want to go alone so I said I'd go with her, just once, no more than that. I was pretty clear. I didn't like to dance. Dancing embarrassed me. I was so clumsy, I couldn't walk in a straight line without tripping. I was sure if I danced everyone would laugh at me.

"It was October eleventh. I remember the date because it was the day I met Beatrice. I wrote the date down in my parents' Bible, Oct. 11, 1956, a very fine day. I wrote in the book of Matthew, on the same page as the Beatitudes. I wrote it in red ink. My mother was furious. 'Why are you defaming the Bible,' she said? It was raining really hard that night. By the time I got to the building from my car, I was drenched. All the men wore suits and ties but me. I said to my sister, 'Why didn't you tell me to wear a tie?' 'I didn't know,' she said.

"Dick Couture, the president of the club, he died maybe fifteen years ago, greeted me and my sister. 'Welcome, welcome, welcome,' he said. He shook my hand real hard. I didn't think he'd ever let go. He was very nice. Everybody was so nice. I didn't want to dance so I sat in a chair against the back wall and listened to the music and watched everybody dance. It was almost like watching a movie or a play. Then the music stopped and Dick said, 'And now from our musical family to yours and for all you first timers, it's time to learn to a waltz.' He tried to sound like Lawrence Welk with an accent and everything. He even had a conductor's baton that he tapped three times against his left hand just like Welk did. Everybody laughed. I didn't get the joke then because I'd never seen the show.

"There were eight of us beginners, my sister and me and four other women and two other men. The five women all jumped right up and moved to the center of the dance floor. They were immediately joined by five men, all club members, who bowed to them as if they were in a royal court. Me and the other two guys, we didn't move. That's when I met Beatrice. She had volunteered to dance with a newcomer and she got stuck with me. I had noticed her when I walked in the door. She was beautiful. She had on a pink dress and black shoes and she wore a blue ribbon in her dark brown hair. She grabbed my right hand with her left and said, 'Shall we dance?' I said, 'I'd rather not,' and she said, 'Just this once' and I said, 'I'll probably step on your feet,' and she said, 'You won't be the first man to step on my feet.' When she placed her fingers on my hip I almost fainted. My heart was beating so hard I was pretty sure she could hear it beat. I felt my pulse in my throat.

"She was very patient with me. Every time I screwed up she stopped me and said, 'Slow down Mr. Rogers, stop thinking so much, just move with the music.' 'Easy for you to say,' I said. We had name tags on our shirts so that's how she knew my name. I told her to call me Tim. I said, 'My father's Mr. Rogers.' She laughed and said I was very funny.

"I don't know how long we danced but the next thing I knew it was closing time, midnight, maybe a little later. 'Are you coming next week?' she said. I said, 'Maybe, depends if I'm busy or not.' I knew and she knew that yes was the real answer. Then she said, 'I saw you look at me when you came in the door.' I lied and said, 'No I didn't look at you,' and she laughed. I must have blushed really hard because she said my cheeks matched her lips. I came the next week and the week after that and every week for the rest of the season.

"When I told my sister I wanted to go the second week she laughed at me and said, 'I thought you said only once.' I said "I changed my mind.' 'You mean the sexy dancer with the beautiful brown hair changed your mind,' she said. I got mad and said "No, I just like dancing.' And she said, 'Yeah, you and Elvis.'

"We were engaged in March and married in June. We couldn't

afford a real honeymoon so we spent the next day walking through the woods in the Providence town forest. We saw a black bear eating berries."

Tim walked to the kitchen sink, turned on the faucet and drank from the faucet stream. He wiped his wet face dry with his right sleeve and walked back to the living room. "So that's about it, I guess. It was great while it lasted."

"When did you last dance?" Sarah asked.

"Funny you should ask. I danced just last week, right here in my living room. I am teaching one of my home health aides how to waltz and foxtrot. She's kind of a clod but she'll learn. She wears heavy men's work boots, just about all the time, can you believe that? Why do young women wear men's boots?"

Sarah laughed. "I hope you can make it to our event on Saturday," she said.

"I'd love to go but I have no way to get there and it's my birthday and my daughters are coming to Providence to celebrate with me."

"Not a problem, we've talked to them, everything's all set. We'll come and get you," Bob said.

"I don't think I can walk down the stairs. I haven't done that in over a year."

"Don't worry about that Mr. Rogers, we'll get you to the church on time," Bob said and smiled.

"I don't have anything to wear."

"It doesn't matter what you wear as long as you are there," Bob sang and laughed at his joke.

"Can I wear my tux?"

"I'll be in a tux."

"Then it's a date."

. . . . .

IT IS TIM'S ninetieth birthday. He is wearing the same tux he wore the night he and Bernice won the bronze medal. The pant legs are too long and too loose and the jacket and cummerbund are stretched tightly across his generous belly. With his skinny legs, fat belly, stick thin arms and legs, and a long beak nose, he looks like a large bird.

"Dad, you can't wear that," his daughter Anne says.

"I can, and I will."

"Nobody wears a tux anymore, especially one that smells like a wet dog who rolled in mothballs. You look silly."

"It doesn't smell," Tim says.

"Dad, please," Anne says.

There is a light tap at the door. "Hello, it's me, Bob Barrett." He opens the door and peaks inside. He is wearing a tux.

"Come right in," Tim says.

Barrett, Sarah Morrison and two large men enter the apartment. "We're here to take Tim to his big night," Barrett says.

"Are you all set to go Mr. Rogers?" the taller of the two big men says. He is at least six-five and has huge shoulders and arms.

"I'm Tim," Tim says.

"You're Mr. Rogers to us, the legendary dancing champion, Mr. Timothy Rogers." He and the other man create a chair with their arms for Tim and lift him off the floor.

The hallway is so dark the two men carrying Tim worry they will trip over an unseen object. A tall, slender man wearing black jeans and a gray T-shirt is sitting on the top step of the stairs, smoking a cigarette. "If it isn't Fred Astaire himself or is it Gene Kelly," he says. His cigarette bobs up and down as he talks. "Congratulations old man, who knew we had a celebrity right here in the Blanchard Hotel." He stands up, turns to Tim and extends his right hand to him. "We're all proud of you."

Tim shakes his hand. "Thank you."

The slender man removes the cigarette from his mouth, drops it to the floor, crushes it with his shoe and says to the men holding Tim, "Do you need any help?"

"Thanks, we're fine," the taller man says.

The slender man points to the door at the bottom of the stairs. "Just so you know, it's twenty-two steps from here to the bottom and there's three steps on the other side of the door. I know, I've counted them a thousand times."

"Thanks," the shorter man says.

A stretch limo is parked at the curbside in front of the building. "Your chariot awaits," Barrett says to Tim. Inside the limo there are two bottles of champagne in an ice bucket and several champagne glasses on a silver tray. Barrett opens the champagne. The plastic top pops against the window between the driver's seat and the passengers' seat, startling the driver.

"Keep it down back there, let's not get too crazy," the driver says in jest.

Barrett fills the glasses and hands them to Tim, Tim's daughters, and Sarah Morrison. "To Tim and Beatrice," he says. Everyone clicks their glasses together.

"To Mom and Dad," Anne says.

"To Mom and Dad," Kara and Beth say together.

The limo drives to the Holiday Inn. The sign in front of the building says, 'Tim Rogers, 10 Time Providence Dance Club Champion.' At the entrance door to the ballroom there is a life-size, color poster of Tim and Beatrice. The picture is the same one that was in the newspaper when they won their fifth club championship. He and Beatrice are in a dance pose, similar to how figure skaters end their routines. Her back is almost parallel to the floor. Tim is holding her with his right arm. His left arm and her right arm are pointing to the ceiling. Tim is wearing the same tux he has on now and Beatrice is wearing a blue gown.

"Oh my goodness," Tim says to no one in particular. "Where did they get that picture?"

"I gave it to them," Anne says.

"When?"

"Three months ago, maybe four."

"You never said anything."

"I did not." She smiles.

Tim walks into the ballroom. Everyone at the ten round tables, about one hundred people, stand up and clap loudly for him. One man shouts, "Tim." A silver dance globe is spraying colored light beams around the room. There are three candles at each table. The dance floor is at the far end of the room, opposite the door. Tim spots Alice Hammond standing at the table to the left of the door. She waves to him and pumps her right fist. Phyllis Karin, Tim's physical therapist, Aliyah Taylor, his social worker, Emily Ross, one of the home health aides, and Jennifer Mason, his nurse, are standing at the same table with Alice. They wave to him.

Barrett and Morrison escort Tim to the table at the far end of the room, next to the dance floor. His daughters' husbands are at the table, clapping. "Way to go Dad," one of the three husbands says.

Barrett grabs a program from the table and gives it to Tim. The cover picture on the brochure is the same as the one on the poster. The back page of the pamphlet is a reprint of the story from the *Providence Herald* about when he and Beatrice won their tenth club championship.

"I don't know what to say," Tim says.

"You don't have to say anything," Anne says.

Tim is trying to suppress his tears but he is failing.

Barrett steps to the center of the dance floor. He taps the microphone three times. "Can I have your attention please?" It takes a few minutes for the clatter to stop. "You all know why we are gathered here tonight, to honor Tim Rogers, Providence, Vermont's greatest ballroom dancer."

The crowd gives Tim a standing ovation.

"Before we start our evening events, I would like Tim, whose ninetieth birthday is today, to grace us with the first dance."

The crowd roars approval when Tim's birthday is mentioned. Tim whispers to Sarah, "I don't think I can do this."

"Yes, you can Mr. Rogers." She lifts him from his seat and walks him slowly to the center of the dance floor. Alice joins them from her table. "I can't do this," he whispers to Alice.

"Yes, you can, Mr. Rogers, you can do this better than anyone." She grabs his hand with hers and gently pulls him toward her. She nods to the disc jockey. The music is a waltz from *Swan Lake*.

"That music was playing when Beatrice and I won the bronze medal." His eyes are filled with tears.

"I know." Alice says.

"Remember Alice, when I step forward you step back."

"I know Mr. Rogers, I'm your mirror image."

"Let's dance." He steps forward with his right foot, she steps back with her left. He slides his right foot, she slides her left.

"One, two, three; one, two, three," Tim says as they dance.

"One, two, three; one, two, three," Alice says.

"By George Eliza, I think you've got it." He smiles.

The crowd is standing and clapping.

CHAPTER 29

SUSAN YOUNG

SUSAN YOUNG CHECKS the calendar on the left wall of her cubicle. The box for tomorrow is marked with a big, red, angry X. Two months ago Charles Connor told her all the home care aides must be using the new computer charting program by tomorrow, no exceptions. When she marked the calendar she pressed the felt marker so hard against the paper, she knocked it off the wall. When Connor gave her the two month deadline he said, "How hard could it be?" She wonders if he remembers the deadline, probably not.

Her cell phone rings. It's her daughter Colleen. "Mom, my car broke down and I'm on the interstate near Burlington."

"What exactly do you want me to do, I'm at work?"

"I don't know, I just thought you should know."

"Okay, I know. Next time call Triple A, not me."

Colleen has been a college student for five years and there is no end in sight. She has changed her major three times and is considering another change. Susan has lost track of what her daughter is studying now, possibly psychology, she isn't sure.

Last week, her older daughter Cynthia moved back to Susan's house with her two-year-old twins, a boy who breaks everything he touches and a girl who throws the food she doesn't like to the floor, and a big, lazy, smelly dog who loves to roll in mud and then jump on the couch, and a furniture-scratching cat who hates everyone but Cynthia. Cynthia's husband Gordon can't keep a job and constantly loses his temper at the slightest provocation. He calls her every night and cries, "Why won't you come back home? Please, please, please come back home."

"I will when I'm damn good and ready," Cynthia tells him each night.

Susan checks her work schedule for the day. She is barely awake. She had forgotten how often and loud babies cry. She calls her mother.

"How's Dad doing?"

"Just fine." Her mother always says her husband is doing fine whether true or not. Last week he wandered eight blocks from his house and had no clue how to get back.

Susan would quit if she could but she can't afford not to work. When she considers quitting, which is usually at three-thirty in the morning, she frets, who would hire a fifty-nine-year-old nurse with a two-year nursing degree? She's not even sure nursing schools still grant two-year RN degrees. Even if she could find a job, she is pretty sure she doesn't remember enough nursing to be safe. It's been eight years since she's done direct care, and it's unlikely she could handle the physical demands of a nurses' aide's job. Even if she could, the pay for a home care aide is too low.

Her cell phone rings. It's her daughter Colleen. "What now Colleen?"

"Just thought you should know, everything will be okay, no need to worry, Triple A will be here soon."

"Good to know."

Her cell phone rings again. She checks the screen. This time the call is from her daughter Cynthia. "Oh my god, what now," she says out loud.

"Your daughters again?" says Gail Rivers, the supervisor for the homemakers, from the other side of their common wall.

"Who else would it be?" She slaps her forehead with her right palm.

"Mom, I think my children hate me," Cynthia says.

"They don't hate you."

"Yes, they do."

"No, they don't hate you. I hate you, but they don't hate you."

"Very funny, Mom. They won't stop fighting. How do I get them to stop fighting?"

"You don't, they're kids, that's what kids do."

"They're driving me crazy."

"That's their job."

"I can't stand it. I tell at them all day to stop fighting but they don't. I'm a failure."

"No, you're not."

Charles Connor is standing at the entrance to Susan's cubicle. "We need to talk," he says. He leads her to his office. Charles Potter is sitting at the conference table, rubbing his eyes with his thumbs. Ruth Patterson, the human resources director, Doris Lang, the agency lawyer, and Mike Dean, the president of the agency, are with him. Patterson and Lang are sitting at the table. Dean is sitting on Connor's desk, fumbling with his car keys.

"What's going on? Is there a problem?" Susan says.

"Yes, there is a problem, a very big problem. Bill Nason has threatened to file a three-million-dollar lawsuit against the agency and he will name you, me, and Mike in the suit. He says we should have fired Alice Hammond two years ago," Connor says.

"That's nonsense, she's one of my best employees," Susan says.

Lang grabs a folder from the table, pulls several documents from it and shows them to Susan. "Have you read these?" The documents are the three evaluations of Alice.

"Of course I have, I wrote them."

"Why didn't you fire her?" Lang says.

"Why would I? She hasn't missed a day in three years. She fills in on her days off, just about anytime I ask. Her patients love her and her work is top notch. If I had ten more employees like her, I'd be thrilled."

"That may be so, but Alice has serious boundary issues," Lang says.

"If I fired every home health aide with boundary issues I'd have to fire half the staff," Susan says.

"What about you, why didn't you fire her?" Connor says to Patterson, "You read the evaluations."

Before Patterson answers him, Susan's phone rings.

"Is that your daughter again?" Connor asks. He shakes his head.

"I don't know." She checks her phone. The screen says, 'Cynthia'. She turns the phone off.

"We'll talk more about this tomorrow. Don't tell anyone," Connor says to Susan and sends her away with a hand wave.

Back at her cubicle, Susan sends Alice a text. 'After your last visit, stop by the office, we need to talk.'

Alice's phone pings. She is dancing a slow foxtrot with Tim Rogers. She stops, grabs the phone from her nursing bag, and reads the text. She writes back, 'I'LL BE THERE AT FIVE!'

Susan's work phone rings.

"My car broke down, I can't make my afternoon appointments," Yvonne Dotten says.

"Yvonne, please tell me this isn't a real call, I am home asleep, it's midnight, and I am having a bad dream."

"It's really me, sorry."

"No kidding Yvonne, that was a joke. I'll deal with it. How about tomorrow, can you work tomorrow?"

"I don't know."

"Tell me soon, by noon today, at the latest."

Susan's phone rings again. It's her daughter Colleen. She considers not answering it but hits the talk icon. "What?"

"Nothing, thought you should know I'm now at the Toyota dealership, all's well."

"Didn't you tell me that a half hour ago." She ends the call and sends a text to Alice. 'Don't bother meeting with me this afternoon. Can you pick up an extra patient later today at 4:30? Mrs. O'Reardon, 39 Park Street. Should be quick, vital signs, check the wound on her arm, and check her food supply. Make sure she has enough food to feed herself for at least three days. She tends to forget to buy food.'

Alice answers the text, 'Sure, no problem.'

CHAPTER 30

MICHAEL WAINWRIGHT

MICHAEL WAINWRIGHT IS frustrated with his inability to tie his brand new, blue necktie the right length. The first try was too long, the second too short. Four tries later, still the wrong length. He rips the tie off his neck and throws it to the ground.

"Relax, you're just nervous," Alice says to him as she picks the tie off the pavement and ties it correctly for him.

"I'm not nervous. I'm just mad," he says.

"Michael, you're very nervous. You're a cat in a dog park nervous. If you don't relax you'll explode, thousands of Michael Wainwright body parts all over the church. It will be disgusting."

"Very funny." He tugs the tie knot closer to his neck. "Why am I doing this? Why am I getting married? This is the dumbest thing I've ever done."

"No, jumping off the cliff and breaking your neck, that was the stupidest thing you ever did."

"All right, this is the second dumbest."

"I don't think so, there's a lot of competition for the dumbest thing you've ever done. This isn't even in the top ten, not even in the top one hundred. What about the time you dropped down into a sewer and couldn't get out and the police had to save your sorry ass or the time you ate ten goldfish on a dare and you were sick for days? Those were brilliant."

"You're a regular comedian."

"I try."

"Why would Rita marry me? It makes no sense. She's too good for me."

"Just a guess here, because she loves you."

"Why would she love me?"

Alice kneels in front of Michael's wheelchair and puts her hands on his knees. "If Rita didn't want to marry you, she wouldn't have said yes. You're going into that church and you're getting married and that's the end of it."

"Michael, Michael, wait up," Michael's mother shouts from the side of her car, which is parked at the far end of the parking lot, near the church rectory. She and her husband trot toward Michael and Alice. "Hi, I'm Sylvia, Michael's mother." She is winded from the run.

"Mom, I think Alice guessed who you are."

"I'm Justin, Michael's father." He also is winded. He gives Alice a timid wave.

"Same for you Dad, Alice knows who you are."

Sylvia grabs her cellphone from her pocketbook. "Let me take a picture of the two of you," she says.

"Mother, please."

She takes several pictures. "Alice, we've heard so much about you, in fact when Michael said he had a girlfriend, we thought it was you."

"I'm a girl and a friend, but not his girlfriend."

Alice wheels Michael to the ramp entrance at the back of the church. The pavement is cracked and bumpy.

"The ramps are always at the back of the building, it's as if we aren't worthy enough to enter in the front with everybody else," Michael says.

"Cut them some slack, this church was built long before anybody gave a shit about people in wheelchairs," Alice says

"They could have put the ramp in the front."

"Whatever you say." Alice helps wheel him to the vestry. "Why are you getting married in a church? I don't remember you ever going to church."

"I don't. I'm a modern Christian, marriage, funerals, Easter, Christmas, five bucks in the basket, that's about it," he says.

The pastor peeks his head through the doorway. "It's time," he says. He walks toward Michael and Alice. "You must be Alice."

She nods.

"I've heard a lot about you."

"All good I hope."

"All good."

"Not from me," Michael says.

"Don't listen to him, he thinks you're pretty special," the minister says. He shakes Alice's hand. He looks at Michael. "You are one lucky man, you've got a great friend and you're marrying a wonderful woman."

Alice guides Michael to the altar. He reaches back and grabs her right hand. "Thank you," he says.

"Thank me for what"

"For when I'm an asshole, letting me know."

"You, an asshole, never."

She laughs and squeezes his fingers.

The minister is waiting for them. There are eighteen pews in the church, nine on each side of the center aisle. The pews are half full. Michael's parents are in the front pew on the right. Both of them are crying.

"Oh, for God's sake," Michael says when he sees them. The sun is streaming through the rose window. Michael looks toward the front of the church. The sun's glare forces him to shade his eyes with his hands.

Rita is standing at the entrance door. The minister nods to the organist who begins playing the 'Wedding March.' The fifty people in the seats, stand. Rita and her bridesmaid walk slowly toward the altar, their steps in pace with the music.

"She's so damn beautiful," Michael says.

"She is," Alice says.

"Blessed be God, the father, son and the holy spirit," the minister says. About half of the people answer him. "And blessed be his kingdom, now and forever, amen."

"Oh damn, I don't have the ring," Michael says.

Alice opens her hand and shows him the ring. "You gave it to me an hour ago, relax."

Rita kneels on the marble floor facing Michael, her head even with his, and grabs both of his hands. "Are you nervous?" she says.

"Big time."

"Me too, I couldn't sleep all night," she says.

"I couldn't either. Two sleepwalkers getting married. Is that even legal?" Michael says. Rita remains kneeling.

"We have come together in the presence of God to witness and bless the joining of this man, Michael Wainwright, and this woman, Rita Ives, in holy matrimony," the minister says. Someone shouts, "Whoop, whoop, whoop."

"That's got to be Randy," Michael says.

Michael and Rita say their vows. "Rita Ives, you are too good for me, way too good for me, everyone here knows that." He looks to the congregation to see if they agree. Several do. Everyone laughs. "I'm a very lucky man. I will honor you forever."

"Sometimes, Michael Wainwright, you are a total pain in the ass but mostly you are a decent man," Rita says.

"Tell it like it is," Randy shouts when she says ass.

Rita pulls a paper from her left sleeve and reads from it. "Michael, there is no one but you who I want to spend my life with. You are my partner, my lover, and my best friend. I can't promise to obey you, I'm not a lap dog, but I do promise to love you and to honor you forever."

The minister lifts his arms. "Into this holy union this man, Michael Wainwright, and this woman, Rita Ives, now come to be joined. If any of you can show just cause why they may not lawfully be married, speak now or forever hold your peace."

Another, 'Whoop, whoop, whoop,' from Randy, much louder than before.

"I object," Michael says quietly, smiling.

Alice swats his head. Rita, the minister and the people in the first few pews who heard him and saw Alice swat him, smile.

The minister addresses the congregation. "Will all of you witnessing these promises do all in your power to hold these two persons in the marriage."

There is a loud and enthusiastic "We will" from the congregation. Michael's parents are crying even harder than before. Michael rolls his eyes.

"Looks like we're a team," Rita says.

"Go Sox," Michael says.

Rita leans to Michael and kisses him. Everyone claps. She grabs the wheelchair from Alice. "He's mine now."

"That sounded like a threat," Michael says, smiling. "Let me guess, you've purchased a huge insurance policy on me and you're going to drop me off a cliff?"

"Exactly, ten million bucks, I'll be rich."

"You heard her Alice, when they find my dead body in the gorge, go to the police. I've got my phone in my pocket, I've recorded everything she said, I'll send you the audio."

"I can't, I'm in on it with her, I get half the money."

"Figures."

"Michael, you are one lucky man," Alice says.

"I am indeed."

Rita wheels Michael down the aisle. Everyone claps. His parents are still crying.

CHAPTER 31

HAROLD DOTY

ALICE IS KNEELING on Harold Doty's living room floor, washing the stump end of his left leg. He tugs the wet cloth away from her and tosses it to the floor.

"Squeeze my leg," he says.

She gently squeezes his leg.

"No harder, squeeze it harder."

"Why would I do that?"

"Because my leg is totally healed. I wanted to show you. When you squeeze it, it doesn't hurt, hasn't for the past week."

"I know it's healed Mr. Doty, I can see it, your leg looks great."

"Yes, it does. Doc Merriam said I can get fitted for a fake foot in three or four months, maybe sooner. It won't look like a foot but if I put a shoe on, nobody will know, just like that old joke when you call the store and ask them if they have pigs' feet." He chuckles at his story. "Doc says I probably will always need a cane or crutches but hey, I thought I'd be stuck in this wheelchair for the rest of my life."

"Are you sure he said that?" Alice says.

"Yes, I'm sure, why would I make that up?"

"That's not what he said and you know it," his son Ron says from the kitchen. He is washing the breakfast dishes.

"He did too, you don't know nothing."

"What he said was in three or four months he will reevaluate whether you can try a prosthetic foot. He wasn't optimistic, that's for sure."

"He said I could get a new foot. You don't know your ass from your goddamn elbow."

"That may be true but I do know what I heard."

"What do you think?" Harold asks Alice.

"Well, it's complicated."

"How complicated could it be? My leg is healed, it feels good, it doesn't hurt. Three months from now I'll be ready to go. I'll be dancing by next winter, cha, cha, cha."

"Maybe," Alice says.

"No maybe about it."

"I wish it were that simple, but it's not. Not everyone is a good candidate for a prosthesis." She rinses Harold's leg with a clean towel and dries the skin. "First off, you're not young."

"Tell me something I don't know. What's that got to do with anything?"

"A lot, and there may not be enough soft tissue left to cushion the bone."

"Looks like plenty to me."

"Could be, I don't know, I'm not a doctor or a physical therapist. And you'll need a strong right leg. I'm not sure your right leg is strong enough."

"It's plenty strong. I could kick your ass with it. Maybe I should kick your ass."

"Maybe you should, but not today, I'm running late."

"You're always running late, what else is new?"

Alice rubs Harold's leg with a dry cloth, spreads lotion on his skin and slips a tube sock over the stump. She carries the washbasin and cloths to the kitchen and hands them to Ron.

"He's delusional," Ron whispers to her.

She returns to the living room and tells Harold to hold his arms at a ninety-degree angle at shoulder level, palms facing down. "Push your arms straight out in front of you and curve your fingers as if you were riding a bicycle."

"I don't want to, you can't make me."

"No, I can't, but.."

Before she finishes Ron says, "Cut the crap Dad and do what she says, she's here to help you."

Alice tells Harold to bend his elbows and pull his arms back until his elbows are slightly behind his torso and squeeze his shoulder blades together. He does what he was told.

"That wasn't too bad now was it." She tells him to sit up straight in the wheelchair and tilt his toes on his right foot toward the ceiling.

"That was a stupid exercise. Why are we doing it?"

"Because Phyllis wants us to, that's why."

"Who is she, God?"

"No, she's your physical therapist and she knows what's best for you."

"I doubt that."

"Time for your knee exercises," Alice says.

"They're even stupider, what a waste of time."

"You got anything better to do?" Ron says.

Alice tells Harold to lift his left leg as high as he can and hold it in the air for ten seconds.

"I can't do it."

"Don't be a pain in the ass," Ron says as if he were the parent. He is in the living room standing next to Alice. Harold lifts his leg, holds it for about ten seconds, and then lifts his right leg.

"Truth is Alice, I don't think I'll walk again, maybe, but I doubt it," Harold says.

"You never know," Alice says.

"Now you're finally talking some truth," Ron says. He walks to his bedroom and returns wearing a McDonalds shirt and hat. "Time to sling burgers, living the dream." He exits the building.

"I bet you didn't know I was once in the circus?" Harold says.

"You'd win that bet," Alice says.

"When I was sixteen, I ran away and joined Keller Brothers Circus. Sounds like I'm making this up, but I'm not, I was a regular Toby Tyler."

"Who?"

"Toby Tyler. You're too young, Disney movie in the sixties. Toby ran away and joined a circus, just like me, except I didn't actually run away. My father wanted me out of the house. He was sick of me. 'Time to get a job, be a man,' he said. I was pretty much done with school anyway. I was a terrible student and a trouble maker. Most of my teachers were hoping I'd quit, so I did. The circus was in town and they hired local boys to help clean up the mess after each show. I got a job selling popcorn and cotton candy. When they were set to leave I asked the manager if he needed help and he said sure, so there I was, a sixteen-year-old circus boy. I went home to get my clothes and say goodbye to my parents. I thought my mother would cry but she didn't. I did, later that night, I bawled like a freaking baby. I've never told anybody about that, not even Donna.

"It was a pretty big circus, not as big as Ringling Brothers or anything but pretty damn big, three rings, elephants, lions, acrobats, clowns, the whole nine yards. Mostly we toured the South, North Carolina, South Carolina, Georgia, Florida, Texas, Louisiana, Mississippi. Goddamn those states are hot. My job was to clean and feed the animals and sell popcorn during the show and clean up the mess. Worked fifteen hours a day. Made almost nothing but it was great, best eight years of my life."

"I got to fill in for the knife thrower for almost a month. He was showing off his knife skills to one of the acrobats and sliced his fingers so bad he couldn't throw. What an idiot."

"What did you throw at?" Alice asks.

"A woman, what else? She was tied to a round board that was painted like a large target. Her arms and legs were shackled to the board. The board turned in a slow circle, clockwise I think, fast enough to be scary but slow enough so the audience could see the knives hit the board. I'd throw the knives at her moving body and just barely miss her. The audience would gasp every time I threw, positive I would to kill her. But I didn't kill her because I didn't actually throw anything. I'd go through the throwing motion and when my arm was fully extended, I'd tuck the knife in my sleeve and step on a button on the ground which released a knife from behind the board. What the audience thought they saw was the knives smashing onto the board but what was really happening was the knives was springing out from behind the board itself. I was always afraid one of the knives would slip out of my hand and go flying at her head but that never happened. You can't do that trick now days because everybody would film it on their cell phones and realize it was fake.

"I traveled with the circus for eight years, one month and six days. My last day the clowns showed up at my tent with their little car and sang 'Auld Lang Syne' and gave me a dozen balloon animals. That made me cry even harder than when I left home.

"A week later I joined the army, that's when I met Donna in Tucson. She was so beautiful she took my breath away. She didn't want me at first but I didn't give up. Every day I had off I'd show up at her house and beg her to go out with me. I had to hitch a ride to get to Tucson. Some days it took me almost all day to get there. It was pretty obvious her parents thought I was poor white trash, especially after I told them I'd worked in a circus. They thought she was way too young for me. She had just graduated from high school and I was an army guy and an ex-circus worker. Eventually she did go out with me. On our first date I took her to the movie *Sounder*. I wanted to go to *Deliverance* but I figured that movie probably wouldn't ta been a good first date. I saw it two weeks later with some of my army buddies. Good thing I didn't take her to that movie, she probably would a left me.

"I got transferred five months later and asked her to marry me. She said yes and we got married that weekend. Her mother cried like a six-year-old. It wasn't happy cries. After I got out of the army we moved back to Providence. I guess the rest is history."

Alice takes Harold's vital signs. "Everything looks good." She stands up and starts to pack her nursing bag.

"This may be the last time I see you," Harold says.

"Why?"

"Next week I'm moving to Sunset Ridge. I just can't do this by myself, it's too damn hard, I need help. Sunset Ridge has people that will help me. I can get lunch and supper every day and they'll do my laundry and I can play bingo or do nothing, if I don't want to do nothing. Ron is leaving in November. When he leaves, I'll be all alone. I can't do this alone."

"I thought he had two years left on his parole?"

"He did but that changed. Too many men on parole I guess. He'll be a totally free man November first. I'm selling my house. You want to buy it, cheap? You got the money, you're rich."

"I haven't got anything yet Mr. Doty, and I may not get anything, who knows, it's all up in the air."

"You will. Bill's not stupid, he'll offer you something, don't know what, but something, otherwise he could get nothing and he knows it. You should buy my house, it's got ta be better than that dump you're living in now. Three bedrooms, a half-acre and a garage for a hundred fifty thousand dollars, you can't beat that. The payments probably would be less than what you're paying for rent."

"How do you know my apartment is a dump, you've never been

there?"

"Your neighbor, Brian Lester, he's my grandnephew, he told me."

"I wondered what his last name was."

"He likes you, likes you a lot. He'd like to, um, date you."

"Date me, I don't think so."

"Well, you know what I mean."

"Yes, I do, and no, that's not going to happen."

"You think you're too good for him?"

"No, I'm just not interested in men right now."

"Why not?"

"Just not?"

"Something bad happen?"

"No."

"Every woman needs a man."

"Actually, no we don't." Alice walks toward the door.

Harold stops her. "Before you go, I want you to do one last thing for me. I want you to take our picture together. Get my phone." He points to the television. His phone is on the top on the TV.

Alice grabs his phone, steps behind his wheelchair, bends down to his level, extends her arm as far as she can, and takes their picture.

"Not bad, I look pretty good, if I say so myself."

"Yes, you do Mr. Doty, a handsome devil you are."

"Give me your phone." Alice hands her phone to him. He types his telephone number and his name into her contacts list. "There, now you won't forget me."

"I definitely will not forget you Mr. Doty."

CHAPTER 32

CHARLES CONNOR

CHARLES CONNER AND Charles Potter are in Connor's office. The door is shut and the blinds are closed. Connor is sitting at his desk, his feet are on the desktop, and he is tossing a baseball into the air, trying to just miss the ceiling. There are dozens of scuff marks on the ceiling from previous tosses. The baseball is signed by David Ortiz. Ortiz wrote, 'Boston Strong' on the ball. Potter has a stack of charts and spreadsheets in his left hand and a ballpoint pen in his right hand.

"So give me the bad news, but make it fast, Bill Nason and his nitwit lawyer, and Alice Hammond and her lawyer, and Mike Dean, my favorite board president, are coming in a half an hour," Connor says.

"Don't forget the dragon lady Doris Lang."

"How did I forget Cruella De Vil?" He smacks his forehead in mock surprise. "I think she kicks puppies for fun."

"No, she kicks babies, babies and old ladies."

Both men laugh.

"So what do you want first, the bad news or the good news?" Potter asks.

"Good news first."

"The agency lost only three thousand dollars last month, our best month in five years. We took in more donations than we had in losses, first time since we've been here. I think we've turned the corner." He hands Connor the spreadsheet that proves what he just said.

"Let's see what happens next month before we declare victory. It's pretty sad when losing three thousand dollars is our best month. Unless Medicaid pays more, which isn't going to happen anytime soon, nothing's ever going to change. Good thing for the hospice donations, we'd be sunk without them. Got any more so-called good news."

"The recreation committee has finally set the date and place for the fall picnic, took them long enough."

"Will the good news never end? Let's pop the champagne, I've got a bottle in the fridge. So, what's the bad news?"

"We lost two nurses last month and we're now down four. One retired and one left to work for the hospital and we still can't find a speech therapist to beat the band. As far as I can tell, they don't actually exist, at least not in Providence, Vermont."

"Let me guess, the nurse who left was young," Connor says.

"You are correct."

"What's the pay gap between our starting pay and the starting pay at the hospital?"

"Seven thousand and change." Potter hands Connor a spreadsheet that shows the pay differential between the agency, Providence hospital and several nursing homes.

"At least we're higher than most of the nursing homes," Potter says.

"Who'd want to work in a nursing home?"

Connor shakes his head no. "Any other bad news?"

"It's worse for the home health aides. We were down four last month, lost six, picked up three new ones, so now we're down seven. If we lose any more we might have to close the program," Potter says.

"What the hell happened?"

"Not totally sure. I think McDonalds and Burger King upped their starting salaries. They're paying fourteen bucks an hour, we start at thirteen."

"We give benefits, they don't. That should account for something."

"Benefits don't pay rent," Potter says.

"Any chance we can raise the starting pay?"

"None. If we raise their pay we'd have to raise everybody else across the board. Even the janitor would want a raise. By the time we were done it would cost the agency a million bucks a year or more." He hands Connor three more spreadsheets.

Connor grabs a Nerf ball from the top of his desk and throws it toward a basketball hoop that is attached to the top of the coat closet door. The ball hits the rim and bounces to the floor. "Sooo close." He retrieves the ball.

"Any other bad news?"

Before Potter answers him there is a soft tap at the door. Lisa Parker, the agency's receptionist, opens the door and peeks her head inside Connor's office.

"Mr. Connor, Bill Nason, Raymond Hebert, Alice Hammond, William Keough, Doris Lang and Mike Dean are here for your nine o'clock meeting," she says.

"Send them to the conference room, I'll be there in a minute." He grabs the remaining spreadsheets and graphs from Potter and places them on his desk. "I'll read them later."

Both men bump each other on their way through the office door.

. . . .

"SO, LADIES AND gentlemen, what brings you all here on this fine Tuesday morning?" Connor says to the group. He points out the window to the light blue sky. He sits at the table next to Mike Dean.

"Let's cut to the chase, we all know why we're here." Hebert says. His bowtie is slightly crooked.

"Great idea, I love cutting to the chase. What exactly is chase anyway?" Connor says. Potter laughs. Lang shakes her head.

"We've got a great compromise, a win, win for everyone, for Alice, for Bill and for the agency," Hebert says.

"That may be so but we're not agreeing to anything here today," William Keough says. He presses Alice's left arm to make sure she says nothing. "So what do you got?"

"Alice gets one hundred twenty-five thousand in cash, the agency gets its twenty-five thousand and the stocks, and Bill gets the house and the land and nobody goes to court."

"That's your win, win. The property is worth two million dollars, that's hardly a win, win. It's a you win, we lose," William says.

Alice starts to speak but William grabs her arm and shakes his head, no.

"Raymond, have you read the will? There is no ambiguity, Clyde Nason left everything to Alice, period, end of story."

"Have you read her evaluations?" Herbert says. He reaches into his briefcase, removes several copies of the evaluations and holds them up for everyone to see. He looks to Mike Dean and Doris Lang. "Believe me, you don't want to go to court, it will get ugly, real ugly and fast and, I assure you, the agency isn't going to look good, not good at all. Sorry Alice but they should have fired you two years ago."

Alice wants to respond but William squeezes her arm and shakes his head.

"It's no secret, you're bleeding money, all you need now is for your donor money to dry up. You'd be in deep trouble," Hebert says.

Keough stands up and tugs on Alice's arm. She stands next to him. "We'll let you know by Monday but what I can tell you now is, this offer is a joke." They walk out of the room.

When Hebert is sure Alice and her lawyers cannot hear him, he says, "If Alice is smart she'll take this offer."

"I don't know about that," Lang says. She looks at Hebert. "This is not a slam dunk Ray, you could win, but you could lose. No guarantees one way or the other."

At her car Alice says to William, "I just want this nonsense to end. One hundred twenty-five thousand is a hell of a lot of money."

"Hebert has no case. He's trying to scare you. He might as well spit into a fan because he cannot win. Read the will carefully. Clyde wanted you to have everything and he wanted Bill to get nothing. He hated his brother. What he wanted is clear as crystal." He strums his fingers against the top of her car. "By the way, who is Harold Doty?"

"Why do you want to know?"

"He called our office yesterday and said his son Ron would beat Bill Nason up if I wanted him to. His language was rather colorful."

"That sounds like Harold."

"Alice, if you want to honor Clyde's last wish, take everything. No decision needed today. Sleep on it. I'll see you in two days."

Alice sighs. "Can't wait."

CHAPTER 33

MARIA GALLO

ALICE IS STUMBLING on the sidewalk trying to balance two bags of groceries. Tony Gallo sees her struggling, darts from his porch and grabs one of the bags, just before she drops it.

"You didn't need to bring food," he says.

"I wanted to make sure I had everything I needed."

Tony places the bag on the hood of Alice's car, reaches into his back pocket, grabs his wallet, pulls out three, twenty-dollar bills and gives them to her. "Is that enough?"

Alice nod. "More than enough." She tries to give back one of the twenties.

He refuses to take it. "Give it to charity. Alice, I know you promised my wife you'd show me how to cook, but you really didn't need to do this."

"Yes, I do. You don't break a promise to a dying woman."

"No, I suppose not."

Alice empties the contents from her bag onto the kitchen table. "I assume you have salt and pepper and flour?" she says.

"Salt and pepper, yes, flour, I don't know, don't have a clue, don't even know where Maria kept it," Tony says.

"I don't know either but my bet is, it's in that container labeled flour." She points to the canister next to the toaster.

"You must think I'm totally incompetent."

"No, I think you're a man."

"Same thing?"

"Sometimes."

"Where did you learn to cook Italian? You're not Italian."

"You don't have to be Italian to cook Italian. I learned from one of my patients."

"Who?"

"You know I can't tell you that." She cuts the pepperoni free from the package. "Pepperoni is the key. We're going to simmer the tomatoes and water for five hours in pepperoni and spices. It will taste great, believe me."

Alice slices the pepperoni into several thick chunks and pulls the skin off the meat. She covers the bottom of the pan with a thin coating of olive oil, turns on the left, back burner and lightly browns the garlic. She adds tomato paste and stirs the paste in the hot oil. She adds the tomatoes from the two cans, fills each empty can with water and dumps the water into the pan. She tosses the pepperoni into the pan and sprinkles in salt, pepper, Italian spices and basil. She crumbles a bay leaf into the sauce and half covers the surface with oregano. She stirs the spices. She waits for the water to boil, lets it boil for a few minutes and turns the burner dial to low.

"That's it, now you let it slow boil for about an hour and then simmer for three or four hours."

"That's it?"

"Pretty much. You should stir it every forty-five minutes or so to make sure it's cooking correctly and adjust the temperature if it's cooking too fast or too slow."

"How will I know?"

"If the sauce is bubbling all over the stove, that's too hot and if it isn't bubbling at all, that's too low. The key is to use good pepperoni and don't use too much. Ten inches is on the high end. Fresh tomatoes work better than canned but we'd have to skin and crush them and that's kind of a pain in the butt." She grabs one of the eggplants.

"We can't make eggplant parm without sauce, so I'll walk you through what to do."

"Before you do, I've got something I need to show you." He starts to walk out of the kitchen, stops at the entrance and turns back to Alice. "Come with me."

He opens the top drawer of the credenza in the living room, pulls out eight drawings and places them, side-by-side, on the top of coffee table in front of the couch. "What do you think?"

"I assume Celeste did them, they're fabulous, she has real talent, I'm impressed."

All eight drawings are pictures of Celeste, her family and her friends.

"Look closer."

"Okay. They're still great. The detail is amazing."

"Look closer."

"Clue me in, what am I looking for?"

"Look at the hands." He picks up one of the drawings of him, Celeste and Maria, and taps the page with his right index finger. "Look closely, Maria doesn't have any hands. I have hands, Celeste has hands, but Maria doesn't have hands in any of the pictures."

He drops the picture to the table and grabs another one. "This one is of her and grandparents and Maria and me. Just like the last picture, she has hands, her grandparents have hands, and I have hands, but Maria has no hands. Her pictures scare me. What do they mean?"

"I have absolutely no idea. Have you talked with Emma? She's the professional."

"Yes, she's the one who had her draw this nonsense."

"I assure you it's not nonsense. Talk to Emma, she'll help you through this. I'm not qualified to comment."

"Emma says I shouldn't worry, this is normal but I am worried. I know Celeste is grieving but she's driving me nuts, she's gotten so mean, it's not like her. Before her mother's death, she was the nicest girl in the world. Now she's angry all the time. Everything I do disgusts her. Yesterday, she looked at me and said, 'Are you going to wear that? If you want to look like a clown, that's your business.' She mocks everything I say. She constantly corrects my grammar. This morning she said, 'Less people Dad, are you serious? It's fewer people, it's always fewer people, only ignorant people say less people.' She rolled her eyes and looked at me as if I had open sores on my face. Well, excuse me Miss Merriam Webster. She is driving me totally insane."

"She's thirteen?"

"Yes, she'll be fourteen in three months."

"She's pretty normal. When I was thirteen I told my mother not to go to a Girl Scout picnic because she eats too fast and too loud and she'd embarrass herself. I wouldn't worry if your daughter insults you, that's what teenage girls do."

"I guess so but it sure is annoying."

"It will get better."

"When?"

"Not anytime soon, maybe when she's eighteen."

"I can't wait that long."

"Yes, you can. You don't have much choice."

Tony puts the drawings back into the drawer. "Don't tell Celeste I showed you these drawings, she'd bite my head off if she knew."

He walks to the kitchen and stirs the sauce. "Smells good." He dips the stirring spoon into the pan, takes a sip of sauce and burns his tongue. "Fuck that's hot."

Alice laughs. "Bubbling sauce usually is."

He lowers his head under the kitchen faucet, turns on the cold water and cools his tongue in the cold stream. Alice talks him through the steps to cook eggplant Parmesan.

"Make sure you buy local eggplants if you can, California eggplants tend to be hard and chewy. And cut the slices real thin. You realize I haven't told you anything you couldn't have learned on the internet. If you can read, you can cook."

"Dad read directions? That's not going to happen," Celeste says from the living room.

"When did she get here?" Tony whispers to Alice.

"I don't know." Alice checks the time. "It looks like I've met my promise to your wife. I do have to leave. Don't forget, if you can read, you can cook almost anything."

"Before you go, I need your help," Tony says. He points to the stairs. "Follow me."

He leads her to his bedroom, to the walk-in closet. The left wall, back wall and half of the right wall are filled with his wife's clothes. "I want you to have these. And see that bureau over there," he points to a dresser across the room, "I want you to take what's in it."

"I can't do that."

"Yes, you can."

"No, I can't. Take everything to Goodwill, they'll be thrilled to get these clothes," Alice says.

"I tried but it's just too damn hard for me. Every time I pick up one of her dresses my body shakes."

"I guess I can do that for you, I can take everything to Goodwill."

"I hoped you'd say that."

He picks up a box of garbage bags from the closet floor and hands it to her. "Make sure you keep some for yourself, you're both the same size."

"Same height Tony, not the same size."

"Then keep what fits."

"I really don't need anything."

"Oh yes you do, believe me Alice. As far as I can tell you own four shirts and they're all flannel. If I didn't know better, I'd think you were a logger."

"I own way more than that."

"Then they all look alike."

"That's probably true." Alice pulls a half dozen dresses from the left rack, carries them to the bed and drops them on the mattress. She folds two dresses and stuffs them into a garbage bag. She starts to fold the third dress but holds it up to her shoulders as if she were in a fashion shop buying a dress.

"This is really beautiful."

"Yes, it is. I remember the day she bought it. We were on a cruise in the Caribbean. She bought it at the gift shop on the very first day. She said she needed it for the ball. I didn't even know there was a ball. The dress was way too expensive, more than we could afford. She bought it anyway. It was the fourth year of our marriage. It was a really bad time for us. Celeste was seven months old and Maria and I were fighting constantly. I think Maria resented the fact that I went to work every day. It didn't help that Celeste was a crier, she'd cry from morning to night, every day, all day. We were convinced she hated us. We blamed each other.

"Her parents sensed we were having trouble so they bought us a seven-day cruise. This will spice things up, if you get my drift, her mother told me. That really embarrassed me, my mother-in-law shouldn't be talking to me about sex, that was none of her business.

"The trip didn't help, it made things worse. The cabin was so small, more like a closet than a cabin. We couldn't get out of each other's way. I spent most of my time in the movie theater or watching fat people belly up to the food tables. People on cruises sure eat a lot of food. I watched *Avatar* four times. I didn't even go on the excursions her parents had paid for, she went by herself. One woman, who was on the cruise with her girlfriends, thought I was alone and asked me to join her and her friends. I showed her my ring. 'Trouble in paradise,' she said. I nodded yes. If you change your mind I'm in room whatever. I didn't go but I did think about it for the rest of the cruise.

"On the last morning, when we were packing our bags, Maria said if things didn't get better soon, we should get a divorce. She gave us one year. I didn't say anything. It did get better eventually, but not in a year. I don't remember when or how, but it did. What helped was when Maria went back to work six months after the cruise and she finally had a life beyond diapers and baby talk. Some women, and some men too I suppose, are made to stay home, everything they need is right there in front of them, but not Maria, a stay-at-home mom was not for her. We didn't get a divorce after the year deadline, even though things were still awful, mostly because neither of us had the energy to get it done. Good thing because by the time Celeste was ten, she and Maria were my whole life."

Alice grabs three plastic bags and Tony grabs the other six bags. They walk carefully down the stairs.

"You can't have my mother's clothes, those aren't your clothes, you can't take them, who do you think you are?" Celeste says.

"She's taking them to Goodwill," Tony says.

"Who says she can take them to Goodwill? Maybe I want them."

"Do you really want them Celeste?" Tony says.

"No." She turns her back to him and huffs.

Alice throws her three bags into the backseat of her car and Tony tosses four of his bags in the trunk and the other two in the backseat. "Take these bags home first before you go to Goodwill and see if there is anything you want. Next time I see you I want to see you in something besides a man's shirt."

"Will do."

"I'm not sure I've ever thanked you, you've been very kind."

"No need to, I was just doing my job."

"Well, thank you anyway. You and Jen and Emma and everybody else helped make our last few months bearable. Not sure if we could have done it without you."

"Thank you, that means a lot to me. I'll tell the others."

Tony steps back to the porch, turns around to Alice and waves. She shifts the car into reverse and starts to back out of the driveway.

"Wait, wait," Celeste hollers. She runs to the car and pounds on the hood. "Stop."

Alice stops the car. Celeste opens the passenger door and sits on the seat.

"I'm so sorry, I didn't mean what I said. Don't take mom's clothes to Goodwill, keep them for yourself, my mom would have wanted you to have them."

"Maybe."

"Definitely. Did you know Mom was hoping you'd marry my dad?"

"She didn't want me to marry your father Celeste, what she wanted was for me to teach him how to cook and do laundry, and to talk to you about girl things, but not marry him."

"I'm pretty sure she was hoping you'd marry Dad so I'd have a good mom. I think you'd be a good mom."

"Thank you."

"Not going to happen is it?"

"No, it's not."

Celeste kisses Alice cheek. "You could do worse." She smiles.

"I could do much worse."

"Do you think my father will be okay?"

"Yes, I do. How about you, are you okay?"

"I think so. Some days are better than others."

"It will get better, not today, and not tomorrow, but it will get better."

Celeste hugs Alice, exits the car and joins her father on the porch.

Alice drives out of the driveway, watching them wave to her as she backs her car into the road. She nearly hits a man on a bicycle. He has to swerve to miss the back end of her car. "Watch where you're going you stupid idiot," he says. He shakes his fist.

"Sorry."

"Maybe you should take some driver's lessons," Tony says from the porch.

"Maybe I should." She waves to him and Celeste.

CHAPTER 34

BILL NASON

BILL NASON IS taping shut a washing machine box with duct tape. The box is filled with Clyde's winter coats. He has spent three days cleaning Clyde's house and packing everything Clyde owned into boxes, taping them shut, and labeling each box. There are about three dozen filled boxes on the floor in the kitchen and the living room. On the top of the washing machine box he writes, 'Winter Jackets'.

The smell of death in the house is gone but the air is stale. He opens all the windows that will open. On the kitchen table there is a chess set with the game completed. Black won. Bill wonders if black was Alice or Clyde.

He left the living room closet for last. He opens the door and scans the contents. A birthday package is on the top shelf. He grabs the package and carries it to the couch. A blue envelope is taped to the gift. 'To my brother Bill' is written on the envelope. Inside is a birthday card. The cover of the card is a picture of a bear in a rowboat. The words above the bear say, 'Happy Birthday Brother.' Clyde had added the word Brother with a black marker. The card makes him smile. His birthday was eight days after Clyde's.

The message printed on the inside says, 'Have a Grrrreat Birthday.' The message from Clyde says, 'I hope you like this gift. Things have been rough between us lately, but you are my brother and I love you.

Happy 50th birthday.' *If you had loved me you would have left me your damn property.*

The gift is a photo album filled with pictures of him and Clyde and their parents. There are two pictures on the first page, a picture of him and Clyde and their mother, taken by their father Carl, on Clyde's nineteenth birthday, and the team photo of Clyde's high school baseball team, Clyde's senior year. Clyde was team captain and Bill was the ball boy. Clyde is sitting on the team bench, Bill is sitting on the ground at his feet. Clyde's right hand is resting on Bill's shoulder. Bill's head is tilted slightly. He is looking up at his brother. He has a big smile. Before every game, all the players rubbed Bill's head for luck. He pretended he hated it when they rubbed his head, but he loved it.

He returns to the closet. The trophy Clyde won for the caber toss at the Highland games is at the back wall, behind a set of golf clubs. The trophy is dented. Bill bought the golf clubs for Clyde's thirty-second birthday. Clyde hated golf. He could hit the ball well over three hundred yards but he rarely hit it straight. He spent more time in the woods than he did on the fairway. "If I wanted to walk in the goddamn woods, I'd go to work," he said every time he hit his ball into the trees.

Bill reaches for the trophy. He trips over Clyde's typewriter and nearly falls into the back wall. *I can't believe Clyde still used that stupid typewriter.*

Clyde bought the typewriter when he started his logging business, an IBM Selectric, with the letters on the ball. It made sense when he bought it because computers were expensive and unreliable. Clyde never switched even after everyone else had.

He grabs the typewriter case and carries it to the couch. There are two envelopes in the case, one is addressed to him and the other to Mike Dean. The envelopes are held together by a thin, pink, rubber band. Each envelope includes a letter and a new will. The will in Bill's envelope is a carbon copy.

Neither the letters nor the wills are signed. Both envelopes are stamped. The letters are dated March thirty-one, the day before Clyde died. The first letter says, 'Dear Bill, I really screwed up big time. Two months ago I wrote a will and I gave everything to Alice Hammond, one of my home health aides. That was a mistake. I wrote the will the day after you came in here and yelled at Alice and me. I was stuck in the tub and I couldn't get up without help. You yelled at me like I was a six-year-old. I was humiliated and so damn angry. I wrote the will to punish you. That was stupid. You've been good to me Bill. Without you I don't know what I would have done. I probably would have ended up in a nursing home with a bunch of old people. I owe you everything. You are my best friend.'

The new will leaves Bill all the property and one hundred thousand in cash, twenty thousand to Alice, five thousand each to nurse Jen Mason, home health aide Eva Driscoll, and physical therapist Phyllis Karin, and fifteen thousand to the Providence VNA.

He reads the letter addressed to Mike Dean.

'Mike. Here's a new will. Please tear up the old one. I know you think I hate my brother. I don't, I love him. Sometimes he drives me nuts but I love him even when he's a jerk. He's done everything for me. I owe him my life. I wrote the first will because I was angry. It was a knee-jerk reaction. My mother always told me, think about what you do, don't make any decisions angry. I should have listened to her. Nobody has seen the first will but me and you and the people in your office who came here when I signed it so it should be pretty easy to rip up. I've ripped up my copy. This will is the right one. If you need a witness to see me sign it, you'll have to come here, like you did last time. I tried calling your office today but I called too late. Anyway, tear up the old will and use this one and tear up the letter I wrote to Alice Hammond.'

He wipes tears from his eyes. He sends a text to his lawyer Raymond

Hebert. 'Raymond, I've found a new will. It leaves the property to me. I'll bring it to you this afternoon.'

He pumps his right fist. He drives to Alice's apartment building and parks on the side of the road in front of her building. He rereads the two letters and the will. He folds the letter to him and places it in the cup holder between the seats.

Brian Lester is in her apartment, looking out her front window. "Bill Nason is parked out front of the building. I think he's coming in here. You want me to leave," he says.

"Yes." Alice says. She waves him out the door. She opens her door before Bill knocks and greets him. "I haven't decided what I want to do yet. I've got until Monday," she says.

"The offer is off the table. I've found a new will. It leaves me the property and most of the money. I found it in Clyde's typewriter." He holds up the will. "Thought you ought to know."

He doesn't wait for her to respond. Instead he turns around and exits the building. A few seconds after he drives away.

Brian returns to Alice's apartment. "What the hell was that all about?"

"Nothing, absolutely nothing."

CHAPTER 35

ALICE HAMMOND

THE CONSTANT DRIP from the kitchen faucet is annoying Alice. She places a washcloth under the spout to muffle the sound. She called her landlord four days ago. "I'll be there first thing tomorrow morning," he said. She doesn't expect him for another week or more. She had to use a wrench to turn on the cold water in the bathroom for nearly two months before the handle got fixed.

Brian is watching hockey in his apartment. Things must not be going well for the Canadians because he is complaining about how stupid they are, even his grandmother could do better. She hears him through their common wall.

She is sitting at the table reading an email from William Keough. The email includes a copy of the new will and the letters from Clyde Nason to his brother Bill and Mike Dean. The note from him says, don't worry, this is garbage, no court will honor this will, it's a fake. The money and property are yours.

"This is a nightmare that will never end," she says to her dog. Ella licks her ankles. She rereads the will and the letters and sighs. I hate this, I hate everything about this stupid will. She pounds the kitchen table three times. A glass near the edge falls to the floor and shatters.

"Damn it all to hell," she says. Ella runs and hides behind the couch. "Come here little buddy, I didn't mean to scare you." The dog crawls out from under the couch. Alice rubs its ears. "I'm so sorry." She kisses Ella's nose. "Let's go for a walk." She cleans the glass from the floor and grabs the dog's leash. When she returns she checks the date and time on her phone. It's seven-thirty. It is her birthday. She is twenty-nine today. Last birthday she watched the first season of *Weeds* on Netflix. She'll watch the sixth season tonight. There is a knock at her door.

"Alice, it's me," her mother Lesley says.

Alice opens the door. "Mother, why are you here?"

Lesley is standing in her doorway holding two bags of groceries. She pushes past Alice, walks to the kitchen, and places the bags on the table. "You're too thin. You need real food." Ella licks her shoes.

"I have food," Alice says.

"You need meat."

"I'm fine."

Lesley returns to her car, grabs a birthday cake, and a gift package.

"What's all this?" Alice says.

"It's your birthday. You're twenty-nine today."

"I know that Mother, so what."

"It's your twenty-ninth birthday, it's Saturday night, and you're alone. That's not right. You're a beautiful, smart woman. You should be having fun. Whatever happened to fun Alice?"

"I like being alone."

"No, you don't." She points to the table. "Sit. We need to talk"

"Talk about what?"

"About you. Are you okay?"

"Yes. Mind your own damn business."

"You're not okay. You don't have a single friend."

"I have plenty of friends."

"I've talked to Jessica, Christine and Lauren. You four were as tight as tics in high school. They told me you ignore them."

"High school was a long time ago. We're not friends anymore."

"What about Nicki from college?"

"I haven't talked to her since I left Baltimore."

"You need friends."

"I have friends."

"Who?"

"I don't know. My patients, they're my friends."

"Your patients are not your friends."

The Canadians must have scored because Brian is cheering and throwing pillows against the wall and screaming, "Yes, yes yes."

"Is he always that loud?" Lesley says. "How do you sleep?"

"You get used to it."

"Tell me what's wrong? I'm your mother, I know when something is wrong."

"Nothing's wrong, I've already told you."

"I don't want to sound like your father but what do you want to do with your life?"

"I don't know?"

"You've wanted to be a doctor since you were a little kid.

"I'm not a little kid anymore.'

"Remember when you'd pretend to be a surgeon and you'd pull off your dolls' leg so you could fix them but the legs never went back on right. You'd get mad and throw them at the wall and cry. You must have had a dozen dolls with one leg."

"More like two dozen."

They both laugh.

"What do you want to do five years from now?"

"I have no idea. What is this, a job interview?"

"You've been in a funk for three years. You need to get your head together."

"My head is fine."

"No, it isn't. You're lonely. You know it and I know. You need to get your old life back. You were always the life of the party. What happened?"

"Nothing happened, I'm fine."

"No, you're not. What do you want to do with your life?"

"I've been thinking I might want to be a home care nurse. I've spent twenty-eight years wanting to be Dad. I think I want to be you, Mom. Don't tell Dad."

"Why not?"

"He'll be disappointed."

"No, he won't."

"Don't tell him anyway, I haven't decided one way or the other. I still might go back to med school. What was it like being a home care nurse?"

"You should know, you've been a home health aide for three years."

"Not the same. I want to know about home care nursing."

"It's just like any other job, there are good parts and bad. On the good side, you get to know your patients intimately, sometimes too well, of course you already know that. Weren't you the best man recently for one of your patients?"

"Yes. So what."

"That wasn't a good idea."

"Why not? He was my friend."

"Was he your friend before he was your patient?"

"No."

"Then he isn't your friend."

"It's hard keeping distance."

"It is but if you want to last, you have to, otherwise you'll burn out."

"I'm close to that now."

"I know you are. It's obvious."

"How did you like working in the homes?" Alice asks.

"It was harder in the beginning when I was a new nurse and not confident of my skills. When I had a question I couldn't just walk down the hall and ask for help. It was pretty nerve-racking, at least at first. And, as you know, some of the homes are pretty scary places."

"And dirty," Alice says.

"One of my patients, an old guy, ninety plus, had cut his leg with an ax. I was sent to check on his wound and do a dressing change. I turned the water on in the kitchen sink to wash my hands. The water stunk like rotted garbage. I told the man, 'Your water stinks, something's wrong.' He laughed. 'Must be a dead animal in the well,' he said. I thought he was kidding but he wasn't. We walked a quarter mile to the well. He used crutches so it took a half hour to get there. I was carrying a garden rake and a flashlight. The well was covered with a wire mesh to keep the animals out but there was a hole in the wire. There were two dead woodchucks floating in the water. He told me to fish them out with the rake. 'I can't do that,' I said. 'I can't either,' he said, 'I'm not strong enough.' I did get them out, it wasn't easy. You'd be surprised how heavy a woodchuck is after it's been floating dead in a well for two days."

"I haven't had anything that bad, at least not yet," Alice says. She gets up, fills two glasses with water and returns to the table. "What's the worst thing that happened to you?"

"I don't know if it was the worst thing or not but the most embarrassing was when I fell through a porch, got stuck and couldn't get out. The floorboards were rotten. I wasn't hurt but I couldn't free myself. When the patient heard me crash through the wood, he opened the screen door to see what had happened and smashed my left shoulder with the door. It was sore for weeks. He tried to pull me out but he couldn't do it. I was wedged between two boards. I couldn't move my arms. Eventually the firemen came and cut me free. All the neighbors watched. I felt like a fool. What about you, what are your horror stories?"

"My worst story is mostly sad. One of my patients had fourteen cats, all indoor cats. She kept the litter boxes fairly clean but the smell was so strong it burned my throat. She is a pretty simple person so we told her there was a rat problem in Waterbury and we needed her cats. She was thrilled to help. We got rid of most of them, one cat at a time. We didn't kill them, we found homes for ten of them. It wasn't easy. Each time we boxed a cat to take it away, she was very proud. But then somebody, I don't know who, told her the truth. She was upset and very sad. She blamed me. She called me a lot of awful names. One day she threatened me with a knife. I just left. I think she's okay now but one of the other aides told me she is still mad at me."

Lesley laughs. "You can't be a home care nurse without dealing with at least one crazy cat lady."

"And crazy cat men, they're plenty of them."

"And crazy cat men. And mean dogs. I got bitten three times,"

"I've been lucky so far, no dog bites, although one time was real close, the dog snapped at my legs and just missed me. God, I hate that dog," Alice says.

Have you ever gotten in the middle of a fight between a husband and wife or an adult son and his mother? Never, never, never takes sides when there's a disagreement, believe me, I learned the hard way."

"Easier said than done," Alice says.

"True."

"Mom, how did you keep your distance between you and your patients? I go to bed thinking about them. I wake up thinking about them. I can't even read because I'm thinking about them. That's all I do, I work and I think about them when I'm not at work. Will that get better?"

"I don't know, Alice, only you can fix that. If you want to keep your head on straight, you need to keep a professional distance. Compassion fatigue is real. I'm surprised you've lasted three years. When you cross the line Alice, you put yourself, your patients, your colleagues and your employer at risk. That's what you did with Clyde Nason. You shouldn't have given him those gifts, you shouldn't have accepted any, you shouldn't have stayed late and played chess with him, you shouldn't have done anything outside of the tasks you were assigned."

"I know that. I was wrong. I couldn't help myself."

"I don't think you purposely flirted with Clyde but what you did could easily be misinterpreted as flirting. I'm surprised your supervisor didn't call you on your behavior."

"She did, plenty of times. I didn't listen," Alice says.

"If you really want to be a home care nurse, you need to respect the line between you and your patients. If you can't do that, home care is not for you."

"How did you do it?"

"The most important thing, you need a life outside your job. You need friends, you need your family".

"I have friends."

"Alice, please. I don't know what happened to you in Baltimore and I don't need to know but if you want to be a home health nurse, or a physician, or do your current job well, you have to put Baltimore in the rear view mirror. Can you do that?"

"I think I can."

"Good, because I'm tired of the new Alice."

"Me too."

"So let's eat," Lesley says. She removes the cake from the box. The wording on the top says, 'Happy Birthday Alice.'

"Thanks, Mom. This is a nice surprise."

CHAPTER 36

CLYDE NASON

ALICE IS DRIVING to Barbara Fermonte's apartment. Her phone pings a text message from Susan Young. She pulls to the side of the road. 'Alice you started working here three years ago today. Congratulations! Stop by the office, I have a gift for you. Also, there is a surprise for you at Barbara's apartment. You might want to bring a badminton racket.'

Alice smiles. *What is that all about?*

She remembers the first day she worked alone without a supervising nurse at her side. Her patient was Clyde Nason. She had to set the GPS on her phone because she had never heard of Beckley Hill Road. The road to his house scared her. It was very narrow and steep and the trees along both sides of the road blocked the sunlight. It was like driving in a dark, green tunnel. She wasn't sure her car could climb the last half mile. It sputtered several times but did not stall. When she got to his driveway she opened the car door and threw up her breakfast. Half the puke landed in her car and half on the gravel.

"Who are you?" Clyde said.

She had never seen a man that big. His dog licked her boots. She patted the dog's head. "I'm Alice Hammond, your new home care aide."

"Are you sick? I saw you throw up."

"Your road scared me."

"It's steep, that's for sure."

He walked to the kitchen and sat on one of the chairs. The dog begged for food. "I didn't want anybody new. What happened to Sue? I liked her."

"She's gone. Hopefully, you'll like me."

"We'll see."

At her last visit with Clyde before he died, he tripped over a broom and fell to the floor. She tried to stop him from falling but she was not strong enough. He banged his left elbow against the kitchen table. Blood oozed from his arm. She grabbed a towel from the sink and pressed it against his skin. The bleeding took longer to stop than Alice thought it should. By the time the bleeding stopped the towel was soaked with blood. Her hand was sore from pressing the towel against his arm. He started to cry.

"Does it hurt?" Alice said.

"No, it doesn't hurt. It's not that."

She helped him off the floor and guided him to the kitchen chair. His breathing was fast and labored. "Anything I can do to help?" Her hands were shaking.

He took several deep breaths. He waved her away when she touched his back. "Not really," he said when he could talk. He wiped the tears from his eyes. "I'm embarrassed, Alice. I shouldn't have cried. I'm a man, not a little boy."

"There's no reason to be embarrassed, we all get sad."

"I wasn't always this fat. I don't know how it happened, one pound at a time I suppose." He laughed at his joke. "When you're this fat, people think you are stupid and lazy. I'm not stupid and I'm not lazy but people who don't know me just assume that I am. How'd you let yourself get so fat? If you had any pride you'd lose weight. Easier said than done, believe me. I'm tired of the nasty looks, as if I was subhuman. One time, when Bill took me to one of his softball games, a bunch of morons were making jokes about me. They spoke loud on purpose so Bill and I would hear them. They were teenagers, maybe fifteen, sixteen at most. They weren't very original, pig sounds, oink, oink oink, beached whale, blubber boy, nothing I hadn't heard before. Bill got up to threaten them. I said, 'Bill don't bother, they're just stupid idiots.' He went up to them anyway and said, 'Cut the shit boys.' 'Who's going to stop us, you and lard ass,' one of the boys said. Bill picked him up and threw him hard against the fence. The boy broke his nose. I didn't know Bill was that strong. 'Fuck you asshole,' the boy said, 'my father's going to sue your ass off.' He was crying like a baby. Bill made a fist and then touched the boy's chin with his knuckles. 'I ought to beat your face in, you little piece of shit,' he said. The four boys ran off. They made pig sounds as they ran away. I thought Bill was in trouble but we never heard from the kid or his parents."

Alice removed the towel and washed and dried his arm. "It looks like you may need stitches. I'll have Jen come by this afternoon." She retrieved a bandage from her nursing bag and covered the wound.

"I don't need stitches."

"So, you're a nurse now. Who knew?" she said. She took his temperature, pulse and blood pressure. His temperature was normal but his pulse and blood pressure were dangerously high. "Clyde, I'm going to call your doctor, I think you need to go to the hospital."

"I don't need to go to the hospital, I'm fine, just a little short of breath."

"Maybe so but let's let your doctor make that call." When she gave the blood pressure numbers to Clyde's physician, he called the ambulance. "Stay with him," he said to Alice. "Do you know CPR?" She said yes. "Good. How big are you?"

"One hundred fifteen, maybe one twenty, why?"

"You probably won't have to do CPR, but if you do, it will be difficult, just do your best."

"Hopefully, it won't come to that."

What was that all about, why did he want to know your weight?" Clyde said.

"I have no idea." She pointed to the chessboard that was on the counter next to the toaster. "Let's play chess."

"Don't you have another visit soon? Aren't you already late?"

"No big deal, I'll call my boss. I want to play chess." She left the building and sat in her car to make the call. "Everything's fine, no more visits today," she said when she returned to the kitchen.

The chessboard was already set up on the table. "You're white," Clyde said. She moved her pawn two spaces to E4.

"The Danish Gambit, bold more," he said. His breathing was loud and labored.

"The what?"

"The Danish Gambit, one of the most aggressive moves in chess."

"If you say so."

Thirty-four moves later the ambulance rolled up Clyde's driveway. "What the heck is that," Clyde said when he heard the siren.

"You need to go to the hospital."

"I do not."

"Yes, you do. Your doctor called the ambulance."

"You should have told me."

"You're right, I should have."

"Watch it boys," Clyde said to the three EMTs. "She's one hundred fifteen pounds of pure mean."

The three men laughed.

"And just so you know Alice, it's checkmate on my next move," Clyde said to her just before he entered the ambulance. "That's four wins in a row, but who's counting."

"Apparently you are," Alice said. She waved to the ambulance as it drove away.

CHAPTER 37

BARBARA FERMONTE

ALICE KNOCKS ON Barbara Fermonte's door. Barbara does not hear her. She knocks a second time. Still no response. She turns the doorknob. The door is locked. The door has never been locked before. "Barbara, it's me, Alice." She speaks as loudly as she can without shouting. She raps the door knocker three times. Several of the other residents open their doors to see what the commotion is all about.

She drops her nursing bag to the floor, runs to the elevator and pushes the down button. The elevator takes too long. She runs down the stairs and sprints to the admissions desk. "Martha, I need the key to Barbara's room, I think something's happened."

"Is she dead?"

"I don't know, maybe."

Martha gives Alice the key card. Alice runs across the hall to the stairway and leaps up the stairs, four and five stairs per step. She slips the key into the lockbox. The lock light blinks red. "Dammit," she says.

Several residents are at Barbara's door, crowding Alice. "What's happened?" says a woman who is leaning on her walker.

"Nothing, the door is jammed," Alice says. She pulls the key out of the box and slips it back into the slot. The lock light is green. She opens the door and steps inside. A small parrot flies at her face. She ducks. The bird circles the room and rests on the ceiling fan in the living room, just above Barbara's head. The television is on. Barbara is wearing earphones. The volume is so loud Alice hears a muffled version of the show. The local morning news host is laughing. Barbara is slumped in her television chair, her eyes are closed. There is a picture frame in her lap. The bird buzzes Alice. She swats it with her nursing bag but misses. The bird returns to the ceiling fan. Alice rushes to Barbara. She grabs Barbara's shoulders and shakes her. "Barbara, are you okay?"

"Alice, what the hell are you doing? One of these days you are going to kill me," Barbara says.

Martha Giroux is standing at the apartment door. "Is everything okay?"

"Yes, everything's fine, she was asleep," Alice says.

The bird flies at Martha's head. "That damn bird," she says. She steps to the hallway and shuts the door. The bird circles the room, flies into the bathroom and lands on the curtain rod above the tub.

"I got a bird," Barbara says.

"I see that," Alice says.

There is a bird cage next to the television. The cage door is open. There are several bird turds on the armrest of Barbara's chair. Alice walks to the kitchen, grabs a dishcloth from the drawer next to the sink, sprays Windex on the cloth, returns to the living room and cleans Barbara's chair.

"Do you think it's a good idea to let the bird fly around the apartment?" Alice asks.

"You sound just like my son. He's an ass-ache. Are you going to be an ass-ache too?"

"I don't know, maybe. Not sure if it's a good idea to have bird shit everywhere."

"He hates his cage."

Alice looks up at the ceiling fan. The rims of all five fan blades are caked with bird shit. She grabs a kitchen chair, pulls it to the living room, places it under the fan, pulls on a pair of rubber gloves, stands on the chair, and cleans the fan blades.

Barbara hands the picture frame that was in her lap, to Alice. The frame holds a newspaper clipping. "Have you seen this?" She reads the headline "Providence woman is one hundred years young. I told you that would be the headline."

"Yes, I saw it. It is a wonderful picture. How was your birthday party?"

"Don't tell Paul, but it was okay. I had fun. The girl scouts were lovely. I got a key to the city and a letter from the governor." She gives Alice the letter.

Alice removes the rubber gloves and reads it. "Very nice letter Mrs. Fermonte." She takes Barbara's blood pressure, temperature and pulse. "As usual, the numbers look pretty good."

"Look pretty good for a hundred-year-old."

"Yes, looks pretty good for a hundred-year-old."

"Before my bath, I want you to cook me some green peppers and onions."

"Mrs. Fermonte, it's eight-thirty in the morning, you sure you want fried peppers now?"

"Yes, I haven't had any in over a month. I've left everything next to the stove."

"I thought they disconnected your stove."

"They did but Paul got me a hot plate. It's got a timer on it and it shuts off every five minutes. My hands aren't strong enough to plug it in anyway so I can't use it but you can."

There is a green pepper, a red pepper, an onion, a bottle of olive oil, three garlic cloves and a loaf of Italian bread on top of the stove. Alice fries the peppers and onions in the olive oil and garlic. She cuts a bread slice and places it on a plate. She scoops the cooked peppers and onions onto the bread.

Barbara is sitting at the kitchen table. "Here you go Mrs. Fermonte."

"This is delicious. You should have some."

"That's okay, I am not sure my stomach could handle fried onions this early in the morning." She washes the pan and the utensils and returns the olive oil to the cupboard. "The bird was a bit of a surprise. Does he buzz everyone?"

"He's just saying hi. He's a very friendly bird. He eats right off my hands. Jen doesn't like him. Yesterday, she got a little bird poop on her shoulder. The bird was on the fan. She acted like a ton of shit had fallen from the sky. I said, it's just a tiny bit of bird poop, no big deal."

"I'm with Jen, bird poop is gross." She checks her watch. "It's getting late, I'll get your bath ready." She walks to the bathroom. The bird flies at her head, circles the living room, and flies into its cage. There are several bird poops in the tub. Alice cleans the tub before she fills it. "That bird's got to go," she says to Barbara. Barbara doesn't hear her.

CHAPTER 38

ALICE HAMMOND

ALICE'S PHONE RINGS. It's six-thirty in the morning. It must be work. Ella is asleep on the pillow next to her head. She brushes the dog aside and grabs the phone.

"Alice, it's me Jessica, your oldest, best friend. You're going out with me and the girls tonight, whether you want to or not. We're sick of you blowing us off and we're not taking no for an answer. Be ready at eight-thirty sharp. We'll drag your sorry ass out of your apartment if we have to. And no flannel, what the hell is that all about, and no shit-kicker boots, we're not going to a barn dance."

"What?" Alice says, half asleep. "Who is this?"

"You heard me, see you at eight-thirty." She hangs up.

Alice's phone pings a message. 'I wasn't kidding. We're picking you up at 8:30. You can run, but you cannot hide!'

Ella is tap dancing across the floor. She needs to go out. Alice sighs and grabs the dog's leash.

Jessica grew up across the street from Alice. They were best friends starting from when they could first cross the street without help. They were so close for so long, people who didn't know them well would mix up their names. Their last night together, before Alice left for the University of Vermont and Jessica for the University of Maine, they promised nothing would ever change. They hugged each other and cried.

On a class trip when they were fifteen, they got frightfully lost in Washington DC. They were staying at the Marriott Hotel on Pennsylvania Avenue and decided to sneak out of the hotel and walk to Ford's Theater, which was only a few blocks away. They got a map from the front desk and were confident they knew where they were going. They would go there and get back to the hotel before anyone knew they were gone.

The map made no sense to them. Three hours later, three hours of aimless wandering, they had no idea where they were. A taxi cab pulled alongside of them. The driver, a tall, Black man, got out of the cab. "You girls aren't from here are you?" Alice grabbed Jessica's arm and pulled her so close their bodies were touching.

"Girls, don't be afraid. It's pretty obvious you're lost."

They nodded yes.

"Get in, I'll take you to your hotel."

"We can't take a ride from a stranger," Jessica said. Her voice trembled.

"Don't be afraid, you need my help. Please get in, you don't want to be here."

There were four police cars waiting for them at the hotel. The chaperons were so angry and frightened their bodies were shaking. What the hell were we thinking? Damn we were stupid. Alice checks the time on her phone. Jessica should be here soon. When Jessica's car pulls up to Alice's building, Alice is ready to go. She has been ready for over an hour. She had tried on eight different tops, three pairs of shoes and five different jeans. She put on a small amount of makeup, eyeliner, mascara, bronzer, and lip gloss. She hasn't worn makeup since she left Baltimore.

"You look good Alice," Jessica says.

"Thanks."

"Got your million bucks from the Bill Nason yet?" She laughs.

"Very funny."

"Lighten up Alice, I was just kidding."

"It's not funny. Some of the comments on-line have been so nasty. People who don't even know me, are judging me. It's awful."

"Don't pay attention to those morons. Can't be any worse than when you plagiarized your grandmother's story."

"Thanks for bringing that up, nothing like rubbing salt on an old wound."

"That's what friends are for." Jessica swats the back of Alice's head. Alice smiles.

The same day the first story about Clyde Nason's will was in the newspaper, Alice started getting texts and social media messages from just about everyone she had ever known from high school. She wondered how they all got her phone number. Most of the notes were a variation of 'I'm here for you,' especially from people she barely knew. But what they really wanted were details. Alice never answered any of the messages, not even the ones from the three women who had been her best friends.

Lauren and Christine are sitting in a back booth laughing. Christine has just gotten engaged. She is showing her ring to Lauren. "It's so beautiful," Lauren says. Christine shows the ring to Alice.

"It is beautiful," Alice says.

Jessica agrees. "Alice, you've been back for three years and this is the first time you've joined us for girls' night out? Too good for us?" Christine says. She punches Alice in the shoulder.

Alice smiles and nods yes.

"So, Alice, you're filthy rich," Lauren says.

"Not yet."

"When you get your money, we've got a great idea. We want a week in Vail, all four of us, no boyfriends, no husbands, no kids, just us.

Deep, soft powder, blue sky, no Vermont ice, it will be great. You can afford it," Christine says.

"I don't think so."

"So what's this bullshit with Clyde Nason? Are you really an evil gold digger?" Christine asks.

"Yes, I am. It was all part of my plan to retire at thirty."

"That's what we figured. You've always been a schemer," Jessica says.

"Don't believe everything you read."

"We don't. Nobody does. When you get the money, I want some, not too much, just about ten thousand, my credit cards bills are killing me," Lauren says.

"Got it. I'll write the check tomorrow," Alice says.

"What the hell have you been doing for the past three years Alice" Jessica says.

"Not much."

"Not much. As far as we can tell you haven't done anything with anyone. We know, we've been watching you. We're the Providence CIA, we've been spying on you since you got home. You need to get a life Alice," Jessica says.

"I have a life."

"No, you don't. My cat has more of a life and he sleeps all day."

"I have a life."

"Alice, I've talked to your mom. All you do is work. She's worried about you. I'm worried about you," Jessica says.

"We're all worried about you. Alice," Christine says.

"Let's talk about something besides my sorry life," Alice says. "What about you, Jessica? What's Providence's most famous dental hygienist up to?"

"Last week I got bitten by a little shit ten-year-old. I was stuffing cotton in his grubby little mouth and the little fuck bit me. I wanted to shove the cotton down his little throat."

"You think that's bad, one of my students tripped me, on purpose. I fell on my face. The whole class laughed, even the suck-ups. I didn't want to shove cotton down his throat, I wanted to kill the little bastard," Lauren says.

"None of you have kids. Try changing a hundred shitty diapers a week if you want to have some real fun," Christine says.

"We should get drunk," Jessica says. She orders beer for the four of them. Alice hands her a ten dollar bill.

"Keep it Alice, you don't make shit. My cousin Tina is a home care aide, I know what you make."

Alice shoves the bill into Jessica's pocketbook.

Jessica holds up her glass. "We should toast. Alice is finally back."

"I don't know if I'm back or not."

"Alice, you're here with us tonight, that's good enough for now," Christine says.

"Thanks. I've missed you guys." Alice taps her glass against Jessica's glass. "To us."

"To us," the three others say.

. . . .

WHEN ALICE GETS back to her apartment she is so drunk she can barely stand. "Jessica, stay with me tonight."

"Do you still hog the bed?"

"I don't know, haven't had anyone in it with me for a while." Alice sprints to the bathroom and throws up.

"You stink," Jessica says.

"I'll brush my teeth."

"This place is a dump."

"It is."

Ella licks the puke off the side of the toilet, trots to the living room and licks Alice's legs.

"That's disgusting. Go wash your legs," Jessica says.

Alice washes her legs and feet, returns to the bedroom and changes into gym shorts and a T-shirt. She grabs a T-shirt from her bureau and a pair of men's boxer shorts and tosses them to Jessica.

"If you hog the covers, I'll throw you off the bed," Jessica says.

"Sounds fair."

"Alice, it's just me, your best friend forever. What the hell happened in Baltimore?"

"Nothing."

"Alice!"

"I had a teacher who drove me insane. He constantly harassed me."

"Did he?"

"No, nothing like that. He just kept touching me, constantly. He'd use any excuse to get next to me and touch me. He'd strum his fingers on my shoulders or in my hair. He'd squeeze my knees and my thighs when he was sitting next to me in the cafeteria and he'd tell all the other students how smart I was. They hated that. One time in his office, when I was there for my first semester evaluation, he told me how beautiful I was. He was so creepy. It's like when you go camping and you have a spider in your sleeping bag. At first you don't know what it is. When you realize there's a spider in your bag, you've got to get it out. I had a spider in my bag and I had to get it out."

"Sounds more like you had a snake in your bag," Jessica says.

"Yes, I had a snake in my sleeping bag."

"You can always go to a different medical school."

"I am not sure if I want to."

"Alice, that was all you ever wanted since you were six years old."

"I'm a different person now. I'm not sure what I want. Maybe I didn't really want to be a doctor, what I really wanted to do was to make everybody happy, especially my dad. The older I get the less I know what I want. When I was eighteen, I knew everything. I don't know anything anymore."

"You were kind of a know-it-all."

"Yes, I was." Alice checks the time.

"You can't let one asshole ruin your life," Jessica says.

"I know that, I really do. But it wasn't just him. Being number one in every class, for nineteen years in a row, was really hard. I never asked myself what I wanted to do. I was too busy trying to be number one. That made no sense."

"Good, so now move on. You're a strong woman."

"I think I can. I'm not sure. One thing I do know, it's two-thirty in the morning and I have to get up at six."

"Do you still snore?"

"I never snored."

"Sure, and I never cheated off your papers."

They both laugh.

"I have to ask you something Jessica and you can't lie."

"I don't lie?"

"Right, and I didn't plagiarize my grandmother's story." Alice pauses. "Did my mother call you?"

"Maybe."

"Damn her."

"What difference does it make if she did or not. Did you have fun?"

"Yes, this was the best night I've had in three years."

"Consider it the first of many."

"I will."

"If you hog the blankets I really will kick you skinny ass to the floor. That's a promise."

"You don't scare me."

"Oh ya." She makes a fist.

Alice grabs Jessica's hands. "Jessica, I need you."
"I know you do."

CHAPTER 39

ALICE HAMMOND

ALICE OPENS THE cupboard under the kitchen sink and reaches for the dishpan. There is a mouse in the pan. She screams and drops the pan. The pan bounces twice on the linoleum. The mouse jumps out of the pan, scurries across the room and dashes under the stove.

"Brian! Brian, I need you, help," she shouts.

"What?" he says from the other side of their common wall.

"I need your help, it's an emergency."

He runs to her apartment. When he gets to her kitchen he is out of breath and panting. Alice is standing on a chair.

"What's the emergency?"

"There's a mouse under the stove."

"That's it, that's the emergency? Are you kidding me? You screamed so loud I thought you had cut off your arm."

"It was huge."

"It's probably the same one that's been in my apartment. He's about as big as my fist, if that. I call him Oscar. I've tried to kill him several dozen times but he's a slippery bugger. I chase him with my basketball." He gives her a sly smile. "What do you want me to do?"

"Capture him and take him outdoors, into the woods, miles from here."

"If I do that, he'll be back next week either that or one of his mouse buddies will just take his place."

"Then kill him."

"Don't you have a cat?"

Her cat emerges from the bedroom, humps its backs and stretches its legs.

"You feed your cat too much." He puffs out his cheeks to imitate a fat mouse. "Where's your broom?"

She points to the closet next to the refrigerator. He grabs it, holds it by the bristles and shoves the handle under the stove. The mouse scurries out, looks at him for a second, and runs behind the refrigerator. The cat ignores the mouse. Brian tries to slip the broom under the refrigerator to swat the mouse but the handle is too wide. "It's too big."

"Move the refrigerator."

"You move it, that sucker's heavy."

"You're the man."

"You're the one wearing combat boots." He struggles with the refrigerator and shimmies it several inches away from the wall. The mouse squirts out from behind the refrigerator, runs across the room, directly under Alice's chair, jumps back into the cupboard under the sink, and disappears down the side of the drainpipe. Alice starts to fall off the chair. Brian catches her.

"He's gone, he took off down to the cellar," Brian says. He points to the small gap between the particle board at the bottom of the cupboard and the drainpipe.

"How'd he fit through that tiny hole? It isn't much bigger than my thumb." She grabs a cloth from the sink and stuffs it in the gap between the wood and the drainpipe.

"That won't stop him, he'll be back."

"What should I do?"

Stop feeding your cat so much, either that or get a mouse trap or poison."

"Where do you get it?"

"The hardware store but no need, there's some in the cellar." He leaves the apartment and returns ten minutes later with four mouse hotels and a box of d-Con. "This should do it. Make sure your cat and dog don't eat the poison. Even if this works, feed your cat less, he's obese."

"It's a she."

"She's fat."

"She's happy fat."

"Santa Clause is happy fat, your cat's obese. You're lucky I was dressed. You screamed so loud, I probably wouldn't have bothered to put my pants on."

"I've seen you in your underwear, remember."

"Right, I forgot. Pretty awesome sight."

"Definitely. You should dance for Thunder From Down Under."

"Who?"

"Nobody." Alice opens the refrigerator and grabs a six-pack of Bud Light. "Here, have a beer, you saved me."

"Bud Light, I would have taken you for an overpriced, local brew type."

"When you make thirteen-twenty-five an hour, you drink Bud Light."

"I thought you snooty types slummed with PBR."

"That's old news." Alice sits at the table. "Sit down, I'm not going to bite you."

"Are you sure? I was thinking you'd kick me." He sits across from her.

"I didn't realize Harold Doty was related to you."

"He's sort of my uncle. He's my grandmother's cousin, so I guess that makes him my uncle or my great-uncle, whatever. I've always called him Uncle Harold. He's a piece of work."

"He is, for sure," Alice says. "How's he doing?"

"It looks like he might lose his other foot."

"Too bad, not surprised."

"He's okay. He's got a wheelchair and rolls around like he's the king."

"Sounds like him. How does he like Sunset Ridge?"

"Much better than we thought he would. He gets the meals every day and plays bingo and he hangs around the rec. room chatting it up with the old ladies. I think he's one of only five men and sixty-five women. He's loving it."

"That reminds me. You seem to be in a bit of a dry spell, nothing since Judy, five months ago? Great for me, I can finally get some sleep, but a twenty week dry spell for you, must be terrible."

"You could help me end my dry spell."

"That's not going to happen."

"Didn't think so. Figured no harm in asking. You should visit Harold, he's hoping you will. He talks a lot about you."

"I will, maybe tomorrow. How's Ron doing?"

"I don't know, he scares the hell out of me."

"He's harmless."

"He beat a man to death with a desk lamp."

"That was thirty years ago. Give the man a break."

"You give him a break, I'll give him some space."

He takes a big gulp of beer and burps. "So what's your story? I know you went to med school. Why are you working as a home health aide for ten bucks an hour?"

"Thirteen-twenty-five, I just told you that just two minutes ago."

"Excuse me, thirteen-twenty-five."

"How do you know I went to med school?"

"Everybody knows. This is Providence, Vermont not New York City." He spins his beer can and sips the beer on top of the can. "Something must be up. Harold thinks something bad happened."

"Nothing bad happened, he's wrong."

"Really, you've got a college degree, you were in med school and now you're wiping butts for a living. Something must have happened."

"Nothing happened."

"How long are you going to work as a home health aide? You're too smart for that job."

"You don't know if I am smart or not. Plus you obviously know nothing about this job. It's complicated."

"You went to med school, they don't let half-wits in."

"You'd be surprised, believe me. You sound like my father. What are you, thirty going on seventy?"

"Come on Alice, something happened?"

"Nothing big enough to even talk about." She finishes her beer. "You want another one?"

"Sure but you're just trying to take advantage of me. I know your type. I bet you slipped a date rape drug into my beer."

"You caught me. You'll be asleep in fifteen minutes, then I'll take your clothes off, cover you with dog food and let Ella lick your body."

"That sounds pretty good."

"You're weird. So, Brian, what's with Judy, is she coming back?"

"Doubt it. She doesn't know you, but she hates you anyway."

"I got that."

Brian pops open the second beer and takes a big gulp. "That whole screaming fit over a tiny mouse surprised me. I didn't take you for a mouse screamer, especially with your combat boots," he says.

"I'm more girly than you think. When I was a kid I played tea parties and dressed like a princess."

"I can't picture that, not with those boots."

"You're obsessed with my boots. Do you have a foot fetish or a boot fetish?"

"Neither. You promised Daisy Duke jeans and tank tops. Daisy

Dukes and tank tops don't go with combat books. What happened?

"We'll go shopping tomorrow. I'll let you pick out my clothes."

"Daisy Dukes it is."

"What's the deal with you and Bill Nason?"

"What do you think it's about?"

"If what I read is correct, in the first will Bill's brother Clyde left you a bucket load of money and property and Bill is not happy. He's saying you took advantage of a lonely old man. In the mystery will, Bill gets the land and most of the money. He found that will in a typewriter case. Is that about right?" he says.

"That pretty much sums it up."

"Well, did you?"

"Did I what?"

"Did you take advantage of a lonely, old man?"

"What do you think?"

"No, I don't think so but I am surprised Clyde left you the money and the land. Bill is an okay dude, a low rent lawyer for sure, but not a bad guy."

"Apparently, Clyde hated him, at least that's what my lawyer told me. I'm not sure why he thinks that. When I saw them together, they seemed to get along just fine."

"Clyde definitely did not hate his brother. Your lawyer is wrong."

"The will is pretty clear, Clyde was angry."

"You mean the first will?"

"Yes, the first will." I played softball with Bill for four years. He talked a lot about Clyde. Sometimes he took him to the games. I don't think I've ever seen a bigger man. They seemed to get along well enough. Clyde was proud of Bill. He called him a big shot lawyer. He said it both as a compliment and a joke."

"I don't know what happened but what I do know is, I don't want to talk about this garbage anymore," Alice says. She tosses her empty can toward the wastebasket next to the closet door. The can bounces on the floor.

"Throwing that away? You're the one making thirteen-twenty-five an hour, not me. Five cents is five cents," Brian says.

"Good point." She grabs the can from the floor and places it in the bag of returnable cans and bottles in the kitchen closet. "Do you want to watch a movie?"

"Depends, what movie?"

"I don't know, whatever's on Netflix."

"Let's watch one of those Hallmark movies where the heroine goes back to her hometown from the big city and falls in love with her high school crush, who's now a widower with a young daughter, and he's trying to save his farm and she's just the big shot lawyer who can do it," Brian says. Ella is licking his shoes.

"That sounds great," Alice says.

"No, it doesn't. That was a joke."

"Gee, I thought you were serious." She stands up from the kitchen chair, walks to the living room and turns on the television. "I'll find something with a lot of car crashes."

"American car crashes, I don't read subtitles. If I want to read, I'll get a book."

"American car crashes it is."

CHAPTER 40

ALICE HAMMOND

ALICE IS AN hour late for her parents' thirty-fifth anniversary celebration. She has been reading anniversary cards at Walgreens for twenty minutes. She has read every card at least twice. She grabs a card with Snoopy and Woodstock on the cover. Snoopy and Woodstock are doing a happy dance. Both are wearing party hats and are being showered with confetti. The words above the two dancers say, 'Happy Anniversary.' On the inside, Snoopy is blowing on a party horn and Woodstock is flying upside down, just above Snoopy's head. "This is perfect," she mumbles to herself. She is not sure why but the card seems oddly familiar.

Alice is in no hurry to get to the party. Her brother David and sister Laura are already there. Starting in January, David will study surgery at the University Medical Center in New Orleans. Laura will stay in Boston and work for legal aide.

"It's the right thing to do for now, I won't stay there forever, I need to do some good," Laura told their father when she rejected an offer from Boston's largest law firm.

"Good move for now but not forever," he said.

Alice turns the car key. The engine grumbles and grunts. "Dammit," she says. She tries again. The car rumbles but does not start. She considers calling her brother but gives the car a third try. It groans and starts. A flume of smoke pours from the exhaust pipe. Before she drives out of the parking lot, she grabs her phone and sends a text to Bill Nason. 'Bill, I called Hebert, Dean and Doris Lang. I'm going with the new will, that is what Clyde really wanted, you know it and I know it. William was furious. He said you probably typed it yourself, he wouldn't put it past you. I told them I didn't care if you did or not, we're going with the new will. Dean and Lang were thrilled. I need the twenty thousand by December 1. And one other thing, don't go to the damn newspaper. Thanks. Alice H.'

She shuts off her phone and tosses it onto the passenger's seat. She pounds her fists against the steering wheel. "I'm free," she says to herself. She steps on the gas pedal. The car hesitates for a second and lurches forward. She drives a mile and pulls into the McDonald's parking lot. She grabs her phone and scrolls through her contacts list. She calls her college roommate Nicki Larson. "Nicki, it's me Alice," she says when Nicki answers.

"Alice Hammond?"

"Do you know another Alice?"

"No, but I haven't heard from you in three years. What happened?"

"It's not worth talking about, at least not on the phone?"

"Anything to do with Thompson."

"Yes."

"That's what I figured. What a total asshole. One time he told me I reminded him of a cool spring day. What the hell does that mean? I thought I would throw up?"

"I did throw up, several times. Where are you now?"

"Portland."

"Maine or Oregon?"

"Maine."

"Only four hours from here. We need to get together," Alice says.

"The sooner the better, I'm seven months pregnant."

"Congratulations. Ron?"

"No, he's long gone. I'm a surgeon at Maine Medical Center. I married a nurse, Rick Morgan, he's a good man."

"Text me your address, I'll be there Sunday morning."

"Alice, I was so worried about you. I must have texted you a hundred times."

"More like four hundred."

"Why didn't you answer?"

"I couldn't."

"Are you okay?"

"I wasn't for a long time but I am now. I'm in a good place. See you Sunday."

She sets her car in reverse, doesn't use the mirrors and rams into the car parked behind her. "Shit," she says. She sees that no one saw what happened. She drives off. Her heart is beating hard. She checks the time on the dashboard clock. She is fifteen minutes late. Not too bad. Alice's father is waiting for her on the porch.

"You're late as usual," he says as he greets her at the top step. He has a bottle of champagne in his right hand.

"Yes, Dad, I'm late as usual."

"You're just in time for our toast," Lesley says from the kitchen.

Dan points Alice to the dining room. On the far end of the table, near the back wall, there are five empty champagne glasses. He removes the foil from the top of the bottle, crumbles it and flicks it onto the table. "All right everybody, let's hope I don't poke out somebody's eye," he says. The top pops into the air and narrowly misses hitting the ceiling. He fills the glasses, places the bottle on a rubber mat on the table, and grabs one of the filled glasses. He holds his glass chest high and waits for the others to grab their glasses.

"To thirty-five years," Dan toasts.

The five of them clink their glasses together.

"To thirty-five years," David says.

David, Laura and Dan sit at the table. Alice and Lesley retrieve food from the kitchen. It takes them four trips to the kitchen and back.

"Before we begin, we should say grace," Dan says.

"It's not Thanksgiving," Alice says.

"It's a thanksgiving day for me. Today, I am thankful that when I asked your mom out on our first date, she said, yes."

"We know Dad, we've all heard the story a few dozen times," David says.

Dan stands up as if he were the best man at a wedding. "Too bad, you're going to hear it again. I was a dirt poor resident at Boston Women's Hospital. I didn't have . . ."

David interrupts him. "Two nickels to rub together."

"A pot to piss in," Laura says.

"Don't interrupt, it's rude," Lesley says.

Dan refills his champagne glass and drinks the champagne in two, loud gulps. "Yes, David, I didn't have two nickels to rub together and your mom, the most beautiful nurse, the most beautiful woman I had ever seen, said yes. Every doctor in the hospital wanted her but she said yes to me."

"Every doctor wanted her, even all the female doctors. Oh wait, there weren't any," Laura says. She laughs.

"Very funny, Laura, there were a few women doctors, not many, but some." He clears his throat. "I took your mom to an Italian restaurant in the North End. I didn't know they didn't take credit cards. When the meal was done, I didn't have enough money to pay the bill. Your mother, she had planned ahead, pulled out forty dollars in cash, one twenty and two, ten dollar bills. She handed me the money and I paid the bill. I was totally embarrassed. 'You think you're the first out-of-state med student who didn't know that half the restaurants in the North End are cash only,' she said in her strong Boston accent. She and the waiter laughed. At that moment I knew I was in love with her and I still am, thirty-seven years, three months and fourteen days from that night."

"And you had ribollita soup, not because you wanted it but because it was the cheapest thing on the menu and mom ordered pork agrodolce, which was twice as expensive. When Mom saw the look on your face she said to the waiter, 'No, I've changed my mind, I'll have ribollita soup also.' I thought that's when you knew you were in love with Mom," David says.

"What I know is, I fell in love with your mother that night and I love her even more now than I did then." He reaches across the table and fills the five glasses. "Thirty-five years."

"Hear, hear," David says.

The five of them reach across the table and clink their glasses together a second time.

"Your turn, Mom," Laura says.

"Well, your father's story is mostly correct. I don't know if I fell in love with him that night or not but I did eventually fall in love with him, even though he was kind of a hick, and I am still in love with him now, thirty-seven years later, and he's still a hick. The boo hoo hoo story about no-two-nickels-to-rub-together, that makes a great story but it's not true. Yes, your father had no money, that is true, and yes, he was living in a total dump on Mission Hill, which was even worse then than it is now, but let's not forget, his father, your grandfather, was the head surgeon at Providence Hospital, not some low paid dishwasher. When your dad was in trouble he could always call home for money, and he often did."

"That's not true, I had no money at all."

"Oh Dan, please, you didn't pay a single rent the four years you were in Boston?"

"I did."

"Four rents, five at most, that's not paying rent. When I was a nursing student I had to live with my parents because there was no way I could afford to live on campus. I worked nights at the drug store near Emerson College, the one by Boston Common, that was a rough area back then. I was a full-time student and I worked the three to eleven shift. Your father thinks he was poor. I was real poor, the kind of poverty the son of a surgeon and grandson of a surgeon could never understand. He was like those kids who sleep out in a tent one night in the winter to bond with the homeless. One night in a four-hundred-dollar tent and a two-hundred dollar sleeping bag isn't exactly the same as being homeless. Your father was in the four hundred dollar tent and he didn't even know it."

"I was poor, Mom just won't admit it. But enough of this nostalgia nonsense, let's eat," Dan says.

"What about grace?" Alice asks.

"You say it, you're the closest to Mother Teresa," David laughs.

"David, stop it," Lesley says.

Alice bows her head. "Bless us, oh Lord, and these your gifts, which we are about to receive from your bounty, through Christ, our Lord, amen."

"Amen," Lesley says.

"So, Alice, have you heard the good news from your sister and your brother?" Dan asks.

"Yes, Dad, I have. David is going to New Orleans to become a surgeon and Laura will stay in Boston to work for legal aid."

"The Big Easy, laissez la bon temps rouler, that means let the good times roll," David says.

"Got it Dave, but I think it's laissey les bon temps rouler, les not la, la is a note that follows sew," Alice says and looks at Laura. "Got to say Laura, I didn't expect legal aid for you, I thought you'd go for some big shot law firm and get your big fat bonus and your six-figure salary."

"Alice, you sure are holier than thou," Laura says.

"Girls, stop it," Lesley says. She uses the same tone she used when they were children.

"Okay Mother Teresa, what's your future, how long are you going to be a home health aide, and don't give us this crap, you're doing God's work, you make a difference and we don't. Anybody with half a brain can do what you're doing," David says.

"David, you don't know anything," Alice says. "Home health aide is a very difficult job. I work with lots of different people and some are extremely challenging, both mentally and physically. For some of my patients, I'm the only person they see all day, no one else, just me."

"We get it, I get it. You do good work. We should all bow to you," David says.

"I do have an announcement. I'm going back to college."

"Great news," Lesley says.

"I've got to agree, that is great news. It took you three years to figure out what you should do but it's still good news. Johns Hopkins, best medical school in the country?" Dan says.

"Nope, I am going to the University of Vermont."

"Good choice," Dan says. He takes a breath and clears his throat again. "Pretty damn good med school. I'm proud of you Alice, it took you a little longer to wake up from your fog than I thought it would, but you did, finally, that's all that matters." He grabs the champagne to refill the glasses but the bottle is empty. "Let's toast Alice, even if our glasses are empty." He stands up and arm motions David, Laura and Lesley to stand. "To Alice," he says.

"I'm not going to medical school, Dad, I'm going to nursing school. I am going to be an RN."

"Are you serious?" he asks.

"Yes, I am."

"Why nursing, why not med school?" Dan says.

"Remember Harold Doty? You said you consulted on his surgery."
"Yes, what about him?"
"Was he married?"
"I don't know, probably."
"What'd he do for work?"
"I don't know Alice, I have no idea."
"Did he have kids?"
"Yes, his son killed a man?"
"What was his son's name?"
"I don't know Alice, what's your point?"
"I want to know those things. I want to know what my patients like and don't like, what their favorite food is, what drives them crazy, what their home is like. And don't worry Mom, I don't want to know too much, just enough to do a good job. I don't want to be their friend."

"Alice, congratulations, it's a great choice," Lesley says. "In case you've forgotten Dan, I was a home care nurse once and I was a damn good one. And you know what Alice, when I was a nurse, I knew I made a difference. You are right Dan, we should toast Alice but not with empty glasses."

She walks to the kitchen, grabs a second bottle of champagne, returns to the dining room, opens the bottle and fills the five glasses. She holds her glass to them and lightly taps it against the other four glasses. "To Alice."

"I'm not surprised, Alice. Nursing is a good choice for you. I always figured you'd join me at the hospital but I guess that's not to be. I'm not disappointed, this is the right decision for you," Dan says.

"I can still join you Dad, I'll be your nurse."

"Maybe, but I suspect home care nursing is in your future."

"Me too." Alice says.

"I'll second that," Lesley says.

Dan clinks his glass against Alice's. "To you Alice, you will be a great nurse."

"Thank you, Dad." She drinks her champagne and looks at her brother and sister. "Let's eat, I'm starved."

"About time," David says.

"It is indeed," Alice says.

ACKNOWLEDGMENTS

I have a lot of people to thank, the most important is my wife Cindy. When I told her I was planning to write a novel, 68-years-old and three years retired, she didn't laugh. She should have. She was also my first reader. I also want to thank my other proofreaders and advisors, my late sister Anne Balk, daughter Colleen LeFebvre, and granddaughter Alice Hammond. Colleen and Alice checked for boomer mistakes. Colleen also helped with the girls' night out chapter. Alice graciously let me use her name. The Alice Hammond in this novel is not my granddaughter, she is totally fictional. What the two have in common, however, is they both are smart and kind.

Also, thanks to my brother-in-law, Dr. Cooper Pearce, who proofread the hospice death chapter. And thanks to my daughter, Leslie Hammond, who set up my various social media accounts related to this book. I'd also like to thank my friend Virginia Fry whose book *Part of Me Died Too: Stories of Creative Survival Among Bereaved Children and Teenagers* guided and inspired me.

About the Author

PETER COBB was the executive director of the VNAs of Vermont, the trade association that represents Vermont's Visiting Nurse Associations, for thirty-three years. Cobb lives in Barre Town, Vermont with his wife Cindy and their two cats. *To Alice* is Cobb's first novel.

Also by J. Peter Cobb

Some Things Aren't Meant to Be (Rootstock Publishing, 2024)

"Cobb ably integrates themes of growth, individuation, and faith, and raises questions about what it truly means to love oneself, to love others, and to love God. Along the way, it engagingly asks readers to explore ideas of commitment, devotion, and family. …A touching work that follows one man's lifelong pilgrimage towards love and selfhood."

–Kirkus Reviews

"*Some Things Aren't Meant to Be* is a lovely, bittersweet romance, grounded in sharply accurate depictions of a hardscrabble Vermont dairy farm and a rural Catholic diocese. It is well-written, believable, and compelling."

–Tom Slayton, editor-in-chief of *Vermont Life* (1986-2007) and author of *Searching for Thoreau: On the Trails and Shores of Wild New England* and other books

🍃 We Grow Our Books in Montpelier, Vermont

Learn more about our titles in Fiction, Nonfiction, Poetry and Children's Literature at the QR code below or visit www.rootstockpublishing.com.

Milton Keynes UK
Ingram Content Group UK Ltd.
UKHW031144311024
450535UK00001B/43